"I Must
I've Been
Attention to That Outfit
You're Wearing," Waine Said.

Francesca looked down at her camisole and fingered the lace. "It's underwear, really. I've never worn it as a blouse like this. The saleswoman said I should. 'It begs to be seen,' was what she said."

"She's right," Waine said.

Francesca put her glass on the coffee table and turned a little toward him. "Touch it, Waine. Feel the silk. It feels like soft skin."

Waine put an arm around her shoulders and a hand on the camisole over her flat stomach.

The light pressure of his hand sent a gentle spasm of pleasure through her body. She raised her face to his and shut her eyes and parted her lips and licked them lightly with her tongue.

His lips covered hers and his tongue, sweet and soft, played with hers. He slipped his hand under her camisole, lightly tracing the line of her ribcage. Francesca broke the embrace of their lips and brought her head down to nibble on his neck. Waine moaned his pleasure, sending a shiver of delight through her.

Dear Reader:

We trust you will enjoy this Richard Gallen romance. We plan to bring you more of the best in both contemporary and historical romantic fiction with four exciting new titles each month.

We'd like your help.

We value your suggestions and opinions. They will help us to publish the kind of romances you want to read. Please send us your comments, or just let us know which Richard Gallen romances you have especially enjoyed. Write to the address below. We're looking forward to hearing from you!

Happy reading!

Richard Gallen Books
330 Steelcase Road East,
Markham, Ontario L3R 2M1

With Eyes of Love

VICTORIA FLEMING

PUBLISHED BY RICHARD GALLEN BOOKS
Distributed by POCKET BOOKS

Distributed in Canada by PaperJacks Ltd., a Licensee
of the trademarks of Simon & Schuster, a division of
Gulf+Western Corporation.

A RICHARD GALLEN BOOKS *Original* publication

Distributed by
POCKET BOOKS, a Simon & Schuster division of
GULF & WESTERN CORPORATION
1230 Avenue of the Americas, New York, N.Y. 10020
In Canada distributed by PaperJacks Ltd.,
330 Steelcase Road, Markham, Ontario.

ISBN: 0-671-43941-3

First Pocket Books printing February, 1982

10 9 8 7 6 5 4 3 2 1

RICHARD GALLEN and colophon are trademarks
of Simon & Schuster and Richard Gallen & Co., Inc.

Printed in Canada

With Eyes of Love

Prologue

~~~~~~~~~~

The Mercedes spun round and round lazily, as if seen in a dream.

Plumes of water arched up from its wheels like spray from some modernistic fountain. The tires left traces of their treads in a sinuous pattern.

Conrad James fought with the steering wheel, trying to control the car. Beside him, his wife, Edith, said with dismay: "Connie? *Con*nie."

In the back seat, Eva James felt as though she were on a carnival ride, like the one she and Becky Morgan had ridden on in Asbury Park, New Jersey where Mr. and Mrs. Morgan had taken them on Becky's eighth birthday. It was different from the ride because there was none of the screeching noise. Except for her mother's sharp cries, there was no sound at all, just the streaking lights.

The spinning stopped and the Mercedes hewed to a straight line.

To Conrad James, the cessation of spinning seemed to mark an end to the crisis. He would now be able to drive on—until he found a place to pull over—to get his breath back, to give Edith a hug, to turn to put a hand on Eva's head—maybe even to laugh about it.

But there was still something wrong. Those lights that stared at him weren't red tail lights, they were headlights, and they were bearing down on him. The Mercedes was traveling backwards.

In the back seat, Eva James noticed how the headlights of the other cars turned her parents into silhouettes. When they glanced at each other, she saw how similar their profiles were to hers.

Eva knew especially well what her profile looked like because only a few weeks before, during the last days of school, Becky Morgan had made a shadow silhouette of her. Eva remembered how hard it had been to sit absolutely still while Becky traced the outline of her shadow onto a piece of paper. When she saw the drawing she wanted it and asked Becky for it, but Becky said no. It was the first time Eva had got mad, really mad, at Becky Morgan.

But a few days later, on the last day of school, Becky handed her a package, wrapped in silver paper and tied with a crimson ribbon. Her silhouette was inside the package. Becky had filled it in, using India ink and a brush her mother had bought her. Becky hadn't gone outside the outline even once, and the coat of ink was so smooth you could hardly see the brush strokes. Then Becky had pasted it on a piece of black oaktag paper. It was perfect, absolutely perfect.

Becky Morgan was Eva James's best friend in the whole world. In fact, Becky was the reason that Eva and her parents were driving to New York on a rainy Sunday night in June. Once school had ended, the Jameses had packed trunks and boxes and suitcases and had pretty much said good-bye to their apartment on Central Park West and to the rest of the city for the summer. Her father would come in once or twice a month from their summer place on Shelter Island, to see his editor at the publishing house that published his novels, or to go to the dentist. Her father didn't like going to the dentist any more than Eva did, but he had to go a lot more often. "That's what happens," he told her, "when you get old. Actually," he would joke, "my teeth are okay, it's the gums that are rotten."

Her mother might not come into the city at all, unless she needed some more paints or canvases. She painted a lot when they were at Shelter Island, pretty pictures of the sea and boats. Eva's favorites, though, were the pictures she painted of the sunsets. Her mother loved Shelter Island, and would just as soon not come into the city, which she hated in the summer.

But tomorrow was Becky Morgan's birthday, —her ninth—and there was no way Eva James was going to miss the party. She would not have missed it even if she had had to come all the way from China.

Suddenly, the Mercedes was going frontwards again —but its rear end sashayed from side to side as it went, slipping back and forth on the wet pavement.

For Conrad James, who had spent his adult life putting fictional characters in positions of jeopardy— sometimes getting them out of them, sometimes killing them off—this was all very disturbing: He was out of control; nothing he could do, certainly nothing he could say, most certainly nothing he could *write* was going to affect the outcome of this episode.

Ironically, out-of-control automobiles were recurring features of Conrad James's novels. He didn't have one in every book, but he had them often enough that his regular readers, of whom there was a multitude, squirmed with pleasure whenever they encountered one, for they knew that they were in for a good several pages of crackling action.

Conrad James's readers trusted the author to get his heroes out of scrapes as much as they counted on him to put the heroes in them. But the fact remained that Conrad James's heroes were figments of Conrad James's imagination. James could, for example, put one of his heroes in an out-of-control automobile, then get up from the typewriter—to make a cup of tea, to take a walk around the block, to play a set of tennis, to go to the Georgia Sea Islands for the weekend or the Caribbean for a week. The hero would still be there when he got back; the skid would be frozen in time.

But though the time of the Mercedes's skid was unreal—it was stretched out, attenuated, like a slow-motion film—the skid itself was vibrant with truth. And in the face of it, Conrad James was helpless.

The rear end of the Mercedes struck the concrete divider. The jolt sent the car sliding across the road.

Edith James thought how odd it was that she felt compelled to read everything—the road signs, the license plates of other cars, the lettering on the sides of trucks. She supposed it was a trick her brain was pulling to distract her from giving full consideration to the certainty that she was going to die. That certainty had come to Edith James with the very first sensation that the Mercedes was no longer obeying her husband's commands.

Edith James turned to look at her daughter, wondering what was so special about her having been born and brought to this time of her life, she no longer needed a father. Or a mother. She reached out to touch her child one last time, but the car jolted, forcing her arm back down to her lap.

The back seat of the Mercedes was in shadow. Lights illuminated Eva's face, though, and made it stark white. Within the white face, Eva's eyes shone with something that Edith James couldn't put a name to.

Eva wasn't frightened. She knew that things were not as they should be, that she and her parents were in some kind of danger, but she didn't feel scared. For one thing, she wasn't seeing events from her life racing before her eyes, like a movie projected at high speed. Becky Morgan had told Eva that drowning people saw their lives race before their eyes; Eva had wondered if the same were true for people who fell from high places or were trapped in burning buildings or tumbling automobiles; Becky had said she didn't know, but Eva had figured that the same was true. And since Eva wasn't seeing her life racing before her eyes, she guessed that that meant she wasn't about to die.

Something curious was happening, though. She could see something in her mind's eye—scenes in which she played a role. They were not scenes like scenes in a movie—they were more like still photographs of movie scenes; she and the other actors in the scenes were frozen in mid-gesture. Eva wondered if she were seeing into the future. She strained to make out where she was in the scenes, and who the other actors were; they were men and women—grownups; but they were not her parents, and not anyone she knew.

The lights shining in Eva's eyes grew brighter and brighter. They seemed to fill the car and to fill her head. Then, very suddenly—more suddenly, even, than that moment when her mother or her father flicked the switch on the wall of Eva's room at bedtime—the lights went out and things were blacker than they had ever been.

Chapter 1

~~~~~~~~~~~~~~~

Francesca Hayward was glad it was summer. It had been a cold spring, but as soon as it had got to be June, the weather had turned sunny and warm, as if on orders from somewhere. Tonight's rain was even a welcome break.

She was glad it was summer because she was able to wear her favorite dress, which she had bought in Guadeloupe. Francesca had gone there with her mother for two weeks at Christmastime, and had got the dress in a small shop in Basse-Terre.

The dress was cotton and had short sleeves and a jewel neck. It tied with a sash at the waist. The pattern was a safari print—tropical flowers with leaves of pink and white and green and thin white zebra-like stripes on a background of black—a black as black as Francesca's shoulder-length hair.

Wearing the dress, Francesca felt as though she were in a jungle—not a steamy jungle rife with danger, but a lush, benign place swept by light breezes from some nearby ocean, full of a sense of flowering and growth.

Wearing the dress, which lightly teased her breasts as she moved and lay gently upon her long, long thighs, Francesca felt lovely—and more than that, lovable.

"That is a man-killer dress," Beatrice Hayward had said to her daughter the first time Francesca had worn it, to dinner at their hotel.

"I'm not sure killing men is what I had in mind," Francesca had said, after first taking a sip of her gin and tonic.

"Just a metaphor," Beatrice Hayward had said. "A man who's had his breath taken away, however, is most likely to give you the attention you deserve."

Francesca had smiled at such worldly advice coming from a woman who had saved herself for the man she had married, had been unswervingly true to him through seventeen years of marriage, and, seventeen years after his death, was still as true to him—as loyal and devoted as if he had been sitting there beside her. "A man who's had his breath taken away is probably going to give most of his attention to getting it back."

"Just a metaphor," Beatrice Hayward had said.

Now, sipping another gin and tonic in the living room of Leeds Cavanaugh's apartment, high above Fifth Avenue, looking out at the gentle rain that fell onto the grateful trees of Central Park, Francesca knew that she—not her mother—had been right. A breathless man wanted to breathe again, and resented having had his breath taken away. The man she wanted—and she didn't know who he was or where he was—would no more lose his breath than he would lose his heart. He would give his heart to her but he would never feel that it had been seized.

Leeds Cavanaugh was certainly not that man, though there had been a time when Francesca had thought he might be. At first, she had been impressed by his equanimity. Leeds was one of the few men Francesca had encountered who had not come unglued when faced with the powerful combination of her beauty, intelligence and seriousness. But recently, Francesca had realized that Leeds's composure was due to his conviction that of all the human beings in the world, none was more beautiful or more intelligent than he.

Right now, for example, sitting next to her on the sofa, sipping gin and tonic, Leeds was convinced, Francesca was sure, that the fact that his apartment looked like an illustration for a magazine article on elegant living was less the result of its expensive, tasteful furnishings than of his presence among them.

And whatever he was saying—she had not paid close attention to him for several minutes—he was, she was sure, saying it with the certainty of one who feels that his words on anything at all are, if not the first, surely the last.

Francesca had stopped listening to Leeds when he had started explaining to her how the human eye *really* worked. Leeds was a photographer of some repute, and had many thoughts on how the human eye worked. That they differed from Francesca's thoughts on how the eye worked, and that her understanding of how it worked was born of the fact that she was an eye doctor, an ophthalmologist, a member of the staff of Lexington Hospital, was of no concern to Leeds.

The subjects of Leeds Cavanaugh's photographs were the victims of calamities—earthquakes, floods, war, volcanic eruptions, tornadoes, urban fires—even of a multi-vehicle accident on a Los Angeles freeway. He had traveled the world in search of disaster: There were photographs from Sicily, the Philippines, the Sudan, Afghanistan, the Pacific Northwest, southern California, Uganda. In most of the photographs, the background contained some evidence of the disruption —a toppled building, a floating house, a pile of bodies, a smoldering landscape, an accordioned car—while in the foreground was some sufferer—a waif with a belly bloated by kwashiorkor, a woman clutching the teddy bear of a missing child, a man standing in what had been the living room of what had been a house, staring wildly at a television set that somehow continued to emit images, notwithstanding that the house itself, all the other furniture and, presumably, the man's family, had been borne away by a tornado.

When she had first seen his work, Francesca had thought that the photographs were meant to be compassionate, but now she was unable to see them as anything but exploitative. She had also been surprised to realize how many of them needed captions, and she had said as much to Leeds when he had showed her some newly framed prints the last time they were together.

"Virtually none of them is clear unto itself," she had said. "The ironies, the tragedies, only become apparent when you know some of the facts behind them."

Leeds had appeared to be listening, but was only, Francesca had realized, admiring his reflection in the glass of one of the photographs.

She had tried once more. "Pictures are supposed to be worth a thousand words. Most of these *need* words —maybe not a thousand, but a few."

Leeds had smiled at her, as if she had been uttering praise.

Now, Leeds was smiling at her again.

Francesca strained to capture the words he had been speaking. She succeeded: Leeds had been outlining the evening that lay before them—a dinner of cold poached salmon with vinaigrette sauce, prepared by Leeds himself, a gourmet cook's gourmet cook; a drive down to SoHo, where one of Leeds's countless friends was giving a small party (small meant fewer than a hundred guests) in his loft; a drive back uptown, stopping at some place worth being seen at for long enough to be seen.

"I'm tired. I worked all day," Francesca said. "I don't feel much like a party tonight."

Leeds sat back and pouted. "You're always working, Francesca. This is the third weekend in a row you've worked. When are we going to get a chance to spend some time together out at the beach?"

"It's June. There's a whole summer ahead of us."

From the pocket of his parquet-weave silk sport jacket, Leeds took his nappa leather Madler cigarette case, extracted a John Player Special cigarette and lighted it with his gold Caran d'Ache Madison lighter—hefting the lighter, at first, as always, as if assaying its value against the current price of gold. The lighter made a rasping noise that Francesca was always able to hear at a distance—a signal that Leeds, who was always resolving to stop smoking, had wavered yet again.

How could he stop? Francesca wondered. Smoking provided him with so many wondrous toys to play with: The gold lighter with its eighty components, the cigarette case, the cigarettes, which were imported from England. Smoking for Leeds was more than a habit; it was a way of flashing his bankroll.

He flicked the lighter shut and ran his fingers through his long, thick blond hair—so sensually that it was an invitation for her to do the same. There was a time when Francesca would have accepted the invitation, but not tonight.

"I'm hungry," she said.

Leeds turned back the cuff of his Ralph Lauren shirt and took a look at his watch. Francesca knew he was annoyed that things were not proceeding as he had planned. Leeds had a highly-developed sense of timing—an instinctual sense, almost, of just how long each facet of an evening should go on. It was the same sense that enabled him to take his well-known photographs—an ability to wait just that moment or two longer in order to capture a quintessential gesture.

The telephone rang, once.

"You have your answering machine on," Francesca said.

Leeds smiled, inhaled on his cigarette, and blew out a stream of smoke, contentedly. "I was hoping we'd be doing something we wouldn't want to be interrupted in."

"It might be for me, Leeds. I left your number on my machine."

"At this very moment, my machine is taking a message. If it's for you, we'll know."

"It might be urgent. It might be the hospital."

"The hospital," Leeds said didactically, "would call you on your beeper."

That was true.

Leeds put his arm around Francesca and drew her close. "So what do you say?"

Francesca planted her feet firmly on the ground and stood up. "I'm starved, Leeds. Let's eat."

Chapter 2

~~~~~~~~~~~~~~~~

Diana Stewart shut her book as the phone rang and reached across the bed to answer it before it woke her husband Charles, who had fallen asleep an hour before —as always, seconds after putting his head down on the pillow.

Diana Stewart had been trying to put herself to sleep by reading, and had dipped into several of the books on her bedside table—a biography of Peter the Great that had come from a book club; a paperback mystery that she had bought six months ago to read on the plane to Aruba and had never got around to; a novel about cavemen that she had bought after reading a good review in a magazine while waiting for one of her thrice-weekly facials at Elizabeth Arden; a Conrad James novel, *The Gold Perplex*, that had been published in the spring but that she had been saving for summer reading.

Nothing had absorbed her. She didn't know Peter the Great from Peter Pan, and didn't care to. The paperback mystery had no more allure than it had had when she first opened it. The novel about cavemen was intractable: She didn't care to read about people named Fawn and Stoat and Elm and Silverbirch. The novel by Conrad James was being saved to be read while sitting in the sun at the Stewarts' summer house in East Hampton. She would rather not have read the book at all, but Conrad James was her brother, and she had a certain obligation to read his books.

She answered the phone on its second ring. "Yes?"

"Uh, Mr. Charles Stewart, please."

"He's asleep." The man had a rough voice. Diana Stewart hoped it wasn't one of the men Charles had said he might have to borrow money from to extricate himself from the financial hole he had dug for himself.

"Uh . . ."

"This is Mrs. Stewart. Can I help you?"

"Uh, my name's McGee. Lieutenant Thomas McGee."

"Police lieutenant?"

"Uh, yes, ma'am."

Diana had always fantasized that it would be the FBI that would phone to say it had uncovered Charles's financial manipulations. It seemed rather pathetic that it might just be the police. She put some bluster in her voice: "Come, come, lieutenant, out with it. You can't say anything to shock me. My husband's with me. I don't have any children. I'm pretty impervious to tragedy. So what's happened? Has my car been towed away?" She laughed, so he could.

But he didn't. "Ma'am, I'm, uh . . . I'm sorry to have to tell you this, but it's about your brother."

"My brother?"

"You do have a brother named, uh, Conrad Rufus James?"

"Is that his middle name? I'd completely forgotten."

"We, uh, called his house and his, uh, housekeeper, Mrs. Wilson—"

"Blanche, yes."

"—she, uh, gave us your number. You see, uh . . ."

"Is my brother dead?" Diana Stewart asked.

"Uh, yes, ma'am. I'm sorry, ma'am."

"How, for God's sake?"

"An accident, ma'am. On the Triborough Bridge. His, uh, wife—"

"Edith? Edith's dead, too?"

". . . yes, ma'am."

"And my niece, Eva? Was she with them?"

"Is that the girl's name, ma'am? She didn't have any ID on her. I mean, being a kid and all."

"Is she all *right*, lieutenant?"

"No, ma'am. I mean, she's alive, but she's hurt pretty bad. She's at Lexington Hospital."

"That's my husband's hospital."

"Ma'am?"

"Nothing. My husband's on the board of—oh, nothing."

"Yes, ma'am. I'm sorry, ma'am. About your brother. We, uh . . ."

"What, lieutenant?"

"Well, we need IDs on the bodies, ma'am. Just, you know, for the record."

"Of course. Tell me where to come."

He told her and she wrote it down, but didn't really listen, and she didn't really listen to his telling her again how sorry he was—twice more.

She hung up the phone. "Charles?"

Nothing.

"Charles."

Charles Stewart groaned and rolled on his back.

"Charles, wake up. The most extraordinary thing has happened."

Clara Hirsch had had to wipe the peppermint-scented oil from her hands in order to answer the phone. She had just squeezed a few drops on her husband's shoulders and had begun to rub them in with her strong fingers. She had already oiled and massaged his lower back and she could feel that she had begun to break some of the tension that seized him whenever his writing was going badly.

Ted Hirsch had moaned softly, giving in to the pleasure of Clara's touch.

"Feel better?"

"Much."

"Maybe you just shouldn't work on Sundays at all. You always seem to wind up depressed. It might be better if you just took the day off."

"Maybe," Ted had said, without conviction. It was the same old problem. Until he could make money exclusively from writing fiction, he couldn't justify not writing fiction in every moment he had left after writing the magazine and newspaper articles he wrote to make money. But fiction didn't come out of him just when he felt like having it come out; it wasn't a facility that could just be summoned up, the way his prowess on the tennis court could, say, in his regular matches with Conrad James, his sister Edith's husband. He had to work at it. But since it was work that was essentially unpaid for, it was all the harder to do.

To be sure, Ted Hirsch had had two novels published. But they had been bought for small advances against royalties that had never surpassed the advances. There was some reward in that his books had received uniformly good reviews, but since notices are not negotiable currency, they didn't sustain him for long. Conrad James, by contrast, was frequently savaged by the critics, who delighted in dissecting his unpolished prose and his inaccurate dialogue. The situation had often led Edith James to wonder how the two men got along so well.

"I can't write the kind of book Ted writes," Conrad James would say. "It's as simple as that. If I could, and he got the good reviews and I didn't, *then* I'd be jealous."

"And I can't write about spies," Ted Hirsch would

say. "There's room in the world for all kinds of writing. If Connie's kind is commercial, well, it just is."

But now, lying beneath Clara's competent fingers, Ted Hirsch had begun to feel a ball of envy forming in his stomach—envy of Conrad James. Ted didn't envy Conrad's money. What he envied was Conrad's freedom, his never having to compromise, his being able to enjoy what he did. For, notwithstanding what he would say when the matter came up, Ted Hirsch was growing to hate the writing of fiction.

"Ted."

Ted shook his head clear of preoccupations and turned on his side to see his wife standing over him, one hand over the mouthpiece of the receiver.

"It's Diana," Clara said.

Ted didn't think he knew a Diana. "Who?"

"Diana Stewart. Connie's sister."

Ted took the receiver. "What does she want?"

Clara gave Ted a look.

Ted wasn't sure in what tone to greet Diana Stewart. He had had little practice. They weren't enemies, but they certainly weren't friends, even if they were related —and Ted wasn't even sure if they *were* related. It was just that Diana and Charles Stewart were very rich and that Ted and Clara Hirsch weren't very rich, at all.

"Hello, Diana? What's up?"

Waine Ryan had been saying goodnight to Bonnie Niles at the door of Winsome Johnny's, her restaurant on Hudson Street in Greenwich Village, when the bartender called to him that he was wanted on the telephone.

Bonnie had rolled her eyes. "Lawyers. Can't you even go out on a Sunday night without telling your service where you are?"

"A client might need me."

"That's what I mean."

Waine had laughed and kissed Bonnie's freckled

forehead and pushed a strand of red hair up off her forehead. "Thanks for the dinner."

"Don't take it personally. We serve it to any customer who orders it."

"Why are you so feisty?" Waine said.

Bonnie looked at her reflection in the mirror behind the bar and saw a good-looking young woman with long, long red hair, high breasts, long dancer's legs. She squinted and the woman got older, the hair lost its gleam, the breasts sagged, the legs got bowed. "Because you're going home alone."

"I have some work to do."

Bonnie looked at Waine's reflection and saw a tall, trim man in his early forties with just enough gray in his brown wavy hair, a handsome face, a broad chest, a flat stomach and strong thighs. She squinted and the man stayed the same. "You can say that you want to be alone."

"I want to be alone. I also should get this phone call."

"It better not be a woman."

"I have women clients. You're one, remember?"

"Umm . . . You've been divorced for two years, Waine. Isn't that alone enough?"

"I was married for eight years."

Bonnie gaped. "So you're going to be alone for six more years?"

Waine laughed. "No. But for a while longer."

"And what am I supposed to do in the meantime?"

"I'm asking for your understanding, Bonnie. If you don't understand, then you'll do something about it."

"Find another man?" She thrust out her chin aggressively.

Waine sighed.

"You think I can't, don't you?" Bonnie Niles said. She poked a finger at her chest to punctuate the pronouns. "I'm not as young as I used to be, but I'm a good catch, Waine. I'm beautiful. I'm sexy. I'm bright.

I'm witty. I'm desirable. I own a very successful restaurant. *Own* it, not just work in it. So don't blow it." *Please, because I'm getting old.*

Waine put his arms around her and held her tightly.

"Get the phone," Bonnie said at last.

Waine kissed her mouth.

"I'm just being feisty."

"You are that." Waine went to the bar and took the phone from the bartender. "Waine Ryan."

"Waine, it's Clara Hirsch."

Chapter 3

~~~~~~~~~~~~

Over espresso and anisette, Leeds was telling Francesca about one of his adventures—something about hunting sharks with scuba gear in the Bahamas. Or had he finished that tale, and moved on to something else?

Francesca suddenly felt very sad. After a moment, she identified her sadness as homesickness. That surprised her, for she wasn't sure where home was, these days. It wasn't here, for this was Leeds's apartment. She had spent a fair amount of time here in the first flush of their romance, but now she found it cold, a home without any heart. How could I have been so taken in by Leeds? she wondered.

Francesca's nostalgia wasn't for her mother's townhouse on West Tenth Street, either, although whenever Francesca referred to it, she called it *home*. It was home inasmuch as it had been where she had lived from two days after her birth until, at sixteen, she moved into a dormitory room at Barnard College. To be sure, while living in the townhouse, Francesca had spent a good deal of time away from it. There had been summers at her parents' home on Shelter Island, and summers that had been divided between Shelter Island and visits to the summer homes of the parents of Francesca's close friends—in Maine, on Martha's Vineyard, on Fire Island, on Cape Cod, on the Outer Banks of North Carolina. And there had been the summer, when Francesca was fourteen, when she had spent six weeks as an exchange student in Florence, Italy—a summer that had impelled her toward her first full-fledged ambition—to be a student of the history of art. And even during the school year, the townhouse had been less a home than a haven—a resting place in the rush of Francesca's daily round, a changing room where she slipped in and out of the assorted costumes of her busy, activity-filled life.

Ironically, the townhouse had become indisputably home for Francesca shortly after she had left it to move into her dormitory room—a move that she had imagined to be a prelude to her leaving home more or less for good. It had happened abruptly—on November 22, 1963, a day that seared itself into history as the day of President John F. Kennedy's assassination, but that was also the day of the death of Francesca's father, Dr. Noel Hayward. On the morning of the following day, Francesca moved out of the dormitory and back into the townhouse. She didn't, strictly speaking, move back into her old room, although she did sleep there, on the narrow bed that was hovered over by reproductions of paintings by Francesca's favorite artists— Verrocchio, Constable, Winslow Homer, Paul Klee, Andrew Wyeth—and, above all, John Singer Sargent. But the bed was to her, very suddenly, a child's bed, and her interest in painting and painters a childish thing. So she spent most of her time in her father's study, reading medical textbooks and journals, beginning to put into action the resolve that came to her nearly simultaneously with the news of her father's death—the determination to be a doctor.

Francesca lived in the townhouse with her mother for two more years. Some of her friends thought she was noble to stick by her mother in a time of adversity; others thought she was morbid—hanging around in her father's study, reading her father's books; still others thought she was in danger of regressing to a state of dependence on her mother (and the ghost of her father) that moving uptown to Barnard had begun to put an end to.

But Francesca didn't feel noble; her mother was tough, and though she was happy to have Francesca around, she would have been just as happy had Francesca decided to continue living in the dormitory. Nor did she feel morbid; her father's study and his books were living things to her, traces of her father's energy, not his end. And most of all, she did not feel she was regressing; on the contrary, she felt that in taking on a share of the responsibility for running the house, she was taking a step toward true adulthood that living in the dormitory would only have delayed.

On gaining admission to New York Hospital-Cornell Medical Center in a program that enabled her to take her fourth year of college as her first year of medical school, she had got an apartment on East Seventieth Street, just a few yards from the hospital. With her schedule, it was impossible to make the long trip to Greenwich Village. And now, sitting on Leeds's sofa, being washed over by Leeds's words, Francesca realized that it was that tiny apartment she missed. Never mind its miniature living room with a miniature kitchen at one end, its bathroom barely big enough to dry off in after taking a shower (taking a bath in the tiny tub was out of the question), its view of a sickly tree in the cement patio surrounded by other, taller buildings that blocked the sun except for an hour or so in the middle of summer—when having the sun blocked would have been welcome.

Whenever anyone asked Francesca why she kept the tiny apartment—given that she spent so little time there—she would say that she liked to have a place to get away from it all. But in her heart of hearts, she knew that the apartment, with her books and records and favorite knickknacks, was *it all*—was her. And she knew that being away from it meant she was turning her back on the things that were important to her, that were her essence.

Francesca suddenly realized that Leeds had stopped talking. He was looking at her in consternation. None of his usual ploys had worked tonight, so he was trying a cold silence on her. Meeting his silence with her own, Francesca got up and removed from her bag the remote device that enabled her to collect messages that had accumulated on the telephone answering machine in the tiny apartment. She went to the phone and dialed her number and listened to her recorded voice. She pushed the buttons on the remote device that rewound the tape and played back the messages. There was a message from her mother, wondering whether Francesca would be coming out to Shelter Island the next weekend; there was a message from Sarah Stein, Francesca's oldest friend, saying she would be in town from Princeton on Wednesday and wanted to have lunch; there was a message from Barbara Harriman, the charge nurse on the eighth floor of the Dwyer Pavilion of Lexington Hospital. She said she would call the number Francesca had left on her message and would try to reach her through her paging beeper. There was another message from Barbara Harriman; she said she had tried the number Francesca had left and had got an answering machine; she said she had tried the beeper several times, but had not got a callback.

Leeds was standing, backing away from the sofa toward the door to the foyer, as if to block her escape—or, perhaps, to escape himself.

"You turned my beeper off." Her stone-cold voice hid the red-hot anger she was feeling.

"W-What?"

"I haven't got time to tell you what I think of you. I haven't got time to find out how you could be so selfish as to do something that could jeopardize someone's life."

"I don't know what you're talking about, Francesca. You must've turned it off." Leeds ran his fingers through his hair, desperately.

"I never turn it off."

Leeds teetered for a moment, then went over the edge. "Don't I know *that?* How many times has that damn thing gone off when we were trying to have a little peace and quiet? In a restaurant. In the movies. At the theater. In the car on the way to the country. 'Let me out, Leeds. I have to go back. You go ahead without me. You stay and watch the movie. You finish your dinner.' What if we had been in bed just now, Francesca? Would you have told me to finish making love without you, too? Francesca?"

But she was gone, out the door and down the hall, not even waiting for the elevator, but taking the stairs.

Eva James was floating through space. Around her streamed bands of bright colors—red, yellow, orange. She didn't know which way was up, nor whether she was falling or traveling forward, propelled by she knew not what sort of force. She had thought at first that this space was the space of *Star Wars* or *Battlestar Galactica* —outer space; she had expected to see droids, or maybe the *Millenium Falcon* swooping past. But this space wasn't cold, the way Eva imagined outer space to be cold—the way the playground in Central Park just off Central Park West was cold in February, say—so cold you put your arms around the chains of the swing so you could keep your hands in your pockets, so cold you forgot to breathe.

This space was warm, like . . . Well, Eva didn't know like what. It wasn't warm like a bath, because even in the hottest of baths you could feel something cold—the side of the tub above the waterline, the handles of the faucets, the draft from chinks in the window. It wasn't warm like the beach near their summer house on Shelter Island, either; the beach was never really warm, it was either cool or very, very hot.

It wasn't warm like a sweater, either, because sweaters were itchy. It was a little bit like the warm she felt when she was with Becky Morgan—a warm that had nothing to do with what the weather was like or what she was wearing—a warm that was centered inside her, somewhere around the indentation between her ribs just above her belly. But it wasn't really warm like that, either, for that warm made her giddy—so much so that sometimes she had to sit down if she was standing up, or stand up if she was sitting down. This warm was . . . Well, Eva didn't know.

"Heaven help us," Tim Ward said when he saw Eva James. He had been told the ambulance was bringing in an auto accident victim and had assumed it would be an adult. It hurt him to see children hurt, made him almost squeamish. A hurt child affected him more than anything he had seen in Vietnam—and he had seen it all there.

Tracy O'Dwyer and Susan Rice, two of the nurses on Tim's trauma team, moved the girl from the ambulance stretcher to the steel table in the center of the room. Tim began to examine the little girl, who whimpered weakly under his touch. At the sound, he took his hands away from her and looked up.

Two med students, a man and a woman, watched from the periphery. The woman had red hair so brilliant it was almost scarlet. She had green eyes. Tim Ward liked that she was watching. He liked her eyes and her hair. He wondered what else there was to like beneath the mask and gown.

Tim knew he was trying to soften the difficulty of the task at hand and told himself not to wonder about the scarlet-haired med student. Besides, it hadn't been his day with the ladies. Earlier, he had tried for the umpteenth time to make a date with Barbara Harriman, the charge nurse on Eight Dwyer, the ophthalmalogy ward where his friend Francesca Hayward was a resident. And Nurse Harriman had told him for the umpteenth time that she wouldn't go out with him.

Peter Davis, the other trauma surgeon, glanced over Tim's shoulder. "I don't like the looks of those eyes," he said to Tim.

"No. Me either. Tracy, get on the phone to Eight Dwyer. See if Ms. Harriman can locate Dr. Hayward. We're going to need her."

Tracy nodded and moved quickly to the phone.

Tim Ward had nothing but admiration for Francesca Hayward. They had met in medical school. Tim had been much older than the other members of his class, thanks to his having done three tours of duty as a medic in Vietnam. Despite being one of the youngest women in the class, Francesca possessed a seriousness that made her seem closer to his age than to that of the rest of their classmates. They became fast friends, because somehow Francesca understood what had happened to him in Vietnam, understood why he had re-enlisted, instead of coming home after his first tour of duty.

He had only gone to Vietnam because he had been drafted. He had been drafted because he flunked out of college. He had flunked out of college because he had spent most of his time pursuing women—and enjoying the ones he caught. Ever since Vietnam, he had had less and less luck with women; he pursued them still, but rarely caught one. Tim couldn't understand it.

He hoped he wasn't paying the price for having been a good, obedient, enthusiastic soldier during an era when soldiering had fallen into disrepute. He hadn't been a killer in Vietnam, but a healer—a repairer of maimed and rent men. A medic by chance, Tim had discovered that medicine came as naturally to him as playing ball had when he was a kid, as chasing women had when he was older. All three were similar: All three required coordination between hand and eye; all three demanded advance planning while putting a premium on the ability to scrap the plans and improvise at a moment's notice; all three were physical—in the sense that you could talk all you wanted and study all you wanted, but in the end it was the doing that mattered.

Nowhere was that more true than in the Emergency Room. Tim Ward loved the Emergency Room, where the challenges came almost as quickly as they had in Vietnam—and were often as violently dramatic. His passion had earned him the nickname—Francesca had given it to him—"Emergency" Ward, a name that mixed equal parts of trepidation at his sometimes rough-and-ready technique with admiration for his undeniable skill.

"Are we getting anybody else?" Peter Davis asked.

"The police said no," Tracy O'Dwyer answered.

"What about the other car?" Peter felt under Child James's arms. "Air blisters."

To Scarlet and her companion, Tim said, "That means punctured lungs."

"There wasn't any," Tracy said. "Car skidded. Hit a girder. On the Triborough Bridge."

"Could've been worse," Peter said. "Rainy Sunday night after a nice day. Lots of people coming home from the beach, from picnics, ball games. Blood pressure, Susan?"

"Sixty."

"That means internal bleeding," Tim told Scarlet.

The male med student edged forward a little, as if worried that Tim would think he wasn't paying attention.

"Just lucky, I guess," Susan Rice said.

"Who?" Peter asked.

Susan shrugged. "Lucky they hit the bridge, not a car full of people is what I meant."

Tim continued his examination in silence. He wanted to say something on the subject of luck, but what he had to say was too complicated for the Emergency Room, where actions were streamlined, treatments the simplest and most efficacious. When you were saving lives, you didn't worry about the finer points. You just did what had to be done.

Still, in Vietnam, the soldiers who got flesh wounds considered themselves lucky—lucky to be wounded, but not seriously wounded. Even some of the seriously wounded considered themselves lucky—lucky not to be dead. They all considered themselves luckier than the unwounded, for being wounded meant going home. To Tim Ward, it had never seemed to be a matter of luck at all; it had been a matter of fallibility. The human body was resilient; the human mind clever. Problems arose when one let the fingers of one's mind slip from the fine tuning of the body's controls. That was what had happened here—not to Child James, of course, but to her father—if that's who he was, if he had been driving the car. Whoever had been driving the car, whatever his or her relationship to Child James, he or she had let Child James down. Luck had had nothing to do with it.

"The police report said this kid's father was Conrad James," Susan Rice said. "Isn't that the writer?"

Tim Ward stood back to let the anesthesiologist slip a plastic tube into Child James's windpipe. He sensed that Scarlet gagged behind her mask; he saw tears in her eyes. "She'll be all right," he said. "We're on top of it."

"I think I read one of his books once," Karen Ludwig said.

Peter Davis probed with a needle in Child James's groin. "How was it?"

"Okay, I guess. I don't really remember. I think I read it at the beach."

"I'm reading *Princess Daisy*," Tracy O'Dwyer said. "It's very long."

"Got it," Peter Davis said, meaning the saphenous vein. The syringe filled with blood. When it was full,

Peter handed it to a lab technician, who hurried away with it, one arm curled protectively over it, like a fullback slanting off-tackle.

Tim Ward inserted a pressure sensor in Child James's right wrist. He felt good; they *were* on top of it; the chitchat was a sign of that. It meant there was no panic, no uncertainty.

"Blood pressure, Tracy?"

"Eighty-five."

"Time for a tap," Tim Ward said.

Below Child James's navel, Peter Davis made a small incision and inserted a plastic tube. Susan Rice held up a bottle of clear saline solution; when it had emptied into Child James's abdomen, she placed it on the floor.

"The liquid will drain back into the bottle," Tim Ward told Scarlet. "If there's internal bleeding, which we suspect because her blood pressure hasn't gone up even though she's getting blood and plasma, then the liquid will come back red."

"Where's the cop who was in the ambulance?" Peter Davis asked.

"In the hall."

"See if they have an ID yet. We're going to need permission to cut her open."

Tim Ward bent over Child James's face; she looked as though she'd gone fifteen rounds with the heavyweight champion. "Where the hell is Dr. Hayward?"

"Right here, Tim." Francesca Hayward's face looked more than usually serious.

At times like this, there was no time. Francesca might have been working for hours or days or weeks. But there was no tiredness, either; if anything, she got stronger as she worked, for the longer she worked the better she understood the peculiarities of the case in question, and was able to move less and less tentatively and more and more aggressively and surely, until she was, as Tim Ward would have put it, on top of it. The tiredness would come later, when it was over.

How beautiful this little girl is, Francesca thought—
for she could see beyond and beneath Eva's wounds to
the face that had been Eva's, and would be again, in
time. And how much life there is in her—so much that
Death had been unable to wring it out of her, despite a
rather extraordinary effort.

This little girl is a survivor, Francesca thought, as she
worked steadily and carefully. She will be bereft when
she learns that her parents are dead, but she won't curl
up into a helpless ball; she'll strike out at the pain and
the sorrow, making room for herself to get on with the
business of living. Francesca didn't know why she was
so sure of that, but sure of it she was.

Francesca bristled when she thought about how
selfish Leeds had been. Of course, there were other
doctors who could have cared for Eva James; they
would have been called had the hospital not been able
to reach Francesca; they would have cared for Eva
well. But Francesca sensed that she was supposed to be
there. She couldn't explain the sense, but she was sure
of it. She didn't think it had anything to do with her
having known the Jameses. The hospital couldn't have
known they had a house on Shelter Island near her
mother's. Damn Leeds. How close she had come to not
being there.

Perhaps, Francesca thought, her certainty about Eva
James's ability to get on with the business of living and
about the fact that she was meant to be the doctor who
would care for Eva James's eyes was born of her
knowledge of what it was like to lose a parent swiftly,
without warning. However, she thought, she knew
nothing about what it was like to lose both parents that
way.

Maybe it was something else, Francesca thought.
Femininity, certainly—femaleness, the condition of
being a woman—had something to do with it. Francesca had always found it easier to care for women—
children or adults—than to care for men; she could
imagine herself inside the skins of women, feel some-

thing of what they were feeling, in a way that she never could with men.

But it's more than that, Francesca thought. The reason I am meant to take care of this child—

A radiologist asked Francesca a question and she lost her train of thought.

Stepping back from the operating table some time later—she thought it was a few minutes, but it was nearly an hour—letting a chest specialist have his turn, Francesca realized that *child* was the key word. Eva James was a *child* whom Francesca was meant to care for.

Interesting, Francesca thought. Very, very interesting.

Chapter 4

~~~~~~~~~~~~~~

Someone was stealing Francesca's shoes from right off her feet.

Things were always being stolen around the hospital, from the patients and from the staff. The joke was that you could leave a boa constrictor out in the open and someone would steal it. The patients suspected the staff of doing the stealing; the staff suspected the patients, and one another. Only very occasionally was someone caught redhanded, or with the stolen goods; the breakdown was about half staff and half patients, but the sample was too small to be really meaningful.

They were her only comfortable shoes, a pair of low-heeled spectator pumps she kept in her office and wore around the hospital. She couldn't let them be stolen—not from right off her feet.

Francesca felt cold. Maybe she wasn't in the hospital. Maybe she was on a bench in Central Park, in which case she supposed she deserved to have her shoes stolen.

No. Whatever she was lying on was softer than a
park bench, and the traffic she could hear was muted by
walls. There was another hum, closer than the hum of
traffic; after a while, she identified it as the hum of an
air conditioner, which probably accounted for the cold.

She wanted those shoes. She struggled up toward the
surface of sleep; it was a long, long haul and she started
to sink back, deeper and deeper. She wanted those
shoes. She made a big effort, bolting for the surface,
risking the deep sleeper's version of the bends. "*You?*"

Tim Ward had a shoe in each hand, like a salesman.
"I think you were having a bad dream."

"What're you doing with my shoes?"

Tim laughed. "Just trying to make you comfortable."

Francesca hugged herself. She discovered that she
was wearing a blue blazer over her shoulders. "Where
did this come from?"

"It's mine. You looked cold."

"I am cold. Where am I?"

He laughed. "You body is in the staff lounge. Your
mind appears to be elsewhere. Back at that party,
maybe."

"What party?"

"Isn't that a party dress?"

Francesca looked down at her safari print. "God, am
I still wearing this?"

"It's a nice dress."

"It's my favorite." Francesca remembered: she had
spent the night doing bloody chores, helping to bring an
eight-year-old girl back from the brink of death. She
swung her feet off the couch. The floor was cold. "Can
I have my shoes, please?"

Tim placed her shoes on the floor and backed away,
bowing extravagantly. "Your shoes, your highness.
How about some breakfast?"

"Breakfast?"

Tim laughed. "Wake up, Francesca."

"I'm trying."

"There's a place on Madison that makes terrific omelets."

"What time is it? I'm on duty at eight."

"It's quarter to seven."

"Damn!"

"That's plenty of time."

"I mean, damn, I didn't get much sleep."

Tim laughed. "You look terrific."

Francesca blushed. Tim's compliments always affected her that way. Even though they had never been more than friends, Francesca sometimes felt that Tim wanted to be something more to her. "You can't have slept much, either."

"It's okay. I'm off today. Are you all right?"

She was all *right*, but not *all* right. She remembered. "Oh."

"What?"

"I had a fight with Leeds. Except I didn't really get to have it; I had to get over here."

"That explains the dress."

"What does?"

"You were with Leeds."

"Yes."

"That explains why you didn't answer your page."

"It does?"

"Doesn't it?"

Francesca laughed. "I'm still asleep."

"How about breakfast?"

". . . omelets?"

"Whatever. Pancakes. The usual."

"What I'd really like is a sauna and a shower. Then an omelet."

"There's time."

"The women's sauna is broken. Or it was yesterday."

"Use the men's. I'll stand guard. There won't be anybody there at this hour."

"Not even Clavin?"

Tim laughed. Dr. Vincent Clavin, the assistant chief of staff, was the man everybody loved to hate. Among other things, they hated him for his ubiquity; he seemed to live at the hospital. It was hard to go anywhere or do anything at any time of the day or night without running into Clavin.

"Tim?" Francesca said.

"Yes?"

"What would you do if a woman you were going with turned off your beeper?"

Tim laughed. "I assume you mean that literally, not figuratively."

"Literally. Leeds turned off my beeper. That's why I didn't answer the page. He thinks I work too much."

"You do."

"So do you. So do we all. It's the nature of the beast. How do you manage your emotional life?"

"Very easily. I don't have one."

"Tim."

Tim shrugged. "As the Arabs say, it isn't written."

"I thought you had a thing for Barbara Harriman."

"Oh, I do. It takes two things to make a thing. She won't give me the time of day."

"You're too nice a man for that, Tim. How about if I put in a good word for you?"

"Well, if you want to . . ." Tim scuffed at the floor with a shoe, not out of embarrassment, but out of hesitation.

"What?" Francesca said.

Tim laughed.

"I know that boyish posture," Francesca said. "It means you have some brotherly advice to give me."

"Um . . ."

"What, Tim? For God's sake."

"Just . . . don't be too hard on Leeds. It's tough to be in love with someone who's in love with her career."

Francesca grunted.

"What does that mean?" Tim said.

"I thought you were going to say something else. I

thought you were going to say I should forget about Leeds."

"Remember, you said that, not me. So which is it going to be? Breakfast or sauna?" Tim changed the subject, not wanting to say anything he would regret. Leeds Cavanaugh was not his kind of person and he never did understand what Francesca saw in him.

Francesca bent over, slipped on her shoes, stood up, sloughed off Tim's blazer, handed it to him, and combed her hair with her fingers. "Breakfast."

The wall phone rang.

Francesca groaned. "It's always dangerous to mention that you're going to eat. Someone hears you and calls up."

Tim Ward answered the phone, listened, then covered the mouthpiece with his hand. "For you."

"Naturally."

"It's Leeds."

"Oh, hell."

"You should talk to him, Francesca."

"I know. I know. Can we go to breakfast another time?"

"Absolutely."

Francesca came to Tim and kissed his cheek. "You're a nice man, Tim."

"Umm." Tim went out the door and down the hall and out of the hospital. He thought he'd walk through Central Park to his apartment on West Eighty-sixth Street. Waiting to cross Fifth Avenue, he saw Barbara Harriman getting out of a taxi. The low morning sun put a touch of red in her blond hair.

Leeds was wearing a white Merino crew-neck sweater, white duck bellbottom pants and Sperry Topsiders with no socks. "I've decided to go sailing for a few days."

"I can see that," Francesca said.

"I'd like you to come with me. We could go up to Newport."

"I have to work."

"Take some time off."

"I want to work. There's an interesting case. Do you remember the Jameses, who have a house near mother's on Shelter Island?"

"Francesca, I want to talk about us."

"Well, I'm part of us, and I'm talking about me, so you can listen."

She said it sharply and Leeds looked worriedly around the dining room of the Pierre, where they were having breakfast. Francesca had wanted to go to the coffee shop Tim Ward had recommended on Madison Avenue, but Leeds had said he was depressed enough without going to a greasy spoon.

"Who said it was a greasy spoon?" Francesca had said.

"I don't have any money," Leeds had said. "I have to go some place where they'll take plastic." Leeds never carried money, which was touched by too many fingers for his taste.

"I'm waiting," Leeds said.

"I'm too tired to talk," Francesca said. "I was up all night."

"Look, the thing with the beeper? That was an accident. I moved your bag off the bed and I must have turned it off accidentally. I'm really sorry."

"Sure."

"I *am.*"

"Oh, I know you're sorry. But it was no accident. It's impossible to turn that thing off accidentally. It's designed that way."

Leeds hung his head.

"It's probably just as well," Francesca said. "We were going along in a rut. Some changes are necessary."

Leeds perked up, and took her hand. "Marry me."

Francesca slid her hand free, and used it to pour more coffee. "I wasn't thinking along those lines. I was thinking more about seeing less of each other—a lot less."

"But why?"

"I don't know why. But the fact that I've been thinking about it is good enough reason for me."

"You were just making the point that you were part of us," Leeds said. "Well, I'm part of us, too, and I think I deserve more explanation than just that you've been 'thinking' about seeing less of each other. And what does that mean, anyway? It's not as though we see each other every day. You're always working."

"Which is a problem for you, isn't it?" Francesca said. "You'd rather that I didn't work at all, wouldn't you?"

Leeds took her hand again, and tried poignancy. "Francesca, I want to have your children."

She thought about that for a moment, and thought that the man was supposed to say that he wanted the woman to have his children, but she didn't quibble. "I'm not ready for children."

"Francesca, you're getting to be the age where—"

"And besides," she interrupted, "why does having children mean I wouldn't work?"

Leeds let go of her hand and sat back in his chair. "I think it's important for me to be a father. I think it would help me work out some of the problems I have."

"Such as?"

He waved a hand, as if to say they weren't *big* problems.

"Such as that you're selfish, vain, egotistical, inconsiderate and unemotional?"

Leeds looked pained. "If that's the way you feel . . ."

"Leeds, last night wasn't the first time you've done something that indicated you thought my work got in the way of our relationship. I have no reason to think it'll be the last time—"

"I told you I was sorry."

"Why don't you just face up to the fact that I'm not the kind of woman you need?" Francesca said. "You need someone who's devoted to you, who'll spend all her time with you, who'll travel with you on your photographic safaris, who'll . . . have your children, who'll cook for you—"

"I can cook," Leeds said. "I cook all the time."

"I know you do. And you cook the way you do everything else—to be in control. When you make love, you want me to know that you're a gourmet lovemaker. When you cook, you want me to know that you're a gourmet cook. You never just let me have a good time—fool around, be playful. And you never just let me eat—eat what I want, when I want, how I want. It's always, 'Take a bite of this and a sip of that, then dip this in this and put it in your mouth for thirty seconds before swallowing it, then take a sip of this, but not out of this glass, out of *this* glass that's been chilling in the refrigerator for six weeks.' It's not what I want, Leeds. I feel stifled and angry all the time. Lately, I'm always annoyed with you. It's no good."

There were a few more customers, now, and some of them had probably heard most of what she said. Leeds looked around and blushed beneath his tan. "Look, you're tired. Why don't I take you home so you can get some sleep?"

"I'm due back at the hospital at eight. And when I do go home, it's going to be to my apartment."

"Not . . .?"

"Yes. Oh, I know it's tiny and dark and doesn't have a doorman, but it's the place I most feel like being right now." Francesca took some bills from her wallet and put them on the table. "Good-bye, Leeds. It was fun for a while, but not anymore."

"I'll take care of it," Leeds said, referring to the check.

Francesca shook her head. Leeds hadn't heard a word she said. She put the salt shaker on top of the bills, got up and walked out.

Leeds didn't see her go. He was looking around for a waiter, holding his credit card aloft.

Out on the street, looking for a cab, Francesca noticed her reflection in the gleaming finish of Leeds's Corniche. It looked like a figure in a funhouse mirror—distorted, but not frighteningly so. Just enough to make her smile.

Chapter 5

Back at the hospital, Francesca went to her office and got some clothes she kept there for emergencies. She showered in the staff washroom and put on the clean things—a simple dark green skirt and a fitted mint-green silk shirt. She was amazed at how clean and refreshed she felt. She'd worked most of the night in surgery, had a few restless hours sleep in the staff lounge, and said good-bye to Leeds over a breakfast she had never got to eat. By all rights, she ought to be tired, hungry and out of sorts, but she felt better than she had in several weeks—more alive, more sure of herself, more excited about her work, especially about the Eva James case.

There had been a message for her from Dr. Finch, the chief of staff, asking her to confer with a lawyer who was working on Eva's case. Probably something about insurance. She would have just enough time for a little paperwork before that meeting. Francesca slipped a white lab coat over her skirt and blouse and set off for the main administration office just off the lobby.

While checking through patients' files, she noticed three nurses twittering over a man who had just asked directions. She heard one of them sigh deeply and utter a long "Gorgeous." Francesca glanced in the man's direction, and caught a glimpse of his trim body and wavy brown hair as he retreated down the hall. She liked the way he walked, with strong and confident steps. If his face is anything like the back of him, that nurse was exactly right in her description. I must be okay, she said to herself, if I'm already looking over other men. Francesca turned back to the file she was reading, a small smile on her lips and in her eyes.

Waine Ryan didn't notice the twittering nurses or the appraising glance of the beautiful black-haired doctor, although at other times he would have been flattered by the attention. But he wasn't the least bit happy to be in a hospital. He hated hospitals, and had from the age of seven, when his mother had spent a year in St. Vincent's Hospital while an army of doctors tried to figure out what was wrong with her. He remembered everything as if it were yesterday—the smells, the sounds, the sight of his mother growing smaller and weaker every day, while the array of tubes pumping fluids in and out of her grew larger; the silences in the apartment, broken only by the clink of ice in his father's glass, or by the sound of more bourbon being poured; the terror of waking to find his father passed out on the kitchen floor or in the hallway by the bathroom—once, on the fire escape, where he had dragged himself to get some air; the awful fear in the pit of his stomach each time he went to the hospital after school that his mother would no longer be there; the grip of the doctor's arms around his chest, restraining his tantrum the day he arrived to find that she had died. He remembered everything as if it had happened only moments before, not even yesterday.

Waine followed the nurses' directions to the office of Dr. Wilson Finch, Lexington Hospital's chief of staff.

While a secretary went to announce him, he went to a window and looked out. The office was on a high floor and had a panoramic view to the east, out across the Upper East Side and Harlem to the East River, the Triborough Bridge, Queens and the Bronx.

The Triborough Bridge: The scene of the accident that killed Conrad and Edith James and sent their daughter, Eva, to this hospital—the accident that had made Waine Ryan the attorney of Ted and Clara Hirsch and that had brought him to this hospital.

The night before, after talking to Clara Hirsch on the telephone at the bar of Bonnie Niles's restaurant, Waine had walked down Charles Street toward his apartment on West Fourth Street. As he had passed the Sixth Precinct station house, he had smiled at the memory of the days when he had always crossed the street when passing the station house; he and the cops had been enemies in those days, and he hadn't liked to use their sidewalk, nor did they like him using it.

In those days, the station house had been on the north side of the street, in a sturdy old building that was now being converted, as were so many old buildings in Greenwich Village, into an apartment house. A sign outside the building listed astronomical rents. Waine had wondered who could afford those rents; but every time a renovation was completed, it was full in no time. He had wondered if his law practice, which was devoted to providing inexpensive legal service for the poor, would one day run out of poor to counsel.

Nowadays, the station house was on the south side of the street, in a building that had been erected in the late sixties. The main entrance was actually on Tenth Street and the rear of the building, on Charles Street, was a service area for white tops and a parking place for the cars of the patrolmen and detectives on duty. As Waine had neared the driveway, a car had pulled out, a battered old Buick.

Waine hadn't slowed down. He wasn't going to let the car make him wait while it pulled out. His ex-wife,

Aura, would have called it a manifestation of his "thing" about cars.

"It's not a thing about cars," Waine would say. "It's a thing on behalf of pedestrians. Pedestrians have the right of way. This city's going to suffocate, in every sense, if it doesn't do something about keeping cars out of midtown. As long as it lets cars in, they have to obey the laws."

Aura would sigh expressively through her nose. *She* had a thing about pedestrians—or rather, the word pedestrian: She never heard it as just a noun—*a person traveling on foot;* she heard it, as well, as an adjective—*commonplace, undistinguished, ordinary.* Commonplace, undistinguished, ordinary things were anathema to Aura. And being a pedestrian was one of the most pedestrian things Aura could think of; she preferred to drive—preferred, above all, to be driven. That Waine didn't drive—wouldn't drive—had been a major contribution to the failure of their marriage. Not the only contribution, however.

"I don't understand you," Aura said once. "All this fuss about who has the right of way. I know you're a lawyer, but you *were* a criminal."

Waine had got a foot and a leg into the driveway before the Buick got completely straightened out. The driver of the Buick had hit his horn.

Waine had stopped and turned to face the car, hands at his sides, like a gunfighter. The driver hit the horn again—but with a difference. He didn't give it another imperious blast; he hit it playfully—da da da dada . . . da da. Shave and a haircut . . . two bits.

"You stupid punk," the driver had yelled out the window, with a lilt in his voice.

Waine had shaded his eyes against the glaring headlights. "Phil?"

Phil Archer got out of the Buick and came at Waine like a boxer, his left up and probing, his right making small, dangerous circles.

Waine got in the same stance and they circled one

another warily, then broke down in laughter and embraced.

"You're not back in this precinct?" Waine said.

"Nah, still in Queens. Just filling in here. They got three guys in the hospital." Archer opened his suit coat and tucked his shirt in. In a moment, it would be out; it was always that way with his shirt tails.

"And you haven't called me, you old son of a gun?" Waine said.

"Today's my first day. I'm supposed to be on vacation, but I need the dough."

"That's right. You said you were going to the Jersey shore."

"Believe me, this is better," Archer said. "Anything's better than seeing Florence in a bathing suit."

Waine laughed and feigned a jab at Archer's pot belly. "I think it's you who doesn't want to be seen in a bathing suit."

Archer shrugged. "Could be. The two of us in bathing suits are enough to empty a beach."

Waine remembered dozens, hundreds, maybe even a thousand conversations like this—standing with Archer on sidewalks around the Village, sitting on stoops, leaning against parked cars, sitting on park benches, strolling out on the Hudson River piers. Could those conversations have been twenty years ago? It didn't seem possible.

Twenty years ago, Waine Ryan *had* been a criminal—of the pesky, urban punk variety. He had been the head of the Hawks, a gang of Irish Catholic teenagers who roamed the Village stealing hubcaps, and occasionally a car in which they would joyride for a night before abandoning it; shoplifting from Italian and Jewish merchants. They would break a window here, overturn a trash can there, deface a building or toss a cherry bomb under a busful of tourists. Nothing major, measured individually, but taken cumulatively a rampage of considerable scope and duration, aimed at taking out on the world an anger that each and every Hawk carried inside him, thanks to home lives that sapped their spirits and battered their bodies.

Phil Archer changed all that—for Waine Ryan, at any rate. Archer walked a beat in the Sixth Precinct in those days. One summer evening, he walked up to where Waine sat on a bench in Abingdon Square, waiting for the evening gathering of the Hawks, lifted him to his feet by the collar of his black leather jacket, got a grip on the seat of his pants with his other hand, and quickmarched him across Bleecker Street into a restaurant, past a roomful of startled diners and into a back room. He sat Waine in a chair, pulled the jacket down over the back of the chair, pinning Waine's arms, and told him he was throwing his life away and was going to wind up in the slammer for a good long time if he didn't get his ass in gear. Archer repeated the message in a number of variations for more than an hour, punctuating it now and then with slaps across the face and cuffs on the back of the head.

A good many more followup lectures were necessary, but Archer kept after Waine, who, it turned out, reminded Archer of his son, who had been killed in Korea. And if Waine didn't exactly leap to the bait, he wasn't deaf to the wisdom of Archer's counsel, either. The short of it was that Waine got a job at a dry cleaning plant, went to night school to make up the high school credits he was lacking, enrolled at Brooklyn College, studied his way onto the Dean's List, was the salutatorian of his graduating class, went to Harvard Law School on a full scholarship, made Law Review, was courted by all the big New York firms, chose Whitesides, Kent, Ross and Keplow, married the senior partner's daughter and lived in baronial splendor in Rye, New York. It can be put that briefly because to Waine it had seemed to happen just that quickly—all but the last two years at Whitesides, Kent, which coincided with the last two years of marriage to Aura

Whitesides; each of those years had seemed centuries long—before Waine saw the light for the second time in his life.

Archer tucked in his shirt. "Still divorced?"

"Still divorced."

"Still doing nickle and dime cases?"

Waine leaned back a little. "What's this about, Phil?"

Archer waved a big hand. "I don't know. I worry about you sometimes."

"Worry how?"

"I don't know. I guess I worry you're trying to punish yourself, or something. I mean, you were living first class and now you're living third class, and I don't really understand it."

"If you mean because I help out ordinary clients, well, I do it because I'm a good lawyer and ordinary people need good lawyers as much as General Electric and IBM. More. If you mean because I moved back to the old neighborhood, well, my father died, the apartment was vacant, it's a nice apartment, it made sense. If you mean because I see Bonnie, well, Bonnie's a respectable businesswoman. People are fighting to get in to that restaurant."

"I don't know," Archer said.

"First class isn't the only way to travel, Phil. You get where you're going just as fast going third class, and maybe you see a little bit more of how the world works than you do sitting up in the front, getting your glass refilled with champagne every five minutes."

"I guess—" But Archer didn't say what he guessed, for he reminded himself that Waine *wasn't* his son, and that he couldn't demand of him, as he might have of a son, that he surpass his father. And besides, he reminded himself, Waine was doing all right for himself, if the number of times he got his name in the paper representing one of his underdogs was any indication. "Ah, what do I know?" He tucked in his shirt.

"You better know you're having dinner with me one night soon, before you go back to the wilds of Queens."

"Sounds good."

"I'll call you tomorrow. It was good to see you, Phil."

"You, too, Waine. Good thing I didn't run over you."

"This is a sidewalk," Waine said. "Pedestrians have the right of way."

Chapter 6

~~~~~~~~~~~~~~~

Looking out the window out over the cityscape, Waine Ryan wondered how people could live and work so high above the ground. When he had worked downtown, in a steel and glass tower on Broadway just north of Wall Street, he had sometimes been made dizzy by the height. It wasn't fear that induced the dizziness; it was a feeling that down on the street was where the real people were, and that he was in danger of losing touch with them if he stayed up so high. The house in Rye where he had lived with Aura had been only two stories high, but Waine had always thought of it as a penthouse atop a sort of horizontal skyscraper that stretched from Manhattan into the suburbs; again, the feeling he had always had was that the action was down on the ground floor.

"Mr. Ryan? I'm Dr.—" The small, white-haired, bespectacled man withdrew the hand he had extended, held it for a moment to his mouth, then offered it again. "I'm Dr. Finch. Excuse me, but you gave me a start. You're the very image of an old friend of mine. Or rather, you look very much as he did when he was your age. That is to say, quite handsome."

"And how does he look now?" Waine said. Finch's hand was tiny.

Finch put his hand to his mouth again. "I'm afraid he's dead."

"Ah. I'm sorry."

Finch wagged the hand back and forth. "It was a sailing accident. He remained the picture of health."

Finch ushered Waine into his comfortable office, furnished with an antique wooden desk and big easy chairs. There was a shelf of books behind the desk, inhabited not only by medical texts but by current fiction and non-fiction, by classics and by a good number of paperback mysteries and spy novels.

Finch motioned Waine to a seat, then went behind the desk and looked for a moment at his appointment calendar, as if to be sure he was giving his time to the right party. "Waine with an I. I questioned my secretary about that, but she insisted that was the way you had spelled it. I don't think I've ever seen that spelling. Is it a family surname?"

"It's short for Gawaine. My mother was a lover of Arthurian legend."

"So is my mother," said a woman at the door.

"Ah, Dr. Hayward, Dr. Hayward. Come in, come in." Finch nearly flew to greet the woman, flapping his arms and quivering happily.

Waine got up and turned to the woman, whom Finch brought to him like a prize. "Dr. Hayward, this is Mr. Waine Ryan. Mr. Ryan, Dr. Francesca Hayward."

Finch stepped in close, like a boxing referee, while the two of them shook hands, than backed toward the door of his office. "Take all the time you need. I'll be making my rounds. Have me paged when you're ready to leave, Mr. Ryan, and I'll say good-bye to you in the lobby." He pulled the door shut, grinning inexplicably.

Francesca stood with her hands jammed into the

pockets of her lab coat, looking at the rug between her shoes, reluctant to look up just yet at this man. It was the man she had seen in the hall a few minutes before. It was disconcerting enough that his wavy brown hair and dark brown eyes and olive skin and strong nose and mouth and brow went so well together; that his lean, long body fitted so well into, and was flattered so much by, his gray double-breasted suit, his blue cotton shirt, his dark red tie with tiny blue figures; that he wore beautiful shoes of soft brown leather. It was bad enough to be confronted with a man who looked like this so soon after resolving not to have anything to do with men for a while. What made it all worse was that he looked so much like her father had that he might have been his ghost.

Waine Ryan wasn't looking at Francesca, either. He was staring out the window. His discomfort was akin to hers; she was jogging his memory, too: She reminded him of Aura. Not physically, for she had black hair, Aura blond; her skin was white, Aura's always deeply tanned; she was tall, Aura petite. But she had, as it were, the same aura—a quality of having been created according to standards more exacting than those applied to the rest of us, an emanation of quality, of a fine nature given the best of nurturing. In short, she looked expensive.

Her eyes flicked up from the floor, his away from the window. They met, ricocheted, returned to their previous targets.

Finally:

"Excuse my surprise," Waine said, "I talked to Dr. Finch on the phone earlier, but you know how it is when you hear someone's name mentioned several times—'Dr. Hayward says . . .' 'Dr. Hayward feels . . .'—how you build up a picture of Dr. Hayward?"

"And you expected a man?"

"I'm just saying that somehow no pronouns ever got spoken—she, her. My misconception was allowed to grow." He smiled, but she didn't. He put it down to a humorlessness like Aura's.

Francesca thought about telling him that it was a common misconception—especially since senior staff like Dr. Finch had known her father well and tended to think of her, at times, less as his daughter than as his reincarnation. She didn't tell him; for some reason, she wanted him to feel that it was his mistake.

She sat behind Dr. Finch's desk, propping her foot on the handle of the bottom drawer. "You're interested in Eva James's condition, is that right?"

Waine nodded. From where he sat, he could see the inside of her thigh through the kneehold of the desk.

Francesca tipped her head back, as if projecting Eva James's chart onto the ceiling. "She's almost a textbook case of ocular trauma."

Waine noticed how deep was the depression at the base of her throat between the collarbones.

"To begin with, she has fractures of the orbital bones—the eye sockets. The worst is a dislocation of the right zygomatic bone and arch and a depression of the lateral canthus. That caused the cheekbone to collapse. In the left eye, the trauma caused a pressure build-up within the orbit that produced a blowout fracture of the orbital floor. The contents prolapsed into the maxillary sinus. Which is just a way of saying that when I first got a look at her, she didn't seem to have a left eye; it had slipped down inside her skull.

"All these things can be repaired; they sound worse than they are. But before they can, the shock has to be completely managed. The internal bleeding in her chest is still the top priority. I have to wait my turn. Meanwhile, we've done X-rays and laminography to determine if there are other fractures, particularly any that could endanger the brain. The radiologists are still working on those."

"So she's not blind, then?" Waine said.

"Oh, I haven't finished," Francesca said. "I've barely begun."

Waine fingered the knot of his tie. Francesca's recita-
tion was a mixture of matter-of-factness and enthusiasm. He knew he could sound that way himself,
at times, when confronted with a case that excited
him with its difficulties but that he knew he could
handle. He also appreciated that she was taking it by
stages.

Francesca went on: "She also has injuries to the eyes
themselves. There's abrasion of the right cornea and
the right iris—"

Waine held out a hand. "It's been a long time since
high school biology. I guess I'm not really sure what the
cornea is." He wondered why he'd put it so apologetically; he was usually frank about admitting what he
didn't know—it made him a good lawyer.

"The cornea is the clear membrane covering the
front of the eye. The iris is the colored portion. As I
was saying, the right iris is very slightly torn away from
the sclera—the white of the eye. This caused bleeding
into the anterior chamber of the eye. Frequently, more
severe bleeding follows twenty-four to forty-eight
hours after such an injury, leading to the possibility of a
secondary glaucoma—"

"Secondary?" Waine said.

"A glaucoma is any increase in pressure within the
eye. Glaucomas can be congenital; they can develop
from unknown causes; they can be produced by infection or injury. One that develops as a result of injuries
like this is called a secondary glaucoma."

"And that results in blindness?"

"It can. If the bleeding does increase, we'll have to
vent the blood from the chamber. It can be done
chemically, or with a kind of syringe. It's a delicate
procedure, in the best of cases; it's complicated in this
case by the damage to the iris. The pupil of the eye is a
hole in the center of the iris. That hole is the way we get
into the eye."

Waine tried to imagine it, and couldn't. He remarked
that throughout this presentation, Francesca had never

once pointed at her eyes, or turned them toward him, to illustrate a point.

"Also, because of the assortment of problems," Francesca said, "we haven't been able to get a real good look at the retinas. But there's a strong likelihood that they're both detached."

"Detached means what, exactly?" Waine said. That was a little better, but not much. There was still a sense that he *almost* knew what detached meant. Again, he was reminded of the way he had talked to Aura, who had spoken of ballet and opera and tennis—her three passions—with an authoritativeness that had rankled him and had made him pretend to know what she was talking about.

Francesca got up suddenly and took a pad from Dr. Finch's desk and pulled an easy chair up to Waine's and drew pictures as she talked. She, too, was aware of how clinical she was being, and she didn't altogether like it; he was just a layman, trying to understand; his questions weren't meant to imply that she wouldn't know the answers. "The retina is the innermost lining of the eyeball . . ."

Waine tried to watch the lecture, and not the space between her breasts, a view of which had been made available to him down the neck of her silk blouse.

". . . images enter the eye through the pupil—"

"The hole in the iris."

"Right."

"It's literally a hole? Why does it look black? Would you mind if I . . .?" She lifted her chin so that he could see her eyes.

Her irises were dark brown. "Now the white is called the what, again?"

"The sclera." His irises were the same color as hers.

"And this sort of clear dome—that's the cornea?"

"Right." He was older than she had thought at first; there were wrinkles of experience at the edges of his eyes. Maybe experience would make a difference; Leeds was such a boy.

"And this black is the pupil?" Waine said. "And it's a hole?"

There was a dismay in his voice that made Francesca sit back and laugh. "Yes, but don't worry. It's protected. Nothing can get in or out—except light."

Waine smiled, grateful that she had taken some of the edge off. Aura had never taken the edge off; she had just pushed it deeper and deeper. "I see. So it's through the pupil that light—" He cocked his head, as if he'd just heard or remembered something.

". . . what?" Francesca said.

"I was just wondering why we say 'see' when we mean 'understand.'"

"Especially since we so often don't understand, even though we do see."

They looked at one another for a long moment, then looked away—Francesca out the window, Waine at her hands in her lap. It had taken him all that time to notice that she wasn't wearing a wedding ring.

"Go on about retinas," he said at last. "Is that the plural? Retinas?"

"Retinae, if you're feeling arch," Francesca said.

Waine laughed. "I'll say retinas."

Francesca bent over her drawing. Though Waine Ryan looked well-born and well-bred, she was beginning to suspect that he was as much street-smart as well-educated, that there was a toughness to him for which his fine clothing served as a velvet glove. "Where was I? . . . Ah, yes. Images enter the eye through the pupil. They're focused by the lens on the retina. The usual analogy is that if the eye is a camera, the retina is the film—with the difference that instead of storing the images it receives, it transmits them, by means of the optic nerve, to the brain.

"The retina is attached to the interior of the eye in just two places—at the optic nerve in the back and at a point in the front called the ciliary body. The rest of it is held against the interior surface by the pressure of the vitreous fluids inside the eye—"

"Fluids?"

"It's a gel, actually."

Waine nodded, not sure why he'd interrupted, unless it was to have her look at him again.

Francesca ducked her head. "Imagine a balloon inside a balloon. Imagine that the interior balloon was filled with water. It would be in apparent contact with the surface of the outer balloon. Now imagine a hole or a tear in the surface of the interior balloon. The water gushes through the hole, pushing the balloon away from the surface of the outer balloon—"

"A detached retina."

"Right." She sat back, but looked toward the window as she spoke. "Tears usually occur near the front edge, where the retina is thinnest. Blunt injuries like the kind Eva suffered are the most common cause. In a susceptible person, though, a sneeze, a cough, vomiting, heavy lifting—they can all cause detachment. Young people are particularly susceptible. So are nearsighted people; their eyes are slightly elongated and the retina is stretched." She looked at him sharply, almost accusingly. "You're farsighted."

Waine laughed nervously. "I am?"

"Slightly, I'd say." She didn't look away. "We all get to be. The lens loses its elasticity, and can't focus on close objects. It's called presbyopia."

"As in Presbyterian?"

"Yes."

"What does it mean—*presby*—?"

Francesca looked away.

"It's okay," Waine said. "I can take it. If I can take having a hole in my eye, I can take anything."

Francesca looked at him directly. "It means 'older.'"

Waine slumped. "I was wrong. I can't take it."

Francesca laughed. "Why am I telling you all this?"

"That I'm farsighted? I don't know. Why did you tell me?"

"I don't mean that. I mean, about Eva James."

"Ah. Sorry. I thought Dr. Finch mentioned it. My

client is her uncle. A man named Ted Hirsch. He's the brother of Eva's mother—or was, I guess I should say."

"Poor Eva," Francesca said. "She was a very pretty girl, I would think. She will be again, once the fractures have mended, but right now her face is a mess . . . Why does Ted Hirsch need a lawyer?"

"It has to do with custody of Eva. He and his wife want to become her legal guardians."

"I thought Diana was her legal guardian."

"Diana Stewart?"

"Yes. Do you know her?"

"I know of her. You sound as though you know her."

"She's active on some volunteer committees around here," Francesca said. "Her husband's on the board of the hospital. The Stewarts have a summer home near my mother's. In fact, so do the Jameses. So *did* the Jameses."

"I see."

Francesca laughed. "What do you see?"

Waine smiled. "Right now, I'm not saying."

"There's some question, then, about Diana being Eva's guardian?"

"Indeed."

"But she's Eva's aunt."

"And Ted Hirsch is her uncle."

"Isn't there a will?"

"No."

"Aha, the missing will."

"It's more than missing," Waine said. "It's non-existent."

"How can that be?" Francesca said. "Conrad James was a rich man, a famous writer."

"He was also very superstitious."

"You mean, he thought if he made a will he might die?"

"Exactly."

"That's pretty silly. Irresponsible, even." Francesca doodled on the pad for a while. "Ted Hirsch. Why do I know that name?"

Aura had said that all the time. Confronted with something she didn't know about, she would wonder why she did; it was a way of getting told without having to admit that she needed to be. Waine wanted to believe that Francesca did know, so he gave her a moment to think it over.

She held up a triumphant finger. "He's a writer, too, right?"

Waine smiled. "Right."

"I read a novel of his about a baseball player. I liked it a lot. I'm a baseball fan."

"You should meet my associate, Keith Rouse. He's the last of the great fans. He was going to come along today, but I don't trust him around pretty nurses. He's also the last of the great wolves."

Now isn't that something? Francesca thought. *This man you don't even know says the nurses are pretty, and you feel jealous.* "So who's going to win? Custody of Eva, I mean."

"Hard to say. It would be hard enough to say, just based on the merits, but there's a complication. Conrad James purportedly asked Ted Hirsch to care for Eva if anything ever happened to him and his wife."

"Purportedly?"

"There were no witnesses. James and Hirsch were out for a walk together one day last summer."

"I see," Francesca said.

They both laughed.

Francesca looked at her watch. "I really should be getting back to my patients. Do you have any more questions?"

Are you free for dinner?

Waine's superego hopped out of him and looked him up and down.

You're asking her to dinner?

Well, I do have some more questions.

You've met this kind before, you know?

I think she's a little different.

Things aren't over with Bonnie, you know.

. . . I know.
Unless you want them to be.

. . .

You know, I think Archer was right.
How do you mean?
You are living third class.
How do you mean?
*That line you gave Bonnie about needing time to get
your act together. That's a lot of crap. You just want to
provoke her into leaving you, so you can say, "See?
Women are all alike." Then you'll get involved with this
one for a while so she can dump on you the way Aura
did, so you can say, "See? Still the same old thing."
You're making yourself into a professional victim, Ga-
waine, old boy. That's a very third-class way to operate.*

Francesca was on the edge of her chair. "You
disappeared."

"I was just thinking. I do have more questions, but
they can wait for now. I'll be in touch with you fairly
often for a while, I suspect. I hope you don't mind."

"It's your job."

Ha! Take that, Gawaine.
Shut up, will you, please?

"I don't suppose Eva can have visitors just yet."

"Not just yet." Francesca flipped the pad to a clean
page. "Let me give you my home number, in case you
have trouble reaching me here. There's a machine on
it." Francesca remembered that she'd have to change
last night's message telling callers to try her at Leeds's.

You're going to take her home number, Gawaine?
I didn't ask her for it.

Francesca thought: *This is just professional.* She tore
off the page and handed it to Waine.

He read it. "Nice number."

She smiled.

Nice smile.
Oh, brother.
Well, it is.

Chapter 7

Waine Ryan called the number two days later. Francesca told herself that she had known from the way the phone rang that it was he.

"I tried you at the hospital," Waine said. "They said you'd gone home early."

"*Mea culpa,*" Francesca said. "I haven't had a day off in weeks."

"I was wondering how Eva was," Waine said.

"Better. Still not good, but better."

There was a pause. They both laughed.

"Did you want to know the gory details?" Francesca said.

"No. 'Better' is fine. Uh . . ."

Perhaps it would be wise, Francesca thought, *to just cool it for a while. Get your bearings, see which way the wind blows—all those boring clichés. After all, Leeds objected to how much time you spend working. Since you aren't planning to cut back your schedule any, there's a chance that another man might have the same objection. There's a chance that this man might.*

"I . . . wondered if you'd like to have dinner," Waine said.

"I'd love to," Francesca said.

Francesca!

Oh, shut up. I never said I was perfect.

Francesca took a long, cool bath. She left the door open so she could hear the Joni Mitchell album playing on the stereo. It was one she had played so often at one time that it was pitted and scratched. The song that had fascinated her in those days—she had been in med school—was one called "Cactus Tree." It was about a woman whom many men loved, but whom none could have, for she was too busy living freely to have enough time for all of them or any of them.

A man had once told Francesca that the song was about her. Even before he had told her that, she had felt that it was so—with the difference that the woman in the song had a cruel side to her that resembled no aspect of Francesca's personality. Francesca had been —and was—merely dedicated to her work. Yet no man she had known—even those fiercely dedicated to their work—had fully understood that; all had either attributed to her that cruel element, or had thought her merely cold and dispassionate.

But she wasn't like that at all. At times, she fairly burned with passion. And if no man had been the beneficiary of it in its fullest flower, it was only because she believed that it was something rare and irreplaceable and not to be squandered on just anybody.

Francesca wrapped herself in a towel of wonderfully thick pile and sat on the edge of the tub and spent a long time polishing her finger and toe nails. Then she rummaged in a drawer she had not explored for a long time and found a burgundy silk camisole with ecru lace and a matching pair of tap pants with high, lacy legs. She put them on and over them put on a pair of tailored black slacks and a white cotton jacket with embroidered and cut out lapels and pockets. The jacket revealed the lace trim of the camisole, but decorously covered her breasts.

She put on white sandals with stacked heels.

In the mirror behind the bedroom door, she saw a woman of undeniable beauty. She also saw something else—something she had seen before but didn't always see—something she had once called independence but that she now knew was merely confidence.

Waine Ryan saw it, too, when he called for her at seven-thirty, carrying a single red rose. He also saw the beauty, and he thought how a man would ache if he were to fall in love with this woman and not be loved in return. He thought how he would ache.

"I made a reservation at—" he began.

"Surprise me," Francesca said. "I have a habit, when people tell me what they've planned, of second-guessing them. I don't mean it critically; I just know what I like. But I also like to be surprised."

The reservation was at Windows on the World, at the top of one of the twin towers of the World Trade Center in Lower Manhattan. The city spread out beneath them like a jeweled carpet, its rough edges muted by the fading light.

"I am surprised," Francesca said. "You strike me as more the Village bistro type."

Waine laughed. "I don't like high places, as a rule. It's not acrophobia; I just like to be in the middle of things. This is an exception, for an exceptional woman."

Francesca lowered her eyes. He was harder to look at than she imagined he knew. He wore a khaki double-breasted suit, a blue madras shirt, a yellow knit tie. His face, in the candlelight, was strong and resourceful. His hands, resting lightly on the white tablecloth, were the most beautiful hands she had ever seen—the hands of a man who got things done.

They began with daiquiris, and each had two. For an appetizer, Francesca had paté, Waine antipasto. They both ordered broiled swordfish for the main course and Waine chose a bottle of Chablis from the wine list.

"I'm glad we're having the same thing," Francesca said. "People often act disappointed when you order what they're ordering—as though you haven't tried hard enough, or don't have a mind of your own. But when people eat at home together, they eat the same thing, and enjoy sharing the experience. I think one should in a restaurant, too—perhaps even more so. It's . . . unifying."

"I'm a little reluctant to say that I feel the same way," Waine said.

"Reluctant? Why?"

"Because it sounds as though I haven't tried hard enough, or don't have a mind of my own."

Francesca laughed. "A mind of your own is something I would bet a great deal that you have."

Waine lowered his eyes. It was all he could do not to just prop his chin on his hands and stare at her. It was all he could do, too, not to stare at the delicate lace between the lapels of her jacket, to know for sure whether that was her skin he could see behind the web-like pattern, or merely some skin-toned backing. It wasn't really a question; he knew it was skin; what he wondered was what the skin felt like, and whether her breasts were as full as they seemed beneath the fitted jacket.

They talked of things of little consequence—the weather, a movie neither of them had seen but about which people they knew had talked, a highly-praised book both had started and neither had been able to finish, the wine, the fish, the asparagus, the salad. Waine pointed out landmarks—buildings, bridges, streets—even ones in boroughs other than Manhattan, boroughs about which Francesca knew little.

"I feel a little ashamed sometimes about how little I know New York," Francesca said. "It's my home; I don't feel I could live anywhere else—not at this point, anyway; yet I don't know it very well. It's not that my life has been sheltered, exactly; it's more that it's been very rigidly structured; I always seem to have to be someplace—" She almost mentioned her beeper, which was in her pocketbook, then decided not to—"That's another reason I like surprises."

"Would it surprise you if I said we shouldn't have coffee here—that we should have it someplace else?"

"No." Francesca laughed. "You know what I mean, of course. I mean it doesn't surprise me that you've thought of a place to have coffee. A place as nice as this."

"Well, anyway, different," Waine said.

They had coffee on the ferry boat that crosses New York harbor from the Battery, at the southern tip of Manhattan Island, to St. George, on Staten Island. It was terrible coffee, drawn from an urn in which the grounds were recycled until the last bit of color and flavoring were gone from them. They doctored the coffee with milk and sugar and ended up having two cups.

"Delicious," Francesca said. "And a delicious idea. What does one do when one gets to Staten Island? I'm embarrassed to say I haven't taken this ride since I was a kid."

"One comes back," Waine said. "Unless . . ."

"Unless what?"

". . . unless one feels like taking a walk."

"Well, one does." Francesca shivered in the wind of the boat's passage.

"Want to go inside?"

"Heavens, no. That would be like riding in a convertible with the top up . . . They don't make convertibles anymore, do they? More's the pity."

Waine took a big breath, then stepped close to her and put an arm around her. "May I?"

Francesca didn't answer, just put a hand over the hand that held her and leaned her head back against his shoulder.

Waine smelled her smell. It was the scent of perfume,

but also of something more—the scent of a very special woman.

Francesca smelled his manly smell. It made her dizzy.

They climbed the hills of St. George until they could go no higher. In the distance, Manhattan looked like an architect's model. Airplanes crisscrossed the sky, heading for one airport or another, or to distant places.

"Allegheny," Francesca said.

"Gesundheit," Waine said.

Francesca laughed. "I traveled a lot, when I was younger, and loved it. Since med school, since starting to work, I've been lucky to take one trip a year. Whenever I see a plane, I get momentarily jealous of the people on it for going someplace new, someplace exciting. Then I tell myself that it's not Air France or Pan Am or Lufthansa or one of those; I tell myself it's Allegheny, and that it's going to Pittsburgh, or Albany."

Waine followed one of the planes with his eyes; he wished they were on it, going to Paris or Athens, or Albany.

Paris? Athens? What is this?

Just daydreaming.

You really like this woman, don't you?

What does it look like? I'm holding her hand.

Kid stuff. I'm talking about what you're going to do if you get her to go home with you.

I'll wait and see. I like surprises.

The hell you do.

I could get to like them.

He got one right then, and liked it—a kiss on the lips.

Francesca unbuttoned the button that held his suit jacket closed and put her arms under the jacket around his waist and stood on tiptoe to kiss him again, pressing the length of her long body against him.

Hey, wait a minute. I thought you were going to take things easy. See which way the wind blows.

I only kissed him. It doesn't mean I'm going home

with him. Look, he's warm and gentle. He cares. And not just about me. He cares about other people, the state of the world. And I need to be cared about. It's been a long time. Leeds only cared about himself.

Okay, okay. I was just reminding you.

Waine held her close and she nestled against him, burying her head against his strong chest. He stroked her hair, quietly breathing in its clean scent. "We could stay here on St. George all night or we could go back to Manhattan. I live in the Village."

You don't need a weatherman to know which way the wind is blowing tonight.

Oh, be quiet.

"Funny how that hasn't come up," Francesca said. "Where you live. We hardly know each other."

"We can trade résumés on the ferry," Waine said.

"Forget the ferry," Francesca said. "Let's fly."

Chapter 8

~~~~~~~~~~~

Waine made Irish coffee and they drank it sitting on the rug in his living room, their legs straight out under the coffee table, like kids playing at being out in a cocktail lounge.

"So what were you telling Wilson Finch about Arthur?" Francesca said.

"Arthur who?"

"*King* Arthur."

"Ah . . . I was just saying that my mother—well, you heard me—that my mother loved the Arthurian legends, and named me Gawaine."

"*Ga*waine? I didn't hear that part."

"It was just before you came in."

"It must've been, because everything I've heard you say since I've paid very close attention to."

"I must say that tonight I've been paying very close attention to that outfit you're wearing," Waine said.

Francesca looked down at her camisole and fingered the lace. "It's underwear, really. I've never worn it as a blouse like this. The saleswoman said I should. 'It begs to be seen,' was what she said."

"She's right," Waine said.

Francesca put her glass on the coffee table and turned a little toward him. "Touch it, Waine. Feel the silk. It feels like soft skin."

Waine put an arm around her shoulders and a hand on the camisole over her flat stomach.

The light pressure of his hand sent a gentle spasm of pleasure through her body. She raised her face to his and shut her eyes and parted her lips and licked them lightly with her tongue.

His lips covered hers and his tongue, sweet and soft, played with hers. He slipped his hand under her camisole, lightly tracing the line of her ribcage. Francesca broke the embrace of their lips and brought her head down to nibble on his neck. Waine moaned his pleasure, sending a shiver of delight through her.

Then his whole hand cupped her breast, her hard nipple probed at the very center of his palm. Francesca lifted her face toward his again and pressed her lips to his. Their tongues met hungrily, as if they might entwine themselves about each other.

With his mouth still on hers, Waine parted her white jacket and slowly lifted the camisole so that her breasts were exposed. He loosed her mouth from his and sat upright.

Francesca let her head fall back on the cushions of the couch, shutting her eyes, enjoying his admiration of her, of her white breasts and their dark nipples and the soft concavity of her stomach. She smiled slightly as she heard the intake of his breath.

With the suddenness of an athlete, Waine was on his feet. He crouched, put an arm under her legs and the other under her back, and lifted her, as easily as if she weighed nothing.

Francesca opened her eyes and looked into his face. Where she had too often seen a kind of contortion, a pain beneath a man's pleasure that meant that he craved nothing but release, there was only a calm serenity—an expression that seemed to say that this was but foreplay to foreplay.

"I'm flying," Francesca said.

"You said that was what you wanted."

". . . Yes."

Still holding her as if she were not a burden but something all the more beautiful for its insubstantiality, Waine carried Francesca through the living room into the bedroom. He set her down before the bed and stood behind her, his body, stunningly hard at its center, pressed against hers from behind. He kissed the back of her neck, and when she had inclined her head forward, moaning softly, he removed the combs that held her hair up.

She shook her hair free, and shook it again and again. Often, in taking her hair down, knowing how it pleased men to see her hair cascading about her face and shoulders, she had thought that it would be nice for a man to do what he had just done. And this man had. It thrilled her to have her mind made love to, as well as her body.

Francesca held her arms out behind her, inviting Waine to help her out of her jacket. He took it by the collar and she slid her arms free.

Francesca lifted her arms. Waine took the camisole by its hem and slipped it over her head.

Francesca turned and put her arms around his waist, pressing her thighs against his. When he put his arms around her waist, she let go of his and leaned back as far as she could, tipping her head back and swinging it slowly from side to side, as if she might enchant him with her slowly swinging hair.

His tongue touched her nipples, first one, then the other.

Francesca lifted her head, and slowly removed Waine's tie and shirt, elongating every movement, stretching out the time in anticipation of what was to come. His chest was broad and smooth, like an athlete's. She slipped the shirt down over his hard shoulders, letting it fall where he had dropped her clothes. With their eyes embracing each other's eyes, they stepped out of the rest of their clothes. The pile of garments was now a small cairn, a testimony to their passion.

Understanding each other, not having to speak, they moved to opposite sides of the bed and with a quick, almost comic flick, pulled back the spread and sheets. They stood for a moment, smiling at one another, admiring what had been revealed, then moved onto the bed and embraced fully, trying to bring into contact every part of their bodies.

They caressed. They probed. They grazed. They kissed. The bed seemed a huge field capable of accommodating them in any configuration. Time stopped. The world ceased to exist. If there were sounds around them—the woosh of plumbing in another apartment, the blare of a radio on the street, the racket of traffic, they did not hear them. They heard only the inarticulate sounds of their own eloquent language—a language in which, though they had only learned to speak it, they were fast becoming fluent.

Francesca lay on her back, her hair spread out on the pillow. Waine knelt between her legs, the light from the street outside the apartment making his skin look burnished, making him look like the bronze statue of a great hero.

They smiled at each other.

Waine gently spread Francesca's thighs.

They waited a moment longer, then joined together, effortlessly.

Their union carried them out of the field that was the bed to another place. It was like a cloud and it carried them to a place so high that they became shorter and shorter of breath; yet it was safe and sure.

They moved with a harmony that could, Francesca thought, have produced music. Note followed note;

themes were perceived, were repeated, were varied; the sounds gathered momentum that not only built a beginning and a middle, but held the promise of the end, a tonic, a resolution.

When it came, it was like water, like electricity, like bursts of pure energy, like sunflowers, like laughter.

They had risen together to a height, and when they reached it, they did not fall. They soared, coasted, glided, gently landed back on earth—enjoying the descent as much as they had the ascent, prolonging it as they had the ascent, so that their return was as much a culmination as had been their achievement.

Francesca lay in Waine's arms, her head on his chest, her thigh across his thighs, watching the patterns of light made on the walls and ceiling by the occasional passing car.

There was nothing to say and she liked that they weren't saying there was nothing to say—and weren't saying that they weren't saying it, and so on.

"Would you like to stay?" Waine said at last.

You knew he was going to ask that.

Yes.

Well?

. . . Right now, at this stage of this relationship, I think it's as important to reflect, to remember, as it is to discover.

That sounds like a cop-out.

Who asked you?

Admit it, Francesca—you're scared.

. . . I admit it.

He asked you if you'd like to stay. You would, wouldn't you?

Yes.

Well, then—tell him that. Tell him you'd like to stay, but that you won't. You don't have to tell him why; you don't have to tell him you're scared. He's scared, too; it's normal. He'll understand that you're scared without your having to tell him. He'll also appreciate being told that you'd like to stay, even if you won't. That's

probably why he put the question that way. After all,
he's a lawyer.

"I'd *like* to stay, and I won't," Francesca said.

"I'd like you to stay, and I won't ask why you won't."

Francesca moved to kiss his cheek. "This weekend.
Can I see you this weekend?"

Waine sighed. "I'm afraid—"

"Uh-oh."

Waine laughed. "No, nothing like that. I have to go
out to Long Island this weekend. Ted and Clara Hirsch
live in Sag Harbor. And there's a service for the
Jameses, on Shelter Island."

Francesca rolled on her back, laughing. She turned
back, putting a hand on Waine's chest. "Don't get me
wrong. Mention of funerals doesn't tickle my funny
bone. It's just that I'm going to be at my mother's
house on Shelter Island this weekend. I was going to
invite you out."

"Oh, dear—to meet your mother? Has it come to
that?"

Francesca laughed. "You'll like her. She'll like you.
If you'd said no, I'd have stayed in town. Now, of
course, since you're going to be out there . . ."

"How about brunch on Sunday?" Waine said.

Francesca rolled on her back. "Brunch on Sunday—
how lovely."

Life, Francesca thought in a taxi on the way home, is
going to be lovely.

Chapter 9

Waine Ryan was on his ninety-eighth pushup when the downstairs doorbell rang. He looked at the clock and knew that it was Bonnie Niles; no one else he knew was up at six-twenty-six in the morning.

Waine thought about not responding to the bell: He could say he had been out of town on business; he could say he had gone to work very early. But he rarely went out of town on business; and he never went to work *that* early. He decided to face Bonnie.

Waine's apartment building was old, and didn't have an intercom, just a buzzer system by which the apartments could be signaled and the downstairs door unlocked. When his parents had moved into the building, in 1934, there hadn't been a buzzer, and not even a lock on the front door. There hadn't been any need; neighbors were trustworthy, and people didn't go into buildings unless they were visiting a tenant. Nowadays, such trust had gone the way of Penn Station and the Third Avenue El.

Waine went to the window and leaned his arms on the sill and waited for Bonnie to come out of the building's foyer onto the sidewalk. He didn't want her to ask how he could be so sure who was ringing as to let him or her in unseen. He recalled his mother's leaning on the sill like this, her arms cushioned by a pillow from the couch, watching him play ball or ride his bicycle, or just observing the comings and goings on the street. He remembered coming down the street for years after his mother died and looking up at the window, expecting to see her, feeling bereft when he saw that there was no one there. He realized that he still automatically looked up at the window whenever he came down the street.

Bonnie Niles came out of the foyer and looked up at the window. "Hi, there." She held up a brown paper bag. "I brought breakfast."

Waine went into the front hall and pushed the buzzer to unlock the door. He unlocked the apartment door and left it ajar and went into the bedroom and quickly made the bed, sure that it still smelled of Francesca. He dressed and went out to the kitchen.

Bonnie had laid the food out on the kitchen table—lox and cream cheese and bagels and fresh orange juice in styrofoam containers. "I figured you'd have made coffee, so I didn't bring any." She looked at the stove, which had nothing on its burners. "But I was wrong."

"I'll make some," Waine said. "This looks like a Sunday breakfast."

"Well, if you recall, we didn't have breakfast last Sunday on account of you were out the door at the crack of dawn to see this alleged client of yours."

"He's a real client. It's what he's done that's alleged."

"He must've done it. Anybody who'd want to see his lawyer at eight o'clock on a Sunday morning must be a crook."

"It was ten o'clock. He's a commercial fisherman. That's when his day ends. He's asleep by noon. And

Sunday was the only day I could take the time to go all the way out to Sheepshead Bay."

Bonnie Niles tapped her foot on the floor. "What're we doing this Sunday?"

"I have to go out to the island—to see a client."

Bonnie rolled her eyes. "Lawyers."

"It's rather early for you to come calling. Did you want anything particular—other than to have breakfast?"

"I want some changes made."

Waine ran some water into a kettle and put it on the stove and measured some coffee into a filter.

"You're probably wondering why I don't get off your case," Bonnie said.

What Waine was wondering was whether there had been anything to what Phil Archer had said—that he was living third class out of some kind of spite.

Except that the building that contained it was antique, there was nothing third class about Waine's apartment. After his father's death, Waine had spent almost ten thousand dollars having the place refurbished and painted and furnished; it was a small apartment, but, in the word of the decorator he had hired to oversee the work, "distinguished."

Nor was there anything third class about Bonnie Niles. For all the complaining she did about the hours he worked, she worked more—showing up at her restaurant around ten every morning except Sunday and staying past midnight most nights. Yes, she had dropped out of high school and had worked for nearly twenty years as a waitress in a string of luncheonettes, each indistinguishable from the others. But she had saved every savable penny during that time and had achieved the American Dream of owning her own business—hardly a third-class achievement.

Third class? Not the way he lived; not the woman he had been spending time with. Then what was it that made what Archer had said seem right, or nearly so?

Waine poured water into the filter and stared at it as it disappeared.

"I want to live with you, Waine," Bonnie said. "Actually, I'd rather marry you, but I'll settle for living with you. It's the first time in my life I've ever compromised on anything. But you know that. And if you can't handle it, I'd rather not see you at all."

"Bonnie, I've told you, it's too soon for me to live with anyone," Waine said, skirting the marriage issue.

"I'm not asking you to live with anyone. I'm asking you to live with me."

"You know what I mean."

"You've told me this before," Bonnie said.

"Right."

"So you're probably wondering why I don't listen."

"Please stop telling me what I'm wondering."

"I have to do something. You never talk."

"That's not true, and you know it."

"You never talk about how you *feel*," Bonnie said.

"For example."

She threw up her hands. "I can't give you an *example* if you never do it. You never do it. That's it."

"You mean I never say what I feel about you?"

"No. I mean, yes—yes, you never say what you feel about me."

"That's not true."

Bonnie slumped. "No, it's not true. But you never say what I want to hear."

Waine laughed and put his hands on her shoulders. "Bonnie, look, I just need some more time."

Bonnie removed his hands from her shoulders and stood up. "Why don't you just say that you want to be free to play the field?"

Waine sighed. "Bonnie, please sit down and have some breakfast."

"You mean sit down and shut up and have some breakfast."

"All right. That, too."

"Oh, I can stay, can I?"

"Of course you can stay. You brought the breakfast."

"I don't want to bring the breakfast, anymore. I want to wake up with you."

"We wake up together an awful lot."

"But not all the time."

Waine went close to her and nearly put his hands on her shoulders again, but stopped himself. "Bonnie, if it's going to happen, it'll happen. But it has to happen in its own time."

"I don't have time. I'm getting old."

"Don't be ridiculous." He patted her shapely behind. "This is old?"

"In jeans, it looks good," Bonnie said. "Naked, it looks like cottage cheese."

"Bonnie, it happens to everybody, it's called—"

"Getting older?"

"We're all getting older. Every second. But getting older isn't getting *old.*"

She turned to him. "How do you know it happens to everybody? How many backsides do you see a week?"

Waine shut his eyes.

"I'm still going to be here when you open them," Bonnie said, "so you may as well open them."

He opened his eyes.

She struck a cheerleader's pose. "Da dum."

Waine poured a cup of coffee.

"You think I'll just give up on this eventually, don't you?"

Waine took a sip.

"That I'll kiss and make up."

He held the pot poised over another cup and looked at her inquiringly.

"Well, you're wrong." Bonnie got her bag from a chair and shouldered it. "Here's the poop, counselor. Either you move into my place, or I move into your place, or we get a brand-new place together—that's probably the best idea—or we forget about this whole megillah."

"Bonnie, I don't think ultimatums are the way to understanding."

"You're giving *me* an ultimatum. You're saying cool it, or else."

"Not or else. I'm asking you to cool it along with me."

"No, thanks. I've done that."

Waine went to the window and looked down at the street. He wished he could see himself down there, at the age of six or so, playing tag, hopscotch, stoop ball, riding his bike.

He heard the door slam and turned away from the window so he wouldn't have to watch Bonnie storm out the front door. He saw that she had taken the lox and bagels and cream cheese with her, leaving just the orange juice.

He brought his cup of coffee to the table and sat. He sipped his coffee, then reached over by the phone and got a yellow legal pad and pencil.

Third class? he wrote on the pad.

Chapter 10

~~~~~~~~~~~~~~~~~~~

It's funny, Eva James thought. *Just because I can't see, people think I can't hear. People have been saying all kinds of things around me that I bet they don't want me to hear.*

Like Aunt Diana. And that Dr. Clever. I know that's not his name. His name is Clavin, but I think of him as Dr. Clever, 'cause that's what he thinks he is. I wonder if Uncle Charles knows that Aunt Diana is such good pals with Dr. Clever—always laughing and whispering, thinking I can't hear them, just because I can't see. The dumbbells.

Dumbbells was a word Eva had picked up from Becky Morgan. Saying it to herself made her unhappy, for it pained her to think of anything connected with Becky Morgan. She couldn't forgive herself for having spoiled Becky's birthday party by winding up in the hospital. Nor could she forgive herself for having wanted so badly to go to Becky's birthday party that her parents had had to drive her into the city from Shelter Island and had wound up in the hospital too.

Eva wondered what part of the hospital her parents were in, and how badly they were injured. She was a little puzzled that nobody had said anything about her parents in her presence, thinking she wouldn't hear them because she couldn't see. That probably meant her parents were badly injured.

Only Dr. Hayward acted as though she were aware that Eva knew everything that was going on in the room around her, even though she couldn't see. Whenever she moved around the room, Dr. Hayward told Eva what she was doing, knowing Eva would hear her and wonder. And she never referred to Eva as *she*—the way everyone else did, as though Eva weren't there.

"How is she?" Aunt Diana would ask a nurse, instead of asking Eva, *How are you?* "Has she eaten? How's her blood pressure? When will she be able to go home?"

Eva wondered when she would be able to go home, and when her parents would. She would have to ask Dr. Hayward the next time she came by. She wondered when that would be. It felt like morning and Dr. Hayward always came by in the morning, but she hadn't yet.

Eva loved Dr. Hayward. Not the way she loved Becky Morgan—or her mother or her father. But she loved the way Dr. Hayward touched her and the way she smelled and the sound of her voice. She sounded like a movie star. Eva was sure she was as beautiful as a movie star. She had even asked her, just the day before.

Francesca had laughed.

"You look beautiful. I know it," Eva had said.

"You're not so bad yourself," Francesca had said.

Eva had touched the bandages on her face. "I bet I look ugly."

"You look mysterious," Francesca had said. "Beautiful and mysterious."

Eva would not be deterred. "I bet you're as beautiful as Miss Grayson."

"Who's Miss Grayson?"

"My third-grade teacher."

"I'm probably not as smart, though," Francesca had said.

"I bet you're as beautiful as Beverly Arnold."

"Beverly Arnold the singer?"

"Yup. She lives in my building. Everybody says she's *really* beautiful."

"She is. I've seen her on television. Well, I don't know about Miss Grayson, but I *know* I'm not as beautiful as Beverly Arnold. Not even close. And I'm not being modest."

Eva had been sure that she was. "You know what's interesting?"

"What?"

"When I think about things—people or things—I can see them inside my head."

"That is interesting."

"But what's *in*teresting is that I can almost see them *better* than if I could see them with my own eyes. It's like when I think about the stuff in my room, I can really *see* everything. *Every*thing."

"That *is* interesting," Francesca had said.

". . . Dr. Hayward?"

"Yes, Eva?"

"When am I going to be able to see with my eyes?"

"You'll be able to see just as well as before."

"But *when?*"

"As soon as the bandages come off."

Eva had nearly asked when that would be, but she had decided it would be better not to know. If you knew when something was going to happen, you started counting the time until it happened—like the days left before Christmas or until school ended. Eva hated when they started saying on the radio that there were only thirty shopping days left to Christmas. What did they mean *only* thirty? Thirty was a lot. Thirty was e*nor*mous.

Then something very strange and wonderful had

happened. Dr. Hayward had sat down on the edge of the bed and had taken Eva's hands and had put them on her face, so that Eva could feel what her face felt like and could get a sense of what she looked like. Dr. Hayward hadn't said a word; she had just done it.

Her skin had felt smooth and her bones had felt strong and her lips had felt soft. Her hair was long and thick and felt clean and shiny.

"Thank you, Dr. Hayward," Eva had said at last.

"You're welcome."

"I'm right."

"About what?"

"You're more beautiful than Beverly Arnold. And Miss Grayson."

". . . Thank you, Eva."

Out in the hall, on the way to see another patient, Francesca had stopped for a moment and wondered about what she had just done. She had realized that it was very important for her to have Eva James know, as much as she could from touching, what she looked like. She had realized that even if Eva had not asked her what she looked like, she would have wanted her to know. Francesca had had blind patients, but none had ever asked to feel her face, to get a sense of what she looked like; perhaps they thought it wasn't done, or that it didn't matter. Nor had she ever thought to have one feel her face, to get a sense of what she looked like. But in Eva's case, it had been important. It had been a question of . . . intimacy.

Diana Stewart and Dr. Vincent Clavin sat side by side on a bench in Central Park.

"It's very expensive to be rich, Vincent," Diana Stewart said. "The overhead is enormous."

"I thought Charles's business was flourishing," Clavin said. "Computers are enormously in demand these days. Soon, all the hospital's record-keeping will be done by computer. Diagnosis, too, in some cases. Why—"

"Charles isn't in the computer business," Diana Stewart said. "He's in the computer *leasing* business. There's a difference. IBM is continually turning out computers that outmode the previous models. But they're extremely secretive about when the new models will be available, and what the innovations will be. The leasing companies play a continual guessing game. A whole sub-industry exists of research companies that forecast what IBM's going to do. Or they try. Charles relied on an inaccurate forecast. He invested in a line of computers that was almost immediately outmoded. He couldn't lease them, he couldn't sell them, he couldn't give them away. It almost completely wiped out his equity. His other leasing divisions—railway cars and containers—are solvent, but he's had to do some clever bookkeeping to keep the computer division from failing altogether. The shareholders don't know a thing, of course, and mustn't. Not to mention the SEC."

Clavin waited until a professional dog walker—a young woman with six dogs in tow—passed by. "Hence your interest in adopting your niece—or rather, your niece's fortune."

Diana smiled. "I love my niece dearly."

Clavin laughed. "The only person you love dearly is you. Everyone else exists to be used by you."

Diana Stewart stroked her silver hair. "If I didn't use them, they wouldn't be used at all. People fall so far short of their potential. They're practically begging to be manipulated."

"Surely the money your niece will inherit will go into a trust? You won't be able to get your hands on it."

"There are ways and there are ways," Diana Stewart said. "That's where you come in."

Clavin glanced worriedly at a squirrel that had approached them, hoping for a handout. "Me?"

Diana Stewart waved a hand and the squirrel fled. "We're going to help each other, Vincent."

"Help? What help do I need?"

"You should be chief of staff, Vincent. You know that."

Clavin brushed some lint from the front of his suit coat. "That's been true for a long time."

"Charles *is* on the board."

"He was on the board when Finch got the job," Clavin said.

"The difference is that Charles is planning to make a major bequest to the hospital," Diana Stewart said. "The other board members . . . Well, it would be most ungracious of them not to let Charles have his way on a matter or two regarding the way the hospital's run."

"A . . . Conrad James wing?" Clavin said.

"I hadn't thought of that, but that would be very appropriate."

Clavin waited for a nanny pushing a baby in a pram to pass. "Where is Charles going to get the money for this bequest—given his business difficulties?"

"Haven't you been listening, Vincent? We're adopting a rich young girl."

"You have heard of trusts, haven't you, Diana?"

Diana Stewart shook her head in sadness at his denseness. "There is no will, Vincent. Oh, some of Conrad's money will go into a trust for Eva. She deserves it, poor thing. But there's so much money, and so much to be done with it. Conrad, the dear, was planning to make a donation to the hospital himself, as it happens. We can only assume that he would want that plan to be carried out."

Clavin looked at her through narrowed eyes. "I hadn't heard about that."

Diana Stewart made her eyes wide. "Oh, no one has. Just me. Conrad told me about it not long before he died. Sadly, it has fallen to me to make his wish known, since he isn't here to do it himself."

Clavin laughed. "Two can play that game, is that it?"

"Precisely."

"And some of the money allocated for the hospital

will accidentally find its way into your private coffers, is that it?"

"Oh, it won't be an accident."

"How is it that you trust me not to blow the whistle on you?" Clavin said.

Diana Stewart turned toward him sharply. "Haven't you been listening, Vincent? I'm going to help you become chief of staff. You want that job more than anything in the world."

Clavin watched another squirrel approaching. Or was it the same squirrel? He waved at it and it turned and ran. "How can you be so sure that you're going to win custody of Eva?"

"I *want* to win custody of Eva. I'm accustomed to getting what I want."

"And how do you plan to go about it?"

"I'm still weighing the alternatives. But when I choose the appropriate one, you can be sure that I'll succeed."

Clavin was sure, and that gave him hope. He could already see himself in the chief of staff's office, where he had hoped to sit for so long.

Chapter 11

~~~~~~~~~~~~~~~~~

Long Island divides itself into two forks out at its
eastern end. If the fork were imagined to be the jaws of
a shark, Shelter Island would be the fish's lunch.

The metaphor fails immediately, however, for the
island is not an imperiled place, but a peaceful one,
accessible only by ferry boats that run from Greenport,
on the north fork, and North Haven, on the south. The
surrounding bays and sounds act as a moat that insu-
lates the island—in particular from the freneticism that
in summer infects the south fork, whose communities
are magnets for hordes of New Yorkers seeking sur-
cease from the inferno that, in summer, the city can
become.

Shelter Island's population swells in summer, too,
but the absence of any "scene" on the island—any
restaurants or bars it is considered ennobling to be seen
at, any shops whose labels confer cachet; the local de
facto prohibition against renting summer places to
groups of young single people—a practice so common

on the south fork that, in summer, it is necessary to distinguish between a grouper, the fish of the genus epinephelus, and a grouper, a lessee; and the fact that the island has few beaches, and none with any surf—all combine to give it the peaceful atmosphere of a place where people go to get away from it all for a while, rather than to take part in an endless round of activities, each one requiring getting dressed up *à la mode*.

It was on Shelter Island that the ashes of Conrad and Edith James were buried. The urns, each bearing a simple plaque engraved with the names of the deceased and the dates of their tenure on earth, were laid in a shallow grave beneath a maple tree on the lawn of the Jameses' house on Ram Island, overlooking a small bay known as Coecles Harbor.

The decision to cremate the Jameses was reached jointly by Ted and Clara Hirsch and Diana and Charles Stewart. So was the decision to bury the ashes on the grounds of the summer house, which had been the Jameses' pride and joy. There was no discord in the brief discussions over the matter, most of which were handled through intermediaries—Waine Ryan and the Stewarts' attorney, Arthur Rothenburg.

Nor was any animosity displayed in the brief funeral ceremony, conducted by an official of the local Quaker Church. The Jameses had practiced no organized religion, but in view of Shelter Island's having been founded by Quakers fleeing from religious persecution, it was deemed suitable to have someone of that denomination officiate. Again, the decision had been reached by consensus.

Attending the ceremony, which was held at noon on the Saturday following the Jameses' automobile accident, were: Ted and Clara Hirsch; Diana and Charles Stewart; Waine Ryan and Arthur Rothenberg, counselors at law; Mrs. Rothenberg; Walter (Whizzer) Wolfe, Conrad James's literary agent; Brent Brolin, Conrad James's publisher; Jean Richards, the owner of a Fifty-seventh Street art gallery that showed paintings

by Edith James; Deborah Freedman, Edith James's art
teacher; Susan Lester, a television producer who lived
a few houses away from the Jameses on Ram Island and
had been a close friend; Arthur Albert, another Shelter
Islander who had been Conrad James's regular tennis
opponent, and Dan Kleinman, the publisher, editor,
columnist, star reporter and, occasionally, photographer of the *Shelter Islander*, a local weekly.

The day was hot and still. Only the smallest sailboats
could make their way over the waters of Coecles
Harbor. The trees were loud with cicadas. The mourn-
ers' feet crackled on the dry grass as they made their
way back up the lawn to the house to partake of some
cucumber sandwiches and iced tea prepared by the
Jameses' housekeeper at the suggestion, and expense,
of Diana Stewart. The men took off their jackets and
loosened the knots of their ties.

"Wonder what'll happen to this place," Dan Kleinman, the newspaperman, said to no one in particular.

It wasn't a question and it might have been allowed
to just melt in the heat, but it rankled at many ears.

Diana Stewart took her husband's arm. "Charles, I
think you should go talk to this Ryan fellow. He seems
a very reasonable man. Maybe there's a way to settle all
this without going to court." She knew he wouldn't,
which would enable her to, which was what she wanted,
since she was the one who was doing the thinking for
both of them.

Arthur Albert, the tennis player (it was nearly his
profession; he had a rich wife who supported him),
sidled up to Arthur Rothenberg, the lawyer. "What's
this about Connie not having a will?"

"He was crazy, that's all," said Walter (Whizzer)
Wolfe, who had overheard. "It's one thing to be
superstitious and another to be crazy."

"It's funny," said Brent Brolin, the publisher, "but I
never knew Connie to be superstitious. I mean, we own
a black cat, and he never said a word about it. And he
visited us lots of times."

"Black cats," scoffed Walter Wolfe. "I'm talking about death. He was superstitious about death."

"Sounds like a healthy superstition," said Arthur Albert. To Arthur Rothenberg, he said, "You were saying, Art?" They had only just met, but Arthur Albert was one of those men who get particular delight in finding someone of the same name.

Rothenberg shrugged noncommittally. "Things aren't all that complicated."

"How so?" said Dan Kleinman, the newspaperman, trying to extract a notebook from the inside pocket of the jacket he carried over his arm.

"Eva James will inherit her parents' estate," Rothenberg said. "Until she's of age, it will be administered by a trustee."

"A guardian?" Dan Kleinman said, looking up momentarily from writing this down.

Rothenberg smiled sympathetically, and pushed his glasses up on his nose. "The trustee will simply administer the trust. Eva's upbringing, education, and so on, will be the purview of her guardian."

"Who is?" Dan Kleinman said, pencil poised.

Rothenberg started to speak, then shut his mouth and put a finger to his lips, as if to seal them. "I'd rather not discuss this matter now. It simply isn't appropriate."

Waine Ryan, meanwhile, felt a hand on his arm. He turned away from Brent Brolin and Jean Richards, to whom he had been talking, and saw Diana Stewart standing close to him.

"Excuse me for interrupting, Mr. Ryan, but I wondered if I could have a word with you."

"Of course."

"Privately." Diana Stewart smiled at the others.

"Excuse me," Waine said to them, and followed Diana, who placed her feet carefully as she walked across the grass, like a cat on new terrain.

Diana Stewart turned to face Waine. "I just wanted you to know that we're not ogres, my husband and I."

Waine smiled.

"It's all so silly," Diana said. "This disagreement. I mean, we're all civilized people."

"If you're proposing that the matter not go to court, Mrs. Stewart, then I'd be glad to discuss it. But in my office, or Mr. Rothenberg's. Not here."

"I should warn you, Mr. Ryan. I'm not accustomed to being denied what I've set my mind on getting."

"In cases like this, Mrs. Stewart, someone's always being denied. So—"

"Say, uh . . ." It was Dan Kleinman.

Diana Stewart turned and strode away.

Before Kelinman could speak, Arthur Albert clapped Waine on the back. "Don't say anything you don't want to see in the paper, Waine, old buddy. Dan here reports on anything that moves." He went off.

"Don't say anything about what?" Dan Kleinman said to Waine. He usually wrote stories about town meetings and epidemics of jelly fish in the surrounding waters, and he smelled a story that was out of the ordinary.

"I'm off duty today, Mr. Kleinman," Waine said.

"So am I. Call me Dan."

"You brought your notebook."

"Never without it. My memory's slipping. You staying on the island overnight?"

"I'm staying with Ted Hirsch and his wife, In Sag Harbor."

"Maybe we could get together for a drink. I can drive over there, or you can drive over here."

"I don't drive," Waine said. "But I don't think so, anyway. I'd rather things just came out in court."

"Oh, and what court is that?" Kleinman said.

"Surrogate Court."

"Surrogate Court? That's like wills and stuff. Child custody."

Waine nodded.

"I used to cover Police Headquarters for the *Daily News,*" Kleinman said. "Got over to Criminal Court, now and then, but never Surrogate Court. I saved a little money and when the *News* went automated, I moved out here and bought the local paper."

"Something against automation?"

"Everything. Changes the whole news gathering business in ways you probably can't even imagine. I could tell you about it over a drink."

Waine laughed. "I don't think so."

Kleinman ran a finger around the inside of his collar. "So how is she?"

"Who?"

"Eva James. I hear she may go blind."

"The chances are good she won't," Waine said. "At least, that's her doctor's opinion. She won't know for sure for a while longer."

"'She?' You mean, a lady doctor?"

"Yes."

"A lady eye doctor?"

Waine nodded. "An ophthalmologist, yes."

"Not Francesca Hayward?"

Waine fought off a smile. "Yes."

"Did I say something funny?" Kleinman said.

Waine laughed. "No."

Kleinman frowned. "She lives out here, you know."

"I know her mother has a house here, yes."

Kleinman got a reminiscent look in his eye. "I just realized it's been almost seventeen years since old Doc Hayward died. Seventeen years in November. Boat accident."

"Her father was a doctor, too?" Waine said. How could he not have found that out? There was so much he hadn't found out.

"An *eye* doctor, too," Kleinman said.

"And something happened to his boat?"

"Fell off it in Noyack Bay. Or was pushed."

Waine remembered Dr. Wilson Finch's telling him about a man he resembled who had died in a sailing accident. It was disconcerting to think that he resembled Francesca's father. "What do you mean—'or was pushed?'"

Kleinman shrugged. "A joke from my days on the police beat. The cops never said anybody jumped out a window, or off the Brooklyn Bridge. They always said 'fell or jumped.' I always used to ask, 'or was pushed?' I mean, a lot of times somebody'd do a swan dive out of some swanky apartment where there'd be a lot of people—or even just one—who was more glad to see him or her splattered all over the sidewalk than he or she was glad to be splattered, if you know what I mean. So I always used to ask, 'Or was pushed?'—just to kind of get the cops riled up a little. It was a joke . . . Except . . ." Kleinman wiped the perspiration from his forehead with the palm of his hand.

"Except what?"

"Well, Dr. Noel Hayward was a crackerjack sailor. Crackerjack sailors don't fall off their boats."

"Do they jump?"

Kleinman smiled. "Seems to me I'm supposed to be asking the questions here, Mr. Ryan—being the reporter and all."

Something in Waine wanted to be rid of this man, and something wanted to make contact. He took a business card from his wallet. "You can call me at my office."

Kleinman took the card, looking at both sides as if he weren't satisfied with what was on the front. "I just might do that. You can call me, too, if you think of anything you'd like to say. I'm in the book. Or you can call the paper. I'm usually there till late at night."

Waine could see him there, stirring things up.

At just about the same time, Francesca was beginning to unwind. She had driven out to Shelter Island the night before, had had an early dinner with her mother, and had gone upstairs with a book, intending to read for an hour or so before going to sleep. She had

fallen asleep after reading just a few pages and had
awakened at ten o'clock that morning; her mother
had come in during the night and had turned out the
light and put the book on the endtable. If Francesca
had dreamed, she didn't remember it.

The house had been empty when she woke, and she
had found a note from her mother saying that she had
gone to East Hampton to do some shopping. Francesca
had made a big breakfast—two scrambled eggs, bacon,
two slices of toast, orange-cranberry juice and coffee—
and had eaten it out on the lawn, among the grove of
trees behind the house. After cleaning up, she had
taken her book out to read under the trees. She had
fallen asleep again. Again, she had not dreamed, or did
not remember.

Now, she was feeling much, much better. The tension of a hard week at the hospital had dissipated; her
limbs felt loose and supple and her mind was no longer
racing. Now, she was dreaming—daydreams of Waine
Ryan. Some of the daydreams were erotic, some were
chaste, all were pleasant and made her feel warm
inside.

The wind rattled the leaves of the big trees and
Francesca tipped her head back and looked up into the
foliage. She remembered her certainty, as a child, that
the trees in the grove changed their positions from time
to time—at night, when people were away from the
house, sometimes when her back was turned. There
were only a dozen trees, yet no matter how hard she
stared at them, she never knew for certain whether they
had or had not moved. Could it have been that they
moved only when she blinked?

Francesca smiled at the memory of her consternation. She remembered that her father had accepted
quite readily her suggestion that the trees hopped about
from place to place. "Wouldn't you?" he had said. "It'd
be pretty boring to stay in one place all the time." But
he had never seen them move, and had resisted her
efforts to enlist him in one of her surveying projects, to

determine once and for all whether there was movement and what its nature was. "It wouldn't work, 'Cesca," he had said. "They wouldn't move if they knew we were watching them, making marks on the ground and all, planting stakes and stringing string. Trees are like cats; they don't like to be watched."

The wind gusted and the leaves rattled more loudly and Francesca felt a little uneasy. Perhaps the trees were admonishing her not to stare at them so. She lowered her eyes and looked out over the water of Noyack Bay. She understood that wish not to be stared at; stares were judgmental, even stares of admiration. Sometimes she had the feeling she was being watched and that marks were being made on some scorecard; it unsettled her. She liked to think that she was a free agent, and could do what she wanted, when she wanted, as long as she didn't encroach on anyone else or break any laws. She told herself that it was that unwillingness to be audited that was behind the fact that she had not said anything to her mother about having met Waine Ryan.

But she wondered if that were so. Or was there something else—some hesitation born of having been disappointed once again? But disappointed how? There had been nothing to be really disappointed about. So what was the source of her uneasiness? The symptom was plain enough, but the diagnosis of the cause was difficult. Sometimes if you didn't focus on a problem, the solution came to you unexpectedly. Perhaps reading would allow her mind to reorganize itself. Francesca turned once more to her book.

Chapter 12

~~~~~~~~~~~~~~~~

Driving off Ram Island to get on the road to the South Ferry Landing, Ted Hirsch stopped so suddenly that Clara and Waine lurched in their seats.

"It was right here," Ted said, and pulled his car off the road onto the sandy shoulder.

"What was?" Clara said.

Ted got out and crossed the road, motioning to them to follow. They were on a narrow causeway that connects Ram Island with the main mass of Shelter Island. Off to the north lay Gardiner's Bay, and across it the low spit of land that extends out to Orient Point, the easternmost tip of the North Fork. In the heat, the spit looked like a mirage. To the south was Coecles Harbor.

Waine looked for and found the Jameses' house, up on the wooded shoulder of Ram Island.

Ted Hirsch stood at the waterline on a carpet of small rocks and dried waterweed. "It was right here."

"What?" Clara said, impatiently.

"Where you buried the treasure?" Waine said.

"This is where Connie asked me to look after Eva."

"Ah." Clara went down to join Ted, her head down, as if looking for footprints.

Ted pointed at the Jameses' house and moved his arm in a slow arc. "We walked down the road, down the hill, right to here. We came to see the ospreys."

"See those poles, Waine?" Clara said. "The ones with the platforms on top?"

Waine looked and saw that two of the telephone poles that rose up at intervals along the causeway were topped off with man-made wooden platforms on which something not human had constructed huge, shaggy nests of grass and twigs.

"Those are osprey nests," Clara said. "They're hawks, I think. Or maybe they're eagles."

"Hawks," Ted said.

"Aren't eagles hawks?"

"I don't think so. I think they're eagles."

"Anyway," Waine said, "ospreys are birds, right?"

"Right."

Growing up in the city, Waine knew sparrows from pigeons; everything else were birds. "Are they in the nests?"

"The babies are," Clara said.

"The parents are out hunting," Ted said. "We could see them if they were here. They're huge."

"Huge," Clara said. "They have these incredibly fierce faces. Like eagles. I think they're eagles."

"We had hamburgers for dinner," Ted said.

Clara looked at him strangely. "We haven't had dinner yet. And we're having bluefish."

"I meant the night Connie and I walked down here. Last summer. We had hamburgers for dinner, then took a walk. Do you remember, Clara?"

". . . no."

"We had hamburgers, and we all had raw onions. Edith wanted them, and we all agreed to eat them."

"We had hamburgers here a lot," Clara said. "And raw onions."

"Hamburgers, yes," Ted said, "but not raw onions. Occasionally Edith would make fried onions, but most of the time we didn't have any onions."

"It doesn't matter, Ted," Waine said.

"What doesn't matter?"

"What you had for dinner. Or whether Clara remembers. Even if Clara remembered precisely the night you were talking about—the menu, the weather, what everybody was wearing—it wouldn't matter."

Ted poked at a rock with the toe of his shoe. "Because she didn't hear the conversation?"

"Exactly."

Clara came to where Waine stood. "What if I had, Waine? What if I'd been there, too? Would it make Ted more credible, or would people just think he was lying and I was swearing to it?"

Waine avoided her eyes, and Ted's, and looked out over the harbor, where a big sailboat was making its way to its mooring under the power of its engine. The piston's throb was unnaturally loud.

"They would, wouldn't they?" Clara turned away.

"It's not that you're not credible, Clara," Waine said. "Or Ted, either. It's that you're not disinterested."

"Damn that Conrad," Clara said. "Why did he have to be so irresponsible?" She kicked some sand in Ted's direction. "And you—why didn't you say anything to me about it? I've been in enough courtrooms to know that verbal promises don't mean much without witnesses. Why didn't you tell me? I would've made him write it down."

"Don't, Clara," Ted said.

"Well, I would have."

"Okay, so you would have. I didn't say anything about it because Connie asked me not to."

"Dumb."

Ted picked up a stone and skipped it—once, twice, three times—scattering some gulls that bobbed on the

water of the harbor. "I wish, in retrospect, that I'd
talked to Edith about it. It was the first time I knew
anything about there not being a will. I wish I'd insisted
that she prevail on Conrad to make one—for Eva's
sake. But I guess I can understand Conrad—when you
start talking about the eventuality of your death, you
start feeling morbid." He skipped another rock; the
gulls overhead wheeled angrily. "It would be different
if I were a success, wouldn't it?"

Clara glanced at Waine.

"Why don't we drive?" Waine said. "It's awfully hot
here."

"It would, wouldn't it?" Ted said. "Or at least
if I were a mediocrity in some other field. But everybody's going to think that I just want to get my hooks
into my niece so I can reap some of the benefits of my
brother-in-law's success in a field I've been a failure
at."

Clara went to Ted and took his arm. "Why don't we
drive? It's hot here."

They drove without speaking—off the causeway, up
Ram Island Drive, along Route 114 to the South Ferry
Landing. There were enough cars ahead of them to fill
a ferry, so they got out and walked beside a pond. Clara
herded Waine away from Ted.

"Maybe we should just forget about it," Clara said.

"That's up to you."

"Damn it, Waine, it doesn't help at all that you're so
noncommittal. In the cases we've worked on together—
environmental cases, consumer rights cases—you've
always been such a ball of fire, an inspiration. With this
thing, you just mope around, or gaze off into the
distance."

"Maybe you should get another lawyer."

Clara stomped a foot. "I don't want another lawyer.
I want you, but I want you at your best."

Waine tried to fit his shoe into a footprint he'd just
made in the sand. He wondered why the print was so

much larger than his shoe. "I'll be at my best when the time comes. I've had a tough week. I have things on my mind. I probably should've just taken the weekend off, stayed around the house."

"It must be miserably hot in the city," Clara said. She touched his arm lightly. "Do you want to tell me about her?"

Waine laughed. "Did I say it was a her?"

Clara made a pained face. "Come on. I wasn't born yesterday. Is it that woman you've been seeing for a while? What's her name—Donna?"

"Bonnie."

"Bonnie. Same number of Ns as Donna. It's such a pretty name, Bonnie. A bonny name. It was one of the names we had in mind for a daughter, when we still thought we could have children."

"Why can't you?" Waine said. "If I may ask."

"You may not. We're talking about you. So does Bonnie want you to settle down? Is that it?"

"In a word—yes."

"And you still want to sow some oats?" She waved her hands. "Don't answer that. I hate that expression— and the concept. It implies that it's only something men can do. A woman can't sow oats; she can only nurture them . . . So, the question is, do you want to stay single a while longer?"

Waine tried a shoe in another footprint. The fit was better, perhaps because the sand was damper there. "I don't know. That makes it sound as though I want to live alone, by my own devices. But the fact is, all the time I've been single, I've been involved with women I've spent a lot of time with—Bonnie and another woman before her. It's hard to call what I've been single, at all."

"But you can spend the night alone whenever you want, can't you?" Clara said.

"I wouldn't say 'whenever.' Bonnie's demanding. As was the other woman."

"How about you?"

"How about me, what?"

Clara laughed. "Don't try to dodge me, counselor. Are you demanding, too?"

"I suppose."

"What happens when Bonnie wants to spend a night alone?"

"She never does—or doesn't say she does. Nor did the other woman."

"Do you wish she would?"

"I guess so, sometimes. As it is, I'm always the bad guy."

"And you'd like to have something to hold against her?"

Waine looked her over, wondering if she'd been bugging his thoughts. "Can we change the subject?"

Clara laughed. "We can call a recess in the subject, to be resumed the next time we convene in a suitable setting. In the meantime, let's get this ferry."

They stood on the deck during the brief ride, looking west along Shelter Island Sound toward Noyack Bay.

"Strange how everybody involved in this thing is so close together," Ted said. "Even Dr. Hayward."

"She lives up there, Waine," Claire said, pointing toward a point of land rising up from the sound several hundred yards from the ferry crossing. "Or her mother does."

"In the white house?" Waine said, trying to sound only mildly interested.

"Not the small one, right on the water. The big one, among the trees on top of the point. You'll be able to see it better from the other side. The small white house is one of several houses on the estate. I guess they're all rented out during the summer."

From the other side, Waine could see that the house had a gabled roof and at one end a tower—almost like a belfry. It reminded him of Aura's parents' house—one of their houses, actually—on a plantation near Winchester, Virginia, where they raised Arabian horses—or rather, watched them being raised for them.

Waine wondered: Why was he looking forward so little to seeing Francesca for brunch the next day? Why had he thought so little about her since their one and only date?

Date? You call that a date? That was an orgy.

Quiet.

And on the first date, no less.

I thought you said it wasn't a date.

And why hadn't he told Ted and Clara about Francesca when they pointed out her mother's house? Did he feel so strongly that he owed Bonnie a chance, or was it something else?

Getting back into the car as the ferry neared its slip, he realized what it was. It was that he and Francesca had, above all, a professional relationship, and he was fearful that by getting to know each other as, as it were, amateurs, they were behaving unprofessionally.

Turning to look back at the house, he wondered about Francesca's ability—about anyone's ability—to escape the effects of that kind of upbringing.

What kind of upbringing is that?

Just look at that house.

So?

That's a millionaire's house.

So?

As someone said, the rich are different from you and me.

You're amazing, Gawaine, you really are. Do you see what you're doing? You're trying to find a reason to get out of this.

I'm not in it, exactly.

Yeah, you are. And you're also still in it with Bonnie, like it or not. And staying in one of those relationships and getting out of the other is something you're going to

*have to take responsibility for yourself. You're not going
to be able to pin it on someone else.*

. . .

Gawaine?
I'm thinking.
No, you're not. You're looking at the scenery.
I can think and look at the scenery.
Oh, brother, Gawaine.

Chapter 13

~~~~~~~~~~

Francesca Hayward looked straight into the sun in search of the tennis ball her mother had lobbed back at her. She had her racquet back and cocked and was ready to swing at where her instinct told her the ball would be.

"Don't choke," Beatrice Hayward called out.

Francesca staggered, swung wildly, and caught the ball on the wood of the racquet. It soared in a ridiculously high, feeble arc, and went over the fence at the end of the court.

Beatrice Hayward let her racquet drop to the clay and laughed heartily, bending from the waist and pressing her hands between her knees.

Francesca rested her hands on the net and glared menacingly at her mother. "That's not funny."

"Oh, but it was. It was very funny."

"It's *cheat*ing."

"Nonsense. It's competitive spirit. There's not enough of it in tennis. Tennis players are so—" she stuck her nose in the air—"sportsmanlike. In every other game, the players are always yelling at their opponents, to try to distract them. Not to mention the crowd."

"In golf?" Francesca said.

Beatrice Hayward made a sour face. "Golf. What a detestable game that is. Several of my friends are always trying to get me to play, but I will not join them. The only time I ever enjoyed golf was on a vacation your father and I took in Hawaii—before you were born. We'd play the first two holes, then duck into this absolutely delightful little oasis off to the side of the third tee. It had a little waterfall and a pond and absolutely the softest, coolest grass I had ever lain on."

Francesca considered her mother's face, still firm and strong and beautiful, like her body, with only a few age lines around her eyes. "You look like you're still enjoying the afterglow."

Beatrice Hayward cocked her head. "Why, I do believe I still am. I can almost feel how it felt to be in his arms."

Francesca went to the bench beside the court and zipped the case on her racquet and took a sip from the glass of tea she had put there when they started playing. It had been iced; now it was nearly lukewarm.

"You're not quitting, are you?" Beatrice Hayward said. "Just because of that little catcall?"

"That was set point, remember? You made a point of shouting it out before you served."

"It's etiquette to shout it out, Francesca. Like it's etiquette to tell someone you've put him in check . . . What was the score in that set?"

"Six-two, mother. Just like in the first set."

"I thought you played quite well," Beatrice Hayward said.

"I did play well. You're just too good."

"Well, I should hope so. I play every day with Kyle. He played on the varsity at Princeton."

Francesca took another sip of tea. "Who's Kyle?"

"Kyle Davis. He owns the new restaurant I told you about in the Heights. We're going there for dinner tonight."

"We're going out to dinner? I can't ever remember going out to dinner on Shelter Island. That's one of its charms; there's no place to eat."

"That was before Kyle opened his place. The food's very simple—fish and steak and chops—but it's delicious. I eat there several times a week."

"Really? How extraordinary."

"Why?"

"You hate to go out in the evening."

Beatrice Hayward shrugged and smiled.

"Mother?"

"Yes, dear?"

"Have you got a boyfriend? Is this Kyle—"

Beatrice Hayward swatted at the notion with her racquet. "Of course not. He's half my age. One-third my age." She sat on the bench and stuck her long legs out next to Francesca's; they compared favorably. "Speaking of boys . . . I've noticed a distinct absence this weekend of any mention of Leeds. Has he gone off snap-shooting again?"

"We broke up."

"Oh, good." Beatrice Hayward put a hand over her mouth, then held the hand out in front of her and slapped at it lightly with her other hand. "What I *meant* was . . ."

"I know how you feel about Leeds, mother."

"Oh, I like Leeds well enough; it's just that I find him vain and rather petty."

"I *said,* I know how you feel."

Beatrice Hayward poked at a pebble with the end of her racquet. "Is there someone else? I don't mean on his part; I'm not interested in whom he might be seeing. The sort of woman who would appeal to Leeds—"

"Mother, lay off Leeds, will you? He's okay. He's everything you say, but he's okay. And I have spent a fair amount of time with him, so I don't think you should belittle him in my presence."

"How about in your absence?"

Francesca sighed.

Beatrice Hayward laughed. "I can't help it if I have strong opinions, Francesca. And I like to share them with people . . . So. You didn't answer my question: Are you seeing anyone else?"

Francesca didn't wonder that she didn't tell her mother about Waine Ryan. What was far more baffling was that Waine was due for brunch in two hours, and that she hadn't told her mother *that*.

"The reason I ask," her mother went on, "is that I think you'd really like Kyle. I know he'd like you. He adores me, after all."

"Mother."

"You'll see. You'll meet him at dinner."

"I'm going back to the city tonight. I don't want to have to drive into the city in the morning."

"I thought you preferred driving into the city in the morning."

Francesca put her head back and shut her eyes. Had she been hoping that her mother would go off somewhere for the afternoon, so that she and Waine could be alone together? Not likely: Her mother rarely left the grounds of the estate. Had she been hoping that Waine would break the date? She had no reason to think that. They had had a brief but warm telephone conversation around midday on Friday, and he had given her no reason to think that there was anything conditional about his plans. Had she been troubled that Waine hadn't moved to see her sooner than the weekend? Quite the opposite: However much they had rushed into things, she had been pleased that they hadn't abandoned control of their lives.

"Do you want some lunch?" Beatrice Hayward said.

Tell her, Francesca.

". . . I . . . I'm going for a swim first. To wash the sweat off."

"I hardly sweated at all," Beatrice Hayward said.

"Don't rub it in, mother. Please don't rub it in."

Beatrice Hayward laughed.

Francesca dozed in the shade of an umbrella on the beach. She had fallen asleep wondering if she were fated to be a loner. Her work demanded so much of her time, and in the time that was left to her she liked to make sure she did the things that kept her from feeling a slave to her work. She liked to exercise—swimming in the hospital's pool or jogging in Central Park or just taking a long, brisk walk. She liked to read things that had nothing to do with medicine: Slick magazines—*The New Yorker, Time, Esquire*—were her favorite reading; books that required more continous reading time only made her feel ill-at-ease over how little time she had. She liked to waste some time every day—doing absolutely nothing, staring into space. She liked to talk on the phone with friends she didn't need to see as much as she needed to talk to. She liked to see friends she didn't need to talk to as much as to be with. She liked to hang out in the staff lounge, gossiping. On some days, if she wanted to get four hours' sleep—the bare minimum on which she could operate—she had about an hour in which to do any of these things. Not much time—especially if she were trying to have a relationship with a man, as well. Not much time for the relationship itself, either, even if she devoted herself to it exclusively, and did without the exercise, the reading, the wasting time, the talking to friends or seeing them, the hanging out.

How had her father managed? He had worked as hard as she—harder, probably, for the staff had been smaller in his day and he had had administrative duties, as well. Yet he had exercised scrupulously (an hour of *tai chi* every morning); had played the cello in an amateur string quartet; was always reading a novel; had been on the board of a Village community organization; had cooked elaborate, spicy meals to which he would invite friends on the spur of the moment, saying he just happened to have a ton of spaghetti that needed getting rid of; and had been there virtually every night to read to her, to tuck her in, or, when she was older, to spend a little time with her, asking how her day had been, telling her something about his. And her mother had confided that he had remained throughout his life an attentive husband and an ardent, enthusiastic, creative lover. Had there been more hours in the day in those days?

Francesca's remembering gave way to a dream: She was in a small sailboat, like a Sunfish, out on Noyack Bay. It was hot, but there were light airs. There was a slight swell on the water, an occasional rising and falling—as if it were not water, at all, but the hide of some slumbering monster.

The boat wouldn't move. Its bow would turn into the wind so that the sail flapped uselessly. She would lift the center-board to reduce the boat's friction and would push the rudder back and forth rapidly so that the boat would get its bow out of the wind and the sail would begin to fill. As she did this, the boom would begin to swing out over the water—as she intended. But it would keep on swinging and she would have to steer under it to keep from capsizing, and would put the bow into the wind again, and the sail would flap uselessly. She did this over and over many times before she saw the problem: The sail had no sheet—no rope running from the stern of the boat out through pulleys along the boom and back into the cockpit just behind the mast; without a sheet, the sail could not be trimmed.

A dark cloud loomed over her and she was filled with terror that a storm would come up and that she would be helpless.

"Francesca."

She tried to see who was calling, but all she could see was water. She was no longer in the bay; she was on the high seas.

"Francesca."

Francesca woke with a start. Her mother stood over her, blocking the sun, clutching a caftan around her, her hair wet from the shower, looking troubled. "Sorry I startled you. You were sound asleep."

"Was I asleep long?"

"I have no idea. I just got out of the shower. You have a caller."

Half-asleep still, Francesca heard it as *crawler,* and looked down at her body, naked except for her black bikini, in search of some insect. There was none. "A what?"

"There's a gentleman here to see you. It's most extraordinary."

Francesca thought her mother meant something she saw, and she turned and looked out over the bay. A Sunfish slipped by on a starboard tack, its sheet in place. "What is?"

"Your friend, Waine Ryan. He looks just like Noel. It gave me quite a start."

Chapter 14

⌇⌇⌇⌇⌇⌇⌇⌇⌇⌇⌇⌇

"You bicycled from Sag Harbor?" Francesca said. He might as well have said he had saucered in from Mars.

"It's an easy ride," Waine said. "Mostly flat. A lot of shade. Not bad at all."

"Still." Waine looked so nice in his white Lacoste shirt and khaki hiking shorts and blue running shoes with white stripes that Francesca wondered how she could not have looked forward to seeing him.

Francesca looked so nice in the white duck pants and pale blue cotton T-shirt she had changed into on coming up from the beach that Waine wondered how he could not have looked forward to seeing her. He took a step close to her, wanting to kiss her, but he heard her mother puttering in the kitchen, which overlooked the back lawn where they stood, and he told himself to behave. "This is very imposing," he said, gesturing at the estate. "It was pointed out to me yesterday from the ferry boat."

"How was the funeral?" Francesca said.

"Somber."

They stood somberly for a moment, each wiping condensation from the glasses of iced tea that they held in their hands.

"Did you bicycle to the funeral?" Francesca said. *What a dumb thing to say.*

Waine laughed. "No, we drove. I didn't have any choice about bicycling over, really, since I don't drive."

Francesca cocked her head. "Don't drive by choice?"

"It's a small gesture I make."

"Toward?"

"Clean air. Conserving energy."

"So of course I feel guilty," Francesca said, "since I drive all the way out here two or three weekends a month—and drive to East Hampton or Southampton or Montauk when I'm out here."

"Don't feel guilty. I don't really think my gesture has much effect."

"Still." Francesca wondered why she was just a little bit annoyed at him.

"Your name came up at the funeral," Waine said. *What a dumb thing to say.*

"It's a small island," Francesca said. "My father used to say that if people weren't talking about you in the Heights—that's at the other end of the island—by noon, it meant you hadn't gotten up yet. By three, they'd be talking about the fact that you still weren't up at noon."

Waine laughed. "How long . . . " He shook his head. "Nothing."

"What?"

"I was about to ask how long your father's been dead, but I realized I knew."

"How on earth can you?"

"It's a small island."

Francesca took him to a group of lawn chairs within a cool grove of trees. They sat and looked out at the water, not speaking, each wondering why he (and she) felt so uncomfortable, each wondering if they had really been so intimate just a few days before.

"Did the gossips tell you how dad died?" Francesca said.

"In a sailing accident, yes?"

"I don't mean doing what. I mean how."

Waine felt some of the discomfort he tried to make people feel on the witness stand, on the run. He just shook his head, as they often did, in the hope that it wouldn't go into the record.

Francesca squinted out at the bay, at the spot she had always imagined to be the precise spot at which it had happened. "My father was a superb sailor. He sailed a boat as though it were part of him. Not even part of him—was him. He didn't have accidents."

"Isn't that the definition of an accident?" Waine said. "Something we don't usually have."

"He never had them—in his work, in his sports, in his life. He was a perfectionist. He was perfect."

Waine felt the burden of his perceived resemblance to the late Dr. Noel Hayward—felt the impossibility of being anything other than a lookalike.

Francesca looked closely at Waine. "Do you ever have a case where you can *feel* the truth of something, but can't prove it?"

"Often."

"Well, I *feel* that something happened to my father— that something harmed him. But I'll never be able to prove it."

"Were there any witnesses?"

"It was in November—past the season for sailing, usually, but it had been a very warm fall. It was a weekday—a Friday. It was the day John Kennedy was killed. My father was taking a long weekend—to get his boat out of the water and close up the house for the winter. My mother wasn't coming out until Saturday. I was at school." Francesca sat forward in her chair and pointed out some features. "This water here is called West Neck Bay. That spit of land across the way is

called Shell Beach. Beyond it is West Neck Harbor—
where those boats are. That's where my father moored
his boat. We used to row across, in a dinghy. It's the
fastest way. It's about nine miles by road to get over
there, because of all the creeks and inlets. . . .

"He rowed across and took his boat out over there—
to Noyack Bay. It was very early in the morning. That
was his favorite time to sail." She sat very still for a
moment, looking out at the imagined spot, then shifted
in her chair and uncrossed and recrossed her legs
hurriedly. She folded her hands in her lap. "And that's
all that's known. The boat ran aground on that land
over there—North Haven Peninsula; it was unmanned.
His body was found late that afternoon. Death had
been by drowning, but he had a contusion on the back
of his head."

"He *was* sailing alone, wasn't he?" Waine said.

"He'd been planning to go out with Dr. Clavin.
Vincent Clavin. Have you met him? He's the assistant
chief of staff."

"I've heard his name."

"Vincent has a house in North Haven. He and dad
knew each other for a long time. They were never
really friends as much as colleagues. Vincent's a first-
class sailor, too. Not as good as dad was, but pretty
good. They raced together a lot—as a team . . .

"Anyway, Vincent was out here on vacation and he
and dad were planning to sail that morning, but Vincent's car broke down and he couldn't get over. Didn't
have a bicycle, I guess."

Waine smiled. He wondered why she was telling him
this; it seemed to be something that was deeply felt but
rarely, if ever, discussed. Maybe she wanted him to
know something about what went on in the depths of
her.

Francesca looked down at her hands in her lap. She
wondered why she was telling him this; it was something she felt deeply, but had never discussed with
anyone—not even her mother. She guessed she wanted

him to know something about what went on in the depths of her.

"The contusion," Waine said. "What caused it?"

"The boom," Francesca said. "Do you sail?"

Part of Waine wanted to say yes. Another part—the part that had listened to Aura talk about sailing as if she were an expert, which she wasn't—wanted to say, *No, never.* "No."

"The boom is a metal spar that runs along the foot—the bottom edge—of the sail. It swings on a pivot from the mast."

"And it hit him on the head—accidentally?"

Francesca shut her eyes, as if to see it. "There's a sailing maneuver called a jibe. It's a maneuver to change tacks—that is, to move the sail from one side of the boat to the other—while sailing before the wind— that is, with the wind behind you. It's simple enough, but it's fairly violent—especially in a big wind. The boom swings from one side to the other—'rather smartly,' is how my father used to put it. It puts a lot of strain on the rigging . . .

"What apparently happened—what the police and the Coast Guard and everyone else seemed to think must have happened—was that my father jibed and was hit by the boom when it swung. It either knocked him out and he fell overboard or he just fell straight overboard and was too much in shock to swim." Francesca opened her eyes and looked down at her hands again and put the one that was on the bottom on top, then put it on the bottom again, as if it were something she didn't like to look at.

"But?" Waine said.

"But what?"

"But you don't think that's what happened."

Francesca put her head back and looked up at the trees. "You start a jibe by steering the stern of the boat through the eye of the wind. You can do it intentionally or you can do it accidentally—if you can't read the wind well, or if it suddenly shifts. My father wouldn't have done it accidentally; he could read the wind . . . perfectly. He might have been caught by a wind shift; that can happen to anybody."

Waine waited a moment. "But? I hear another but."

Francesca shut her eyes. "This is very speculative."

"Go ahead."

"If you were at the tiller—the rudder—and the wind shifted and you jibed accidentally, the boom would hit you, if you didn't duck, in the side of the head."

"And your father was hit in the back of the head."

"Which is what would happen if he'd been standing farther forward, with his back to the tiller."

"And why would he have been doing that?"

"He wouldn't."

"Unless someone else were on the boat—at the tiller."

It wasn't a question, and Francesca didn't answer. She was thinking about her dream—about sailing the small boat without a sheet with which to trim the sail. Did it mean that she was careless—going out without having checked all her rigging? Or did it mean that she was merely short a crucial something that kept her from putting a desire into effect? She hadn't been in danger, after all; she had only been unable to move. The imagined dark cloud had only been the incorporation into the dream of her mother's having blocked out the sun by standing over her.

And there beside them, suddenly, was her mother, who moved on cat feet. "You two are so quiet."

"An angel was passing," Francesca said.

Waine gave her a long look.

"I've seen your name in the paper, Mr. Ryan," Beatrice Hayward said. "And I've often wondered about that spelling—W,a,i,n,e. Is it a family name?"

Waine thought about changing his name—to Sam or George or Joe—or just changing the spelling, changing the *i* to a *y*. He glanced at Francesca, to see if she would help him through this. She was looking distractedly out at the water. "Francesca tells me you're a fan of

Arthurian legend. So was my mother. She named me Gawaine. It never really took as a name—even she called me Waine."

"Your mother's dead, then?" Beatrice Hayward said.

"She died when I was seven. My father brought me up, in his way. He died just a few years ago."

"That must've been difficult. Francesca, at least, was a young woman when her father died."

Waine felt Francesca giving him a look he imagined told him not to mention what they'd been talking about—ever. "You have a beautiful place here, Mrs. Hayward."

"Beatrice, please." She sat in one of the lawn chairs and looked out over the bay. "It is beautiful, I suppose."

Francesca laughed. "You suppose? Several times a day, you drag me out on the porch to see how beautiful it is, how different it looks as the light changes."

"I guess I've started to feel differently about it since I decided to sell it," Beatrice Hayward said. "Reverse sour grapes, or something."

Francesca sat forward in her chair and twisted around to face her mother. "Since you decided to what?"

"I'm glad you're here, Mr. Ryan—"

"Waine."

"Waine. I'm glad you're here, because I've been waiting to tell Francesca that all weekend, but I've been afraid of a quarrel. She won't quarrel in front of a guest."

"I will if you don't tell me what you're talking about."

Beatrice Hayward waved a despairing hand at the house and grounds. "It's much too big, Francesca. The house, the grounds. There's just me here, essentially— except on weekends. It's frightfully expensive to keep up. The rents don't cover the expenses." To Waine, she said, "There are three smaller houses on the grounds that I rent to summer tenants."

"The point, Francesca," Beatrice continued, "is that I've decided it's time I put an end to this noble widowhood of mine and live a little more productively. I mean, look at this place, sitting out on a point overlooking the very place where Noel died." To Waine, she said, "My husband drowned right out there, in a sailing accident."

Waine looked to where she pointed and nodded, feeling Francesca's eyes on him.

"I mean, it's a little morbid, don't you think?"

Waine wondered if she would think it morbid to find that he lived in his late parents' apartment. He wondered if it was morbid.

"What do you plan to do, mother?" Francesca said evenly.

"I want to go to work. I want to work in the city, and when I'm not working, I want to spend more time in the city than I have—going to museums, plays, the works. I don't want a summer place any longer. I won't have time for it, and I don't want the responsibility."

"What kind of work, mother?"

"You sound just like one of my generation—absolutely incredulous that an old woman would want to work."

"You're not an old woman. And I'm not incredulous. I'm just asking."

Beatrice Hayward gestured apologetically toward Waine. "I'm sorry. This isn't very hospitable."

"No, it certainly isn't," Francesca agreed pointedly. "Here I've invited Waine for lunch and nothing has been done about serving it. If you'll excuse me, I'll see to things in the kitchen." Francesca rose and strode across the lawn toward the house.

"I think it's exciting that you want to work," Waine said to cover the awkwardness of the moment. "Have you given any thought to what you want to do?"

"Oh, I've given it thought, but it hasn't gotten me very far. I'm afraid my only qualification is my enthusiasm."

"Let me mention something, then. One of my clients is the director of a community center for senior citizens." He laughed as Beatrice Hayward pulled a face. "No, I'm not suggesting that you're an old woman, either. The director wants to start a creative writing workshop. As I understand it, it's a concept that's catching on in many places that offer programs for older people. It's a way of encouraging them to express themselves, to set down their experiences, in order to get themselves and others to think of those experiences as something worthwhile, and of themselves as repositories of something valuable."

"Well, you stated that very eloquently," Beatrice Hayward said.

Waine laughed. "I guess I've heard Ann say it enough. Ann Morris is the director of the center. She's looking for someone to run the program. The pay would be minimal, but, well, it might interest you."

"It might, indeed. And I thank you for mentioning it. Can I call you for the details? I'll be in the city late in the week."

"By all means. Maybe we can have lunch."

"I'd like that."

"Then I'll expect your call. My numbers are in the book."

Francesca reappeared, carrying a cut-glass bowl of cold shrimp and a smaller matching bowl of tartar sauce. "Lunch."

"We don't have any plates set out, Francesca," Beatrice said.

"I only have two hands, mother."

"I'll help you," Waine said, starting to get up.

Beatrice Hayward beat him to it and put a hand on his shoulder. "You stay right there."

In the kitchen, Beatrice Hayward looked questioningly at Francesca as she noisily assembled plates and knives and forks. "Is something wrong?"

Francesca shook her head.

"What a nice young man," Beatrice Hayward said.

"He really doesn't look like Noel, once you get a second look at him; his eyes are set wider apart."

Francesca had noticed it, too, and had been relieved. Waine's resemblance to her father had disconcerted her. But she knew that was not the entire reason she hadn't looked forward to seeing him more. And just now she had sat on the lawn with him, speaking about her father's death as she had never done before. Perhaps it was the aftermath of the dream. In talking to Waine, she was hoping to find the crucial something she was missing.

But why did she think Waine Ryan was the one who could supply what was missing? Or lead her to it? And why had her mother chosen to announce her decision to sell the house in front of Waine? Not just because he was a guest. The morning's events were making Francesca's diagnosis of the cause of her uneasiness even more difficult than it had been yesterday.

Chapter 15

~~~~~~~~~~~~~~~

That evening, Waine said good-bye to the Hirsches, who had driven him to the Bridgehampton train station, and walked across the parking lot to the platform, which was crowded with suntanned New Yorkers.

One of the best suntans was possessed by a blond woman who was getting into a new Mercedes, apparently having driven someone to the station to catch the train. She wore a white lace blouse that invited inquiry as to whether she wore anything under it, but that cunningly thwarted a certain answer. The blouse—and the Mercedes, which was also white—nicely set off her tan.

Waine saw that the woman was Aura.

She turned away from the Mercedes and came toward him, a hand extended magnanimously. "Waine, Waine, Waine."

He shook her hand. "Hello, Aura."

She kissed his cheek, then stood back from him and looked him up and down. "You look well. You look so very well. I must've been out of my mind to give you up. Do you ever think that we should've just gone on with it, Waine? Made the best of it."

"No. That would've been painful."

Aura pointed toward the crowd on the station platform. "See the young man with the Madras jacket and the white pants? With the tennis racquets?"

Waine only mimed looking, knowing what she was going to say. "Yes."

"He's my lover. He's twenty-six. I'm thirty-eight. That's pathetic, don't you think?"

Waine looked down the tracks, as if he might conjure up the train.

"I hear you're going around with a waitress. That's pathetic, too . . . Or maybe it's not. Maybe we've both just found our levels. Maybe what was pathetic was trying to ever get along. I mean, I don't think the twain can ever really meet—a rich girl and a kid from the streets. I'm not being a snob; I'm just trying to be realistic. I mean, you and your friend—you probably have lots of things that are automatic between the two of you, don't you? I mean, I know she's not a waitress anymore; I know she owns a restaurant—a very successful one, I hear. But that just means the two of you have climbed up the same ladder—from hardship to respectability . . . What are you doing out here, anyway, Waine? I thought you didn't care for the Hamptons."

"Slumming," Waine said.

Aura laughed. "Of course. That's what it is for you, isn't it? Just the way it's slumming for me to go to the Village."

The train whistled in the distance and Waine shouldered his duffel bag.

"Well, Waine . . ."

". . . yes."

"Good-bye."

"Bye."

Waine took three steps toward the platform, then

stopped suddenly as a car braked ostentatiously in front of him.

"Get in," Francesca said.

Waine glanced at Aura, who had stopped her descent into the creamy leather seat of the Mercedes and was looking on curiously.

"Get *in*."

"What're you doing here? " Waine said.

"Driving you into the city. You are going into the city?"

"Yes. I thought you weren't going in till morning."

"Will you get in?" Francesca said evenly.

Waine got in, carefully, as if the car were of uncertain substantiality. Francesca accelerated away before he had the door closed all the way.

"Who's the blonde?" Francesca said.

"Sorry."

"You heard me."

Waine winced as Francesca just beat a changing traffic light. "Are you on an emergency call or something?"

"If you don't like the way I drive, you can get out."

Waine put a hand on her arm. "Could you pull over?"

"What?"

"I'm not going to get out. I'll go into the city with you. I just want you to pull over for a minute. I want your undivided attention."

Francesca pulled over, screeching to a stop.

Waine laughed.

"What's so funny?" Francesca said.

"It's not the blonde, is it? You're not angry about her?"

"I don't know what you're talking about."

Waine laughed and leaned toward her and kissed her cheek.

Francesca put a fingertip to the spot, as if she had been hit by a drop of rain.

Waine laughed.

"What's so goddamn funny?"

"You."

She gripped the steering wheel, as if she were driving at speed.

Waine put a hand on her wrist. "I'm really glad to see you. I'm glad you remembered I was taking that train. I'm glad you came by to get me. I'm sorry you saw me talking to someone and got the wrong impression."

Francesca tromped on the dead accelerator.

Waine laughed.

"Will you stop laughing?" Francesca said between her teeth.

"On one condition."

Francesca waited, then hit the steering wheel with a fist. "Don't make me ask what, goddamn it."

Waine laughed.

Francesca put her head back against the headrest and shut her eyes.

"The condition," Waine said, "is that you let me kiss you."

Afterward, Waine laughed.

So did she. "I'm sorry. I don't know what got in to me. I guess . . . I don't know."

"I understand it," Waine said. "For whatever reason, we're both a little uneasy about how quickly things got started between us. You took a chance on coming to the station to get me, and there I was with a suspiciously beautiful blond lady. It makes sense that you'd feel even more uneasy."

"So who is she?" Francesca said.

Waine looked away.

"Don't say she's just a friend. She gave me a real looking-over."

Waine looked back at her. "She's an ex-wife."

" 'An?' "

"The."

"Ah. And how long has it been?"

"Since I last saw her? I don't know. Maybe—"

"Not since you last saw her, goddamn it. Since you were married."

"Two years."

"Not very long. And how long were you married?"

"Eight years."

"Eight years. That's long. What happened?"

Waine shrugged. "Nothing, really. But then nothing ever really had."

"Any kids?"

"No."

"Why not?"

"We didn't want any."

"They would have kept you together, is that it?"

"If you want to ask, ask—but don't make assumptions."

"You just happened to bump into her in the parking lot, hey?"

"Right. She's staying with friends."

"She just happened to be there dropping someone off and there you were, getting dropped off yourself, right?"

"Right."

"And you just had a few polite words, is that it?"

"A few."

"And how do you feel about it?"

"About what?"

"About seeing her, goddamn it."

Waine shrugged. "I don't feel anything."

"Come on. You can't spend eight years with someone and not feel something when you see them."

"All right. I feel . . . sad."

"Aha."

"Not because I'm not with her. Because I ever was. Because I didn't see what she was—only what I wanted her to be."

"What did you want her to be?"

". . . compassionate."

"And what was she?"

"Selfish."

"She was the one who didn't want to have children?"

"Not just about children. We came from different backgrounds. She was brought up having everything she wanted, always getting her way."

Francesca realized what it was that underlay his refinement—his good clothes and his good looks and his good manners and his good diction. He was rough, and had, through effort, become smooth. "And you grew up not having anything you wanted? Or very little?"

Waine nodded.

"I was brought up having everything I wanted," Francesca said.

Waine nodded.

"Are we alike—your wife and I?"

"Ex-wife."

"Ex-wife."

". . . you work for a living," Waine said. "Aura's a professional heiress."

"Aura? That's a pretty name. I don't think I've ever heard it before."

Waine was stuck by the ridiculousness of their sitting there by the side of the road out at the end of Long Island, talking about things that mattered, when a few days before, when they might have talked about these things, they hadn't. He was also considering what Aura had said to him—that with Bonnie Niles he had found his level.

"Hello," Francesca said.

"Sorry," Waine said. "I was just thinking."

"About?"

"Something somebody said to me the other day."

Francesca waited, draping a wrist over the top of the steering wheel.

". . . he said the only reason I was interested in you was because you're like my wife—my ex-wife. He said the only reason I'd want to get involved with you was so that it wouldn't work out, just the way it didn't with her. He said I didn't want it to work out because I don't really want to have a relationship with a woman; I just want to make it look as though I try, and that there's something about them—the women—that keeps it from working out."

Francesca thought that that sounded like a description of her relationships; she involved herself with inaccessible men so that she wouldn't have to get involved with them—and it was always their fault when it didn't work out. "It's strange . . ."

"I wouldn't say it was normal, no."

"I don't mean that what you're saying is strange. I mean it's strange that you've been talking to a friend about me. I've been thinking about you a lot, but I have very definitely not talked to any friends about you. It's usually the other way around: Women jabber to their friends and men don't say a word to theirs—not for a while, anyway . . . who is he? This friend?"

Waine smiled. "Actually . . ."

"Don't tell me it was some bartender."

Waine laughed. "It was me. I had a little interior dialogue."

Francesca stared. "Really?"

Waine looked embarrassed. "Nobody heard me. I wasn't ranting and raving like those people you see on the street."

"Have you ever noticed that those people on the street aren't talking to themselves? I mean, we'd describe them as talking to themselves, but they're always talking to someone else."

Waine thought about it. "I guess you're right."

"I suppose it's because no matter how lonely they are—no matter how alone—they can't let themselves admit that they have no one but themselves." Francesca sat up straighter, suddenly, and looked around her urgently, as if she'd just noticed where they were. "What're we doing here?"

Waine laughed.

"You're doing it again."

"What?"

"Laughing at me."

"That's easy to fix."

They both laughed and reached for one another. Their kiss was long and deep with promise.

"What *are* we doing here?" Francesca asked again, her meaning far different from the first time she had asked the question.

Waine laughed, then covered his mouth with a hand. "Sorry. Maybe we should just go to the city. Or . . . Well, I suppose there's another train, if you want me to get out."

"Why would I want that?"

"Because of what my . . . my conscience said."

"Don't be ridiculous. We'll just have to show your conscience that it's wrong—that the reason you're interested in getting to know me is that I'm interesting."

"You are that."

"Wait till you get to know me," Francesca said, as she started the car.

Chapter 16

~~~~~~~~~~~~~~~~~

Francesca took a turn that led she knew not where and
they came upon a small inn that she had neither seen
nor heard of in all the time she had spent in that part of
the world. She parked the car and looked at Waine.
Silently, he nodded his assent.

Their room was on the second floor in the back. It
was furnished with antique wooden chairs, dresser and
endtables. The brass bed was covered with a beautiful
handworked patchwork quilt, a star pattern in lemon-
yellow, white and green. The pillows were covered with
cases of a soft yellow floral design, and the shades of
the lamps on the endtables were covered with the same
yellow-flowered material.

A large window looked out on a grove of trees;
beyond the grove was a small pond on which a pair of
swans swam, looking like a stately couple out for an
evening stroll.

They stood before the window, looking out.

"I've never done this before," Francesca said.

"What?"

"Gone to a hotel room for the express purpose of making love."

Waine laughed.

"I thought we had fixed that." Francesca brought her mouth up to cover his.

They spoke no more, and undressed quickly. Lying on the quilt, enjoying its roughness against their skin, they explored each other with a new permissiveness.

Francesca felt more open, more receptive, than she had ever felt in her life. Yet she did not feel vulnerable, did not feel that she was succumbing.

She felt that Waine was becoming a student of her body, and as he learned more about it, so did she. She learned of its length and of its curves and of its rises and of its hollows. She learned that she was sensitive not only to touch, but to remembered touch and anticipated touch; when his hand touched her in one place, she could still feel it touching her in another, and could imagine it touching her in yet another; his hands, therefore, seemed to be everywhere; she felt embraced, enveloped, by his hands.

And she became a student of his body, and felt his joy at discovering his body along with her. His body was a meal to be devoured, and yet was endlessly replenished.

Francesca was sure she would long remember this moment. She would remember the faint smell, like slightly bitter lemon, of Waine's body, and how hard his arms were; she would remember the way he seemed to grow younger as his hair got more tousled, and the care he took to prepare her for everything he was going to do, so as not to startle her; she would remember her effortless orgasm, nearly coincident with his. But most of all she would remember that this time—and the last, as well—had been the first times she had made love to a man without using the prop of fantasy; she had been aroused by Waine and had made love with Waine and had been satisfied by Waine; no wishes or reminiscences had obtruded. She would remember that, and she would remember the yellowy light of the room and the texture of the quilt and the occasional bleat, out the window, of the swans.

After a long time, Waine laughed softly.

This time, Francesca joined him. She laughed because her heart felt light and full at the same time. She had something to laugh about now.

The yellowy late afternoon light had faded and the room was deep in shadow. Waine reached over to switch on the bedside lamp.

"Don't, Waine."

"We should be going soon. I have to be in court at nine o'clock tomorrow, and you'll have to be at the hospital early . . . won't you?"

"Yes, I will."

Spending the night together in this room had been far from Francesca's mind when she drove up to the inn. Only when Waine had reached over to turn on the lamp had she become aware that she wanted to. And at the same instant, she had known she wouldn't. She wondered why. It had nothing to do with the fact that they both had to be at their jobs early in the morning; it had to do with . . . with what? She didn't know. She only knew that her uneasiness, which had disappeared completely during their lovemaking, had returned. It had to do with the same feeling that had kept her from looking forward to their date this morning. It worried her. It was one thing to have a feeling that she should not commit too much too soon to this man. But quite another to feel so drawn to him, and at the same time try to deny the power of their attraction.

Chapter 17

〜〜〜〜〜〜〜〜〜

They drove in silence for a long time, enjoying the warm breeze. Near Babylon, they passed an accident: Two cars had sideswiped and their opposite fenders were crumpled; their owners gesticulated at each other on the apron; their wives or girl friends talked conspiratorially nearby.

"It's funny," Francesca said, "on the way out here, I didn't have a single thought about accidents. With Eva James on my mind, I would have thought I would."

"How are those retinas of Eva's?" Waine said.

"Still too soon to tell. She has a long haul ahead of her. An expensive haul."

Waine tried to glimpse her expression in the light of approaching headlamps. "Any particular reason you mention that?"

"Hospitals are expensive."

We could have a fight over this, Waine thought. I could tell her I know they're expensive because my mother spent two and a half years in and out of them and my father spent fifteen years paying the bills. She would say I sounded bitter and I would say I had a right to be, didn't I, given that they never did find out what was wrong with my mother and that what she died of was hepatitis, contracted in the hospital. She would say that happens, and I would say it happened a lot more in the days before people realized that sick people had rights, too.

We could have a fight over this, Francesca thought. I could tell him I'm concerned that this custody battle not interfere with Eva's getting better. I could also tell him I don't entirely trust Ted and Clara Hirsch. Ted's never made any money from his writing, good reviews notwithstanding. I'm not sure they're not just trying to get their hands on Conrad James's money. "Eva is going to get her parents' money, isn't she? Will or no will?"

"In cases like this, the estate is distributed according to the intestacy statutes of the state," Waine said. "The statutes attempt to distribute the estate in the same manner the deceased would have. In this case, since there are no brothers or sisters, and since Eva wasn't estranged from her parents in any way, we can be practically certain that she would have been intended to inherit her parents' estate."

Francesca heard in his somewhat didactic delivery a love of the law—of its logic and its necessity. "Will the money be hers, or her guardian's?"

"Hers, but it will be placed in trust for her until she's of age."

"And is her guardian the—what's the word?—the trustee?"

"Trustee is the word, yes; but her guardian won't be the trustee, no. Eva is the beneficiary of the trust. She's not entitled to the body of the trust until she's of age. Until that time, the trustee will make payments to Eva's guardian to the extent necessary for her upbringing, for her education, for . . . her hospital bills."

"What's to keep the guardian from inflating the bills?"

"A trustee has a duty to preserve the assets of the

trust," Waine said. "He is personally liable for any loss
to the trust occasioned by his breach of that duty. He
must also invest the trust and make it fruitful and is
liable for failure to make reasonable, prudent invest-
ments. He may distribute some assets to Eva's guardian
for expenses of her upbringing, but if he were found to
have distributed an excessive amount, or to have distributed any amount to any person other than Eva's
guardian, he'd be liable to the trust for any such funds.
It's a grave responsibility to be a trustee for a minor
child, and any trustee who permitted someone to profit
personally from the trust would be in hot water finan-
cially when the breach surfaced . . . Excuse my metaphor."

Francesca laughed. She was glad he had lightened
up a little. "And who bears this . . . grave responsibility?"

"An institution, usually—like a bank that has a trust
department."

The back of Francesca's neck tingled, the way it did
when she was getting her hair cut or her nails done. It
was a sign that she was enjoying having something done
to her—in this case, being taught. "So what about Ted
Hirsch's saying Conrad James asked him to take care of
Eva? Does that have any . . . legal clout?"

"Ted Hirsch is an honest man. He has no criminal
record—no history of fraud or deception. He and
Conrad James were close. It wasn't unusual for them to
spend time together apart from their wives or any other
witnesses. His testimony may move the judge; the
credibility of witness testimony is determined by the
trier of the facts. However, in view of its self-serving
nature and the fact that there's no corroboration, I'd
say it won't have much clout. Admissible, yes. Effec-
tive, no."

Francesca concentrated on traffic, which was thicken-
ing as they neared the city limits. "Suppose there had
been no conversation between Ted Hirsch and Conrad
James, and suppose Ted Hirsch and Diana Stewart each

wanted custody. Would the two sets of relatives have equal claims?"

"Claim is a precise word. If what you mean by claim is the legal instrument by which proceedings are initiated—for example, a petition for custody of a minor child—then both sets of relatives have equal dignity in the eyes of the law, and equal access to the judicial process. They enter the court as claimants on equal footing. In essence, anyone who can keep a straight face can make a claim—"

Francesca laughed, then tried to wipe the smile from her face.

Waine saw the gesture and thought that it was the kind of thing that could make him fall unequivocally in love with her. He didn't feel unequivocally in love with her, and he wondered why. "—however, if what you mean by claim is the whole factual package supporting their assertion to right of custody, then the two sides have distinctly unequal claims. The Stewarts' claim is vastly superior to the Hirschs'—"

"Wait a minute. Whose lawyer are you?"

"Oh, I'll win the case, but it's going to be difficult. The Stewarts are well-established in the community, and so the judge will be. Ted and Clara are . . . well, just folks."

"I hope you're not just trying to make a point," Francesca said.

"What point?"

Francesca drove.

"What point?"

"You'll say I'm making an assumption."

"You've already made it. You may as well tell me what it is."

Francesca drove.

"Francesca."

"I haven't made an assumption."

"But you have a thought."

"A thought, yes. But if I tell you what my thought is, you'll think it's an assumption."

Waine sighed.

"What?" Francesca said.

"Nothing."

"What, goddamn it?"

"I'm just thinking."

"What about?"

"About what you said."

"Don't make assumptions," Francesca said.

Waine shifted about in his seat, ending up with his shoulder turned to her a little. "I took this case because I believe Ted. I also believe he and Clara will make better foster parents for Eva than the Stewarts. Ted and Clara are good people, hard-working people. I like the way they think and live and act. The Stewarts are . . . I don't know."

"Rich?" Francesca gave him a warning look. "It wasn't an assumption. It was a question."

"Forget about whether they're rich or not. It seems to me that they're casual, complacent. They don't strike me as having a lot of compassion."

"Like your ex-wife?"

". . . they don't strike me as very parental."

"Then why do they want to be parents? Why would they bother?"

"That's a good question."

"It can't be the money. They have money. And you said yourself, they won't be able to get at the trust."

"Absent fraud."

"What?"

"I said Eva's guardian isn't going to be able to reach the body of the trust. It's not unheard of, however, for people to try."

"Are you saying the Stewarts are crooks?" Francesca said. "That sounds pretty far-fetched."

"All I'm saying is that my associate is looking into Charles Stewart's business affairs. He may have a lot of money on paper, but it isn't necessarily liquifiable."

The traffic worsened and took all of Francesca's attention, and much of Waine's, too, for he found himself driving sympathetically. They took a guess that there would be less traffic on Queens Boulevard and the Queensborough Bridge, and guessed wrong; by the time they made it to Manhattan, they were weary and frazzled.

"You don't need to drive downtown," Waine said. "You can drop me anywhere."

They were a lane from the curb, but Francesca pulled over abruptly, bringing down on them a rain of horn blasts. She turned to face him. "What's going on? I mean, a couple of hours ago we were making love in a way I've never made love before."

"Nor have I," Waine said.

"And now I'm feeling a kind of tension that I don't think I've ever felt before, either."

"Nor have I."

"What do you make of it?"

"We're still getting to know each other."

Francesca turned to look out the front windshield. "I'm not so sure."

"Not so sure of what?"

"I think you think you already know me," Francesca said.

"And I think you think you know me," Waine said.

"Because I make assumptions?"

Waine nodded.

"I admit I make assumptions," Francesca said. "Maybe it's because of the work I do. Sometimes I have to proceed based on nothing but assumptions. I have to do it to find out if I'm right or wrong. I don't have time to stand around and wait. But I'm good at my work, which means I must be assuming right a lot of the time. I trust my instincts."

"Maybe . . . " Waine began.

". . . what?"

"Maybe the fact that we both feel unprecedented passion and unprecedented tension just means that this is truly unprecedented—that neither of us has ever been here before, never felt like this before."

"That would be unprecedented," Francesca said. She laughed.

Waine laughed, too.

Francesca took Waine's hand and held it in both of hers. "Do this for me—if you find this is all too much for you, please call me and say so. Don't just disappear. Don't make up excuses not to see me."

"I won't," Waine said. "Can I ask the same of you?"

Francesca nodded.

They moved close together and kissed. Their hands moved toward private places, but stopped short of caressing them.

Driving uptown alone, Francesca felt an urge to just keep on driving—north all the way to the North Pole and over it and south all the way to the South Pole and over it and north again to . . . to where? Such a trip would only bring her back where she started. The trip she wanted to take was one that would bring her to where she had never been. An unprecedented trip.

She wondered if she were on an unprecedented trip, as Waine had suggested.

How was she to know? On an unprecedented trip, there were no familiar road signs. There were no road signs at all.

Chapter 18

~~~~~~~~~~~~~~~~~~~

"Lasers?" Eva James said. "You mean like in *Star Wars*?"

Francesca laughed. "Not exactly, but it's the same principle."

"You're going to shoot a laser at my *eye?*"

Francesca sat on the edge of Eva's bed and squeezed Eva's hand. "Let me explain the whole thing to you, so you'll understand it's nothing to be afraid of. Now, you remember what I told you about a detached retina?"

"A balloon inside a balloon," Eva said.

"Bravo. Okay, so—"

"Brav*a*," Eva said. "When it's a woman, you say brav*a*."

"So you do, sweetheart. So you do. Brav*a* . . . Anyway, about attaching retinas—years and years ago, when my father first became a doctor—"

"Your father's a doctor?"

"Yes. He was. He died a long time ago."

"And you're a doctor, too? Wow. I want to be a writer. Like my father. I want to write science fiction

stories. I wrote a short story once. I wish I had it here
to show you. It's about a bumble bee. Her name's
Bernice. How are my parents today?"

Francesca was glad Eva's eyes were bandaged, for
she could feel the flash of dismay on her face. She shut
her own eyes, the better to lie. "They're . . . fine."

"Better? You mean they're better?"

"I'm not really sure. They're not my patients, peanut
—you know that. You can ask your aunt when she
comes later. She'll know." Francesca hurried on, before there could be more questions, or before Eva
could tell her, as she had told her before, that her Aunt
Diana dodged most of Eva's questions as if she hadn't
heard them. "When my father first became a doctor,
people who had detached retinas almost always lost the
sight in that eye. They only operated when the patient
had already lost the sight in the other eye. The patient
was going to go blind in both eyes, anyway, because of
the detachment, so the operation was worth the risk—"

"So at least maybe they could see out of one eye,"
Eva said.

"Right . . . The surgery was very crude. They
drilled a hole in the back of the eyeball—"

"Yuck."

"—and put a tiny chemical stick through the hole—"

"Ooh, ick."

"Eva, you said you were interested in this stuff. If
you don't want to hear it, just say so." Francesca
wondered why her fuse was so short today.

"I want to hear it, but it's still yucky."

". . . the stick was made of potassium hydroxide. It's
a very powerful chemical; it causes burns. But that's
what they wanted; they wanted to touch the stick to the
place where the retina had become detached and
produce a burn. A scar tissue would form that would
seal off the tear and reattach the retina. Or that's what
they hoped would happen. Sometimes the burn was so
severe, it would destroy the eye—"

"But the person was going to go blind, anyway, right,

because their retina was detached, so they had to do it, anyway, right?"

"Right . . . Then, later on, somebody invented tiny little electrodes—electrical wires—that could carry very high-frequency currents—"

"Your father?"

"My father, what?"

"Did he invent the tiny little electrodes?"

"No, sweetheart, but he used them . . . The electrical current caused burn scars, too, but they were much smaller and much less dangerous than with the chemical sticks. Another good thing about them was that they didn't have to drill a hole in the eyeball—"

"Good."

"—because the electrodes were so thin they could be pushed right through the wall of the eye—"

"Ooh, blechy poohy."

Francesca began a count toward ten. At five, she realized what was upsetting her; she was feeling sure she would never have a little girl as clever and pretty as Eva James; she was feeling sure she would never have any kind of little girl, or little boy. She was feeling sorry for herself. "You're right. It is blechy poohy."

"Do you ever get sick?" Eva said. "I mean, when you cut somebody's guts open or something?"

"I'm an eye doctor, peanut. I don't cut people's guts."

"Do you ever get sick, though?"

Francesca tried not to think about her bad dreams—dreams in which she operated on the wrong one of a patient's eyes, or made so many mistakes that she had to keep peeling away pieces of the eye, which would be layered like an onion. She was often sick on waking from these dreams, which, fortunately, she didn't dream often. "Sometimes I get sick when I'm overworked, but otherwise, no."

"I think I'd get sick all the time. I don't think I'd make a very good doctor."

Francesca wondered if she'd make a very good

mother. " . . . anyway, eventually someone invented lasers—"

"What is a laser, anyway?" Eva said. "I mean, what does it *mean?*"

"It's called an acronym. Do you know what that is?"

"Nope."

"It's a word that's formed from the first letters of other words. Laser is formed from the first letters of the words light amplification by stimulated emission of radiation. That's what a laser is—light that's formed by collecting together electromagnetic radiation."

"Say the words again."

"Light amplification by stimulated emission of radiation. L,a,s,e,r—laser."

"What about 'by?'" Eva said. "And 'of?'"

"They didn't count them, I guess. They didn't make as good a word."

"They'd make 'labseor,'" Eva said. She giggled. "That's a silly word."

Francesca rubbed Eva's stomach briskly.

"Hey."

"Sorry. Does that hurt?"

"No, but what're you doing?"

"Nothing. Just . . . Nothing. Anyway, lasers are so accurate, they can cut a single cell in half, a cell that's so small you need a microscope to see it—"

"Am I ever going to be able to look through a microscope again?" Eva said.

Francesca thought she'd make a better mother if she got over her sadness at seeing children in pain. "Of course you are, peanut. Don't you trust me?"

"I can't see at all now."

Francesca laughed. "You have bandages on your eyes."

"But could I see if I didn't?"

"Yes. Not well, but you'd see."

"But I have detached retinas."

"You could still see, even with them, at this stage. The only thing you would notice would be a feeling like there was a kind of curtain, a thin curtain, blowing off in the corner of your eye. Or sometimes you'd see an occasional flash of light. Or dots."

"I see dots sometimes when I rub my eyes. If I can see, how come I have to wear bandages?"

"So you don't rub your eyes."

"Oh."

Francesca laughed, and so did Eva. Eva had decided that while she still loved Becky Morgan best of all, she loved Dr. Hayward best of all grownups—after her mother and father, of course. She decided to tell her. "I love you, Dr. Hayward." She decided to leave out all the qualifications.

Francesca wished that Eva could see her face, for she felt radiant. "Eva, that's sweet. I love you, too." So that she wouldn't cry, Francesca hurried on again. "Anyway, lasers are very accurate and very powerful. They can be shot through the pupil of the eye—that's the black part; it's a hole, really—"

"A *hole?*"

Francesca smiled, remembering Waine's consternation over that information. "Don't worry. Everybody has one."

"Everybody has a hole in their *eye?*"

Francesca smiled more, glad that remembering Waine made her smile, glad that if things were unprecedented they at least induced smiles. "You didn't know that, did you?"

"*No.*"

"Take it from me."

"I bet Becky doesn't know it, either."

"I called Becky's parents to tell them how you're doing. They sent their love, and so did she."

"When is she going to be able to come and see me?"

"When you're a little better. She'll have to come with her parents. It's regulations."

"So are you going to shoot a laser through the hole in my eye?" Eva said.

"I can only do that if the detachment is in the back of

the eye," Francesca said. "If it is, I'll use the laser. You won't even know it happened. It's over in a fraction of a second."

Eva made a swift click with her tongue. "Like that?"

"Faster. Faster than any sound you can make."

"Wow."

"And it causes no pain. I won't even have to use an anesthetic to make you go to sleep."

"Wow."

"The trouble is, peanut, that if the tear isn't in the back, I won't be able to use the laser. And right now, I'm still not exactly sure where the tear is. If it's in the front, I'll have to use the very latest thing that's been invented. It's called a cryoprobe—"

"I know what that is." Eva waved her hand as if at a teacher.

"You do?"

"I know what cryo means. Cryo means cold. In Science, we studied about cryogenics. That's where dead people are frozen and if they ever discover a cure for what they died of, they'll unfreeze them and cure them."

"That's right. Well, a cryoprobe is an instrument that makes very cold temperatures—"

"Zero?"

"Much colder. Fifty degrees below zero centigrade. That's . . . Well, I don't know what it is Fahrenheit."

"It's *cold*," Eva said.

"Very cold. Anyway, the best thing about the cryo-probe is that I don't have to put it inside your eye at all. I just touch it to the place on the outside of the eye opposite where the retina's detached, and it makes a burn on the inside of the eye without burning the outside."

"Wow."

"Wow, indeed."

"Will I have to have asth—anes—an-es-thetic for that?"

"A local anesthetic. Just the eye will go to sleep."

"But won't I go to sleep if my eye goes to sleep?"
Eva laughed, and sang, with a Latin lilt, "Ay yi yi yi."

Francesca put her head on Eva's chest and hugged
her. "I love you, Eva James."

Eva said nothing. Then, she said: "My mother and
father are dead, aren't they, Dr. Hayward?"

Francesca sat up slowly. " . . . yes."

"I thought so."

" . . . I'm sorry, Eva. They died right away. They
didn't feel any pain."

"That's what they always say—in movies and stuff.
That's what my father said about my dog, Judith, when
she had to be put to sleep. But nobody really knows
that for sure, do they?"

"No, they don't. Not for sure. But your parents died
instantly. If dying instantly means you stop feeling
instantly, then they didn't feel any pain. If it doesn't,
then maybe they felt something. But I don't know
what. It might not have been pain. Pain is a warning.
It's the body's way of telling you to stop doing to it
whatever you're doing—holding your hand under hot
water, running too far or too fast—whatever. So maybe
they didn't feel any pain, because what happened to
their bodies wasn't something that could be made
better. So you understand that, Eva? I think it's
important."

"I understand." Eva put her hand to the bandages,
to feel if the tears she could feel on the inside were
soaking through to the outside. "Does that mean I'm
going to live with Uncle Ted and Aunt Clara?"

" . . . is that what you want?"

"It's what my father wanted."

" . . . he told you that?"

"He told me he was going to put it in his will."

"His will?"

"Yeah. He said if anything ever happened to him and
mom, I'd have to live with somebody, and he asked me
who I'd want to live with."

"And you said your Uncle Ted?"

"I said Becky."

Francesca laughed. "And he said it would be better if it was a relative?"

"Yeah."

"So then you said your Uncle Ted?"

"He's mom's brother."

"I know. Your Aunt Diana is your father's sister."

"I don't like Aunt Diana."

". . . do you know what your father did with the will? Nobody's been able to find it."

"It's in my room."

"*Your* room?"

"Yeah. It's *my* will. I mean, it's about me, so it should be in *my* room, shouldn't it? I mean, doesn't that make sense?"

"When you put it that way it does. Not everybody thinks as clearly as you . . . Your room at home or your room on Shelter Island?"

"At home."

"In a desk or . . . where?"

"It's in a box with my important stuff. A metal box."

"In your desk?"

"In my closet."

"Does the box say anything on it?"

"Yes."

"What?"

"Important *stuff*."

Chapter 19

~~~~~~~~~~~~~~

Eva's revelation weighed on Francesca liked a millstone. She dragged it on her rounds; she dragged it to a
staff meeting presided over by Dr. Vincent Clavin,
filling in for Dr. Wilson Finch, who was out of town at a
convention; on her lunch break, she dragged it into
Central Park and carried it up to the cinder path that
runs around the reservoir. She knew that Tim Ward ran
around the path every day at that time, and she wanted
to talk to him.

She hadn't realized how confused she was until Eva
had dropped her little bombshell and confused her all
the more.

She was confused because Waine Ryan had happened into her professional life, and she had let him
step from her professional life into her personal life
without much resistance. Without, in fact, any resistance. That wasn't like her. To be sure, she had had
advances made toward her by the men she worked with
at every stage of her career—from student to specialist.
But she had never responded—out of a feeling that it

would be impossible to be in love with someone she worked with. To men she worked with, she had to be able to give advice, and take it, to say no and be told no, to be brusque or forgetful or overbearing or impatient or tired—to behave, in general, in ways a colleague could always understand but that a lover never could. She had become sure that she would never, could never, love another doctor.

But Waine Ryan wasn't another doctor, and yet she was involved with him professionally. And she was involved with him personally.

And now there was this terrible confusion, brought on by those involvements.

Francesca stood on the cinder path, looking through the chain link fence that surrounded the reservoir at the gulls and ducks swimming on the surface. With the fingers of one hand grasping the links of the fence, and with her millstone around her neck, she felt like a prisoner; yet she was free to go any way she wanted. Or was she?

Something made her turn away from the fence and look down the path. Tim Ward was running toward her, striding easily along the path. She wondered what had made her turn; other runners had come and gone while she stood there, but she hadn't bothered to check to see if any of them was Tim; she had been sure that she would feel his approach; she wondered why she had been sure of that.

Tim Ward slowed as he saw Francesca, and by the time he reached her he was walking, hands on hips, getting his breath back. He looked quite jaunty with a blue terrycloth headband around his forehead, a white singlet, blue shorts and yellow running shoes with bold blue stripes.

"Out for some exercise?" Tim said. "Or did you think I might need medical attention?"

Francesca smiled. She was wearing her lab coat. "I need to talk. I hate to interrupt your workout, but it's sort of urgent."

Tim took her arm. "Walk with me a little, so I can cool down. I was just thinking, when I saw you, about whether I was going to do four times around the reservoir, the way I usually do, or only three. I've never done only three, but lately I've been thinking a lot about it. I'm finding, as I get older, that although I can run as far and as fast as I always could, I don't really want to. I seem to be losing some mental edge."

"Are you really getting older, Tim?" Francesca said. "I've somehow always thought you wouldn't—that you were different from the rest of us."

Tim glanced at her face, trying to read her expression. "Those are the words of someone with a lot on her mind."

Francesca nodded.

They walked a bit farther, without speaking, then turned back toward the steps leading down from the path. They found a patch of grass in the sun and sat, Tim with his legs out to catch the sun, Francesca with hers tucked under her.

"What would you do if—" Francesca began.

Tim interrupted, waving a hand in protest. "Don't give me any hypotheticals. Just tell me what your problem is. What I'd do 'if' isn't the point."

Francesca smiled ruefully. "Yes, sir."

Tim put a hand out to touch hers. "I didn't mean to be rude. I just think if you have something on your mind, you should—"

"You're right," Francesca said. "You're right."

They sat quietly for a moment, each wishing they could start over.

Since she couldn't start over, Francesca started from where she was. "A patient of mine told me something that's relevant to a legal case that she's involved in. It was unsolicited; that is, I didn't ask her about it, it just came out in a conversation we were having. It's an important detail—so important that the legal question would actually be settled if it were known . . . I . . . I don't know what to do."

Tim Ward picked a blade of grass and chewed on it. "That's pretty vague. I'm not sure I understand."

"I don't think I can be more specific," Francesca said.

Tim nodded. "I understand. But let me ask you a couple of questions . . . Why do you have to do anything? That is, won't your patient tell her lawyers what she told you?"

"She doesn't have a lawyer. Or not exactly. There are lawyers involved, but they're not representing her; they're representing other parties."

Tim examined the blade of grass for a moment. "So she might never be called on to testify, or whatever?"

"Possibly."

"But what she told you is so important that it would decide the legal case?"

"Yes."

"And you're concerned that if you tell the lawyers what she told you you'll be violating a confidence between patient and doctor."

Francesca heard that it wasn't a question, and didn't reply.

Tim Ward tossed away the blade of grass and picked another and chewed on it. "It's not a crime we're talking about, is it? I mean, we're not talking about a murder confession or something, are we?"

"No."

Tim lay on his back and looked up through the trees at the sky. "I'd go to Finch," he said at last. "I'd go to Finch and tell him the situation and let him handle it. You don't have to tell him what your patient told you. You can just suggest that he set up a meeting between your patient and the lawyers."

Francesca nodded, even though Tim couldn't see her.

Tim sat up. "That's what I'd do, 'if.' "

Francesca smiled. "That's what I'd do, too. I guess one of the reasons I'm anguishing over it is that Finch is out of town. He won't be back till next week. I hate like anything to go to Clavin about something like this."

"It probably shouldn't wait," Tim said.

"I know," Francesca said.

Tim didn't need to ask Francesca why she was reluctant to go to Vincent Clavin. It was more than Clavin being unlikeable. He knew that Noel Hayward, Francesca's father, and Wilson Finch had been the closest of friends. He knew that Noel Hayward had been in line to be chief of staff of Lexington Hospital and that Vincent Clavin had been in line to be assistant chief. He knew that when Noel Hayward died, Clavin had expected to be named chief of staff. And he knew that the post had gone to Wilson Finch—a gesture, some said, in memory of his late close friend. He knew that Vincent Clavin had hated Wilson Finch ever since and, by extension, had hated Francesca. "I know it's a tough decision for you to make, but it'll only make things worse if you wait, Francesca," Tim said.

Francesca nodded. She got up from the grass and brushed off her skirt. "Thank you, Tim."

Tim didn't get up. He saw how her eyes were clouded. "There's something else, isn't there?"

Francesca poked at the ground with the toe of a shoe. "Yes," she said softly.

Tim waited.

"I guess I can't talk about it," Francesca said. "I guess I need to think it over a little more before I can talk about it."

Tim got up and brushed off his running shorts. "Well, if you need to talk, you know how to reach me." He patted the waistband of his shorts and Francesca noticed for the first time that he was wearing his paging beeper.

She laughed. "I wouldn't do that to you. I'd at least wait till you'd finished a lap."

"I told you, I'm losing my mental edge. I welcome any excuse to stop."

"You're not going to stop now, are you?"

"No. I'd feel guilty just doing two laps. I'll do another. Maybe I'll do two more, but I'll at least do one. I'm losing my mental edge, but I haven't lost it altogether."

Francesca touched Tim's arm. "Thank you, Tim."

"Any time."

"Have a good run." She started to turn away.

"Francesca?"

She turned back. "Yes?"

"You haven't done anything wrong. So don't worry."

She nodded. "Thanks."

Walking back to the hospital, Francesca thought how easily she could talk to Tim—much more easily than to any man she had ever known—except, perhaps, her father. She wondered if she could only talk easily to a man she loved as a friend—or loved as a father.

At Francesca's knock, Dr. Vincent Clavin spun away from the window he had been looking out, day-dreaming; he acted as though he'd been caught in some crime. "Why, Dr. Hayward, what brings you to my little office?"

Francesca remarked on the adjective. Clavin was always dropping subtle complaints about the assistant chief of staff's lack of power and perquisites. "I know that Dr. Finch is out of town—"

"Some AMA thing. The poor chap. Always having to go someplace or other for some boring seminar on God knows what."

It occurred to Francesca that she never looked Vincent Clavin in the eyes, and that that was strange. Eyes were her bailiwick, healthy or ill; they interested her. She wondered if there were something in his eyes she didn't want to know about. "Something's come up that I feel—"

"Something urgent?" There was eagerness in Clavin's voice. He normally had so little authority that he jumped at the chance to exercise any power.

Francesca heard the eagerness, and hesitated for a moment. It was one thing to put this matter into the hands of someone in authority, and another to drop it in the lap of someone inept.

Clavin covered his concern with bluster, spreading his arms wide. "Come, come, Francesca. Out with it. It can't be *that* serious." He hoped.

Had he ever called her by her Christian name before? She didn't think so—not since her adolescence. And even then, she couldn't remember that he'd done it much; he hadn't paid much attention to her when she was young; he had always seemed, in those days, to be doting over her father. Not doting, exactly, but . . . hovering, as if waiting for something.

Francesca went to the visitor's chair in front of his desk and ran a fingernail over its rough beige fabric.

"Do sit down, Dr. Hayward," Clavin said.

Francesca sat on the very front of the chair, as if ready to flee.

Clavin sat behind the desk. "Yeees?"

"It's about one of my patients. A little girl named Eva James . . ."

Chapter 20

~~~~~~~~~~~~~~

Waine Ryan suspected that he was in love with Francesca Hayward when it became important to him that she meet Phil Archer, the cop to whom Waine felt he owed everything.

"Everything? You shouldn't belittle your own talents."

"If it hadn't been for Phil, I'd have put them to work in other areas—less respectable ones. I was what we used to call a juvenile delinquent. Chances are I'd have become an adult delinquent, too. I'd be one of my clients."

"I've heard talk about your clients," Francesca said. "You're a sort of Robin Hood, aren't you?"

Waine laughed. "Some of my clients have accused me of robbery when they've gotten my bills, yes."

"What I meant to say was, I've heard you have a few rich clients to subsidize taking on not so rich clients."

"I do what I can to help as many poor people as I can," Waine said. "The law is intimidating enough without being charged an arm and a leg by someone helping you cope with it."

They were walking alongside the East Drive in Central Park, on their way to a restaurant on Columbus Avenue where they would meet Phil Archer. Beside them, rush hour traffic swept north with an urgent woosh; above them, on the cinder path around the reservoir, joggers crunched and panted. The trees shimmered in the waning light; the sky was a rich blue.

Francesca stopped, a restraining hand on Waine's arm. "We have a little time, don't we, before we meet your friend?"

"A little. I thought we could find a bench somewhere and enjoy the evening."

"Would you come with me to the museum—the Metropolitan? For just fifteen minutes, to see a favorite painting. It's open late tonight."

Waine hadn't been to the Metropolitan Museum in years—not since the days when he'd gone with Aura, to special previews to which her parents' role as benefactors of the museum had gained them invitations—previews that Waine had never understood the purpose of, since everyone stood with his back to the paintings or sculptures being previewed, carefully gripping his cocktail glass, so as to better see who else was there, and whom they were with, and what they and the people they were with were wearing. "That'd be nice. I have a favorite painting, too. It's been a long time since I've seen it."

"Let me guess which," Francesca said. She put her hand in the crook of his arm and tipped her head back and squinted through the trees as they walked on. "I see a landscape painting. English."

"You could call it a landscape. But not English."

"American, then."

"American."

". . . but it's not quite a landscape? It has people in it?"

"Yes."

"A Winslow Homer, perhaps. The one of the women on the beach. With a dog."

"I remember that one, now that you mention it," Waine said. "I like it, but that's not it."

Francesca stopped, letting go of his arm and waiting until he turned to face her. She looked at him closely, almost suspiciously, as if the remarkable thing would not be that she would guess the painting, but that he would admire the painting she would guess. "Thomas Eakins. 'Max Schmidt in a single scull.'"

Waine held his breath, then let it out in a gasp of wonder. "Why, yes—now that you mention it."

Francesca ran her hand up his arm to his muscular shoulder. "I had some clues. You said you rowed on the crew in college."

"Not in college; in law school. And not on the crew; just in a scull, for fun."

Francesca put her arm all the way through his and hugged it close to her and got them moving again. "Eakins painted himself in that painting. He's the man in the boat in the background."

Waine knew, but didn't mind being told, and didn't feel the need to say he knew.

"I started college intending to be an art history major," Francesca said. "I switched to pre-med when my father died. Nothing melodramatic like picking up the flag or anything. I just realized that what he did was important and that what I proposed to do was take it easy—traveling around the world looking at beautiful paintings."

"It makes sense," Waine said. "You went from studying the visual arts to studying the art of vision."

"I like that," Francesca said. "I wish I'd've thought to put it that way."

The painting was a portrait, by John Singer Sargent, of a man and a woman named Mr. and Mrs. I.A. Phelps Stokes. The woman had her hair up in a bun and wore a gray pleated shirt with a white round collar, a blazer, wide belt and big bow-tie all of brown velvet, and a floor-length white skirt. Her left hand was on her hip, her right hand held against her other hip a straw boater hat with a black band. She was in the foreground of the painting, nearly filling the frame, the gleaming truncated pyramid that was her skirt rendered in broad strokes that gave the painting a modern, abstract look. Her husband stood behind her, in a corner of the frame, his arms folded across his chest, wearing a salmon-pink suit, a white shirt with standup collar and black bow-tie. His bearded face was nearly obscured by shadow, whereas his wife's stood out bold and bright.

Francesca leaned her cheek against Waine's shoulder. "There's a story behind it. Sargent was commissioned to paint only the woman. She was going to be posed with her dog. A large dog, I would guess, since the hand that's holding the hat was going to be resting on the dog's head. I remember vividly that in the biography of Sargent I read the writer said, 'the dog wasn't available.' I always wondered what that meant. Did it die? Was it out of town on business? Did it have another gig?—"

Waine laughed. He *knew* he loved her, for wondering about the dog at all.

"—anyway, there was no dog available, and there was all that frame to fill up. So Sargent got the husband to pose. Or maybe the wife insisted. Or maybe he volunteered. I've always thought . . . Well, look. Look how Sargent just sketched the husband, really. And look at those strange shadows on his face; there's no source for them that we can see. I always imagined that what happened was that Sargent was in love with the woman. I mean, look at her; she's so striking. I always imagined that the husband suspected and got the dog out of the picture somehow—" Francesca laughed at the unintentional pun, and so did Waine. "—and insisted that he be painted in its place, so he could keep an eye on things. Sargent had to give in—he was being paid, after all—but he wasn't going to make Mr. Stokes look any too good . . . Do you like it?"

Waine stepped back and looked the painting over from a new distance for a while, crossing his arms on his chest until he realized he was mirroring the man, then slipping his hands into his pockets. "I do. But it also disturbs me."

"Something . . . Oedipal?"

Waine wondered if she'd showed the painting to other men and if they'd said what he was about to. "Yes. My father was like that—dark and in the background. A presence. Ominous."

"Even after your mother died?"

"More so. He sat with the lights out most of the time, with the television on, but no sound, drowning himself in bourbon."

Francesca had suspected that she was in love with Waine when she realized that it was imperative that he see the painting, which she had always thought of as *her* painting. Now she knew she loved him for confessing what the painting made him see. She had always felt that there was something like that residing in it, and had never showed it to any man before, lest she have to listen to him deny that it had any import. "Ah, so that's why your policeman friend means so much to you."

"I never thought of him as my father," Waine said. "More like a teacher, a coach. He's not real fatherly; he's . . . gruff. He's . . . Well, you'll see."

"I'm going to like him," Francesca said.

"I think you will, yes."

"I know I will—" She kissed his cheek. "—because I love you."

Waine held her gently by the shoulders. "I love you."

She got into his arms, with her cheek against his chest. "Yes, it is a case of that, isn't it?"

"Does it frighten you?"

"God, yes. It's new; it's different; it's . . . doubtful."

"Its future, you mean?"

"Of course. That's what the future is, isn't it? Uncertain."

"Nice girl," Phil Archer said to Waine. Francesca had gone to the ladies' room.

"I think they prefer being called women these days, Phil."

Archer shrugged and leaned back in his chair to tuck in his shirt. "Guess who called me the other day."

Waine waited, sure he was going to say Bonnie.

"Your, uh, friend, Bonnie Niles."

Waine waited.

Archer sipped his beer.

"You know what the trouble with you cops is?" Waine said. "You've seen too many movies about cops. You do what the movie cops do—dole out bits of information until you get to the payoff, instead of just getting to the point, which is what ordinary people do." *Sometimes,* he thought.

Archer unwrapped the paper from a sterile toothpick and put the toothpick in his mouth, adjusting it until it sat just right. "What're you ticked off at me for?"

"For bringing this up."

"I thought you'd want to know."

"Know *what,* Phil?"

"Your, uh, friend's in a jam."

Waine waited.

"Some guys with no necks in striped suits paid a call on her restaurant. They, uh, would like to install a juke box on the premises."

"She has a juke box."

"That's what she told them. They said their's was a higher class model. She told them to take a walk. They said something about how she sure had a lot of plate glass windows, how it'd be too bad if they got busted." Archer sipped some more beer.

"And?"

"What do you mean, *and? And,* I called a guy from rackets and told him to go over there and show her

some pictures. *And,* I called the Six and told them to
have their patrols keep an eye on the place, especially
after hours. What do you mean, *and?* I'm a cop, for
God's sake. Somebody tells me someone's leaning on
them, I try to get them to unlean.''

"Why're you telling me this, Phil?" Waine said.

"I told you, I thought you'd want to know. She's
your, uh, friend."

"Stop saying it like that, will you?"

"Saying it like what?"

"'Uh, friend, uh, friend.'"

Archer shrugged and tucked in his shirt. "So I didn't
go to Harvard. So shoot me."

"Did she ask you to tell me this?" Waine said.

"Tell you? No. You're just a lawyer. What could you
do?"

Waine saw Francesca returning, so he let it go.

But his mind was on Archer's motive for telling him
about Bonnie's call. It was the business about living
third class again, he decided. In this case, Archer
seemed to be saying that the third-class thing he was
doing was leaving things with Bonnie so unresolved
that she would resort to calling someone like Archer,
whom Bonnie scarcely knew and with whom she had
never got along very well.

And Archer was right. Waine had left things with
Bonnie unresolved, and had been dodging any attempts
at resolution. He had been giving a wide berth to the
street where she lived and the street her restaurant was
on. He had been keeping his telephone answering
machine on at home, picking up calls only after listening to the monitor to find out who it was, and had been
having his secretary screen all his calls at the office. The
funny thing was, Bonnie hadn't called. And maybe her
call to Archer had been a legitimate plea for help, made
to someone who would be able to provide it; maybe
Bonnie had felt, as Archer did, that there was nothing
Waine could have done about her dilemma. He was just

a lawyer, and Bonnie didn't need counsel, or anything else, from him.

Or maybe Archer was implying that it was third class to throw himself so earnestly into a relationship with Francesca so quickly—things with Bonnie being muddled or no.

Don't you see?

See what?

You're leaving yourself an out. If things don't work out with Francesca here, you can always go back to Bonnie.

Going back to Bonnie would mean being faced with her demand that we live together, which I don't want to do. So I'm not likely to go back to Bonnie. Nor is she likely to have me back.

What about her?

Who?

Francesca.

What about her? You're as bad as Archer.

Do you want to marry her?

. . . eventually.

When's that?

When I know for sure she's someone I want to marry.

What about kids? She's never been married before. She probably wants that.

Have you asked her?

Have you?

. . . I hardly know her.

That's probably why you picked her.

What's probably why?

She probably wants kids and you'll be able to say you're not ready for kids.

. . .

You're getting older every minute, Gawaine.

. . .

Gawaine?

Drink your beer.

Chapter 21

~~~~~~~~~~~

Francesca was sure she loved Waine when she took
him, after saying goodnight to Phil Archer, to her tiny
apartment.

Lying on the opened sofa bed in the tiny living room,
sipping a brandy, waiting for Waine to finish his shower
and join her, she wondered why, if she was sure she
loved him, she was still so troubled. Was it only that it
was unprecedented?

Waine joined her—clean from the shower and
smooth from the shave he'd had with a borrowed razor,
the facets of his body made alluring by the soft lighting,
the towel around his waist modeling what it concealed
in a way that was more provocative than if he had been
altogether nude.

And before the power of their lovemaking, all
thoughts scattered like leaves before a gale. Waine
Ryan's hands were beneficent bestowers of praise and
admiration; they handled her with authority, yet were
never dogmatic, and were ever conscious of what she

wanted and when. *Profuse,* she thought, and wondered exactly what the word meant, for it seemed to her that it was an appropriate word for what his hands were— bountiful, expansive, playing her now largo, now prestissimo, drawing from her more and more beautiful music than any other player ever had, or had ever suspected was waiting to be liberated.

"Wow," was all she could say when they were done.

Waine laughed. "I take it that means you're essentially speechless."

"Essentially? I'm completely speechless."

Waine laughed and stretched and propped himself up on an elbow to look at the books in a shelf on the wall above the bed. "I like this place."

"Don't be silly. It's a closet."

"I mean it. It reminds me of the apartment I shared in Cambridge when I was in law school."

"Shared? Was your roommate a midget?"

"A ladies' man. He was rarely there."

"Ah. And you?"

"I was there most of the time, when I wasn't in class. It was a good place to study."

She poked him in the ribs. "I meant, were you a ladies' man?"

"I remember a date or two in three years of law school. Two, I think."

"What about later?"

"Later, I was married."

"And faithful to your wife?"

"Yes. Sex with another woman wasn't the solace I was seeking."

"And what about now? Have you been a ladies' man since you got divorced?"

"I've had a couple of relationships. I'm essentially monogamous."

Francesca lifted a leg off the bed, flexed her foot, and let her leg down. "I guess what I'm asking is whether you've been seeing anybody lately. Before you can say,

'Why?' I'll tell you that I was—up until the day I met you. Until an hour before I met you, in fact. And before you can ask why I'm telling you this, it's because I've never let a man spend the night here with me. And before you can ask why I'm telling you that, it's because I want you to. I want you to even if it's inconvenient, even if you have to go all the way downtown in the morning to get a clean shirt—"

"I keep some clean clothes at the office," Waine said, "for when I have to meet clients for dinner."

"And for when you spend a night at a lady's?"

Waine didn't say that because Bonnie lived so close by, it hadn't been a problem. He didn't say that before Bonnie he had used the clean clothes at the office for when he spent a night at a lady's. "You seem to be suggesting it's getting to be lifestory-telling time."

"That'll happen gradually," Francesca said. "It's already happened a little. You know, you dodged the question about the clean clothes at your office."

Waine laughed. "I have spent nights at ladies'. "

"Two?" Francesca said.

Waine laughed.

"And your most recent lady? How are the ends?"

". . . loose."

"Umm . . . Well, let's be careful, shall we? I don't feel that either of us is the type to fall in love irresponsibly, but . . ." Francesca didn't finish her sentence. She knew she felt no allegiance to Leeds still, but she was trying to leave Waine an out. Which also gave her an out.

Waine rolled on his back and put his hands behind his head and considered the cracks that were beginning to form in the paint on the ceiling. He realized that one of the things that was troubling him about Bonnie was a feeling that he had been professionally irresponsible in getting involved with her. He hadn't, strictly speaking, been her lawyer for some time, now; most of the help she needed was in the areas of property and tax law, and he had referred her to someone who was more expert in those matters than he. But he had helped her out of a difficult jam once—that was how they met—and he was nagged by the feeling that he should have been of use to her in the matter of the pressure to install the juke box. And he was also just plain worried—about her safety, about the possibility of damage being done to the restaurant. The sort of people who were leaning on her didn't unlean easily, Archer or no. If he had remained just her lawyer, she would have called him for help without hesitation; he knew that. And so she would if he were just her lover. Now that he was neither, yet still both, she saw him as helpless to help her in any way at all. That was certainly third-class behavior—personally and professionally.

Francesca turned on her stomach and stuffed the pillow under her chin. She, too, felt the clash of personal and professional; she was sure she would feel it for at least as long as it took to resolve the matter of Eva James's custody.

She put the knuckle of her thumb in her mouth and bit it—not altogether gently. She bit it to keep herself from saying out loud what was on her mind. What was on her mind was bewilderment that Waine hadn't said a word about Eva James's revelation that a will existed that named Waine's clients as Eva's guardian. Did that mean he didn't know? How could he not know? It had been two days since she had talked to Dr. Clavin; surely word had gone out to the lawyers for both sides. Even if the will hadn't been found or attested or validated or whatever the word was, surely Waine had cause to be outwardly optimistic about, if not to be actively celebrating, the imminent victory of his clients. But he hadn't said a word about it. Something must be wrong. But what?

Francesca bit her knuckle even harder. She didn't like the position she was in. She was sure that she had done the right thing, and was just as sure that she was going to be judged harshly for having done it, from one quarter or another.

"Another angel passing?" Waine said.

Francesca looked at the digital clock; it was eleven minutes after twelve. Angels passed at twenty after and twenty to—didn't they? "Just tired. You will stay, won't you?"

"I said I would."

"I don't think you did, actually. Not in so many words. I said I wanted you to, but that's all."

"I want to. In so many words."

"Do you ever feel that you're being watched?" Francesca said. "I don't mean by a peeping tom, or anything. Not by anything at all—or anyone. Just watched. That what you do is being scrutinized, that the quality of your performance is being judged, that . . . that you're on trial, somehow?"

"I do, yes—"

"I guess you would, being a lawyer."

"It isn't as a lawyer that I feel it—or not only. I feel it all the time—when I walk down the street, when I work out at the gym, when I'm sitting doing nothing, when I'm making love with you—"

"I felt it then, too."

"I've always imagined—I've felt it since I was a kid—I've always imagined that it was a part of me that was doing the watching—a part that was completely moral and all-knowing and wise and . . . and incapable of being deceived—"

"Yup."

Waine turned on his side and waited until Francesca turned on hers to face him. "You're worried, aren't you? About this. About us."

"Not worried worried. Just . . ."

"Worried?"

Francesca laughed. "Yes. But I'm also happy."

"That's nice to hear."

"And you? Are you happy?"

"Oh, yes."

"Then what're we worried about?"

They laughed and embraced and found that they had not reached satiety at all, but had only been resting. They made love again, less lingeringly, and when they were done, and fell asleep, it was twenty minutes to one.

Chapter 22

~~~~~~~~~~

Francesca hitched the sheet of the Sunfish around a cleat on the cockpit and leaned back, resting her elbows on the gunwale, draping a leg over the tiller to steady it. She touched Waine's thigh with a fingertip. "Thinking what?"

They were sailing off Shelter Island. Francesca had come out on Friday night and Waine had come on Saturday evening, after first visiting the Hirsches in Sag Harbor. He hadn't said anything to Francesca about the nature of the visit.

Waine shook himself out of staring at the water. "What?"

Francesca laughed. "I was just saving time. Instead of saying, 'What's wrong?' and having you say, 'I'm just thinking,' and saying, 'Thinking what?' I just got right down to it . . . Thinking what?"

"I heard you and your mother arguing this morning," Waine said. "I was wondering if she was upset that we spent the night in the same bed."

"Not at all. She was delighted." Francesca put a hand over the side and watched it slice through the water. "I was just making another attempt to talk her out of selling the house. It's all your fault, you know."

Waine laughed. "Oh?"

"No, it's not your fault. But your putting mother in touch with that friend of yours at the senior citizen's center was the push she really needed. She's fairly sure she's going to get that job. The house, suddenly, is unimportant to her."

"It bothers you a lot, doesn't it?" Waine said. "The house means a lot to you."

"I suppose I think of it as a memorial to my father," Francesca said. She shrugged. "Maybe memorials aren't necessary."

Waine remembered the wish he had had to erect some kind of memorial to his mother, a wish he had retained for years. Once, he had mentioned it to Phil Archer; Archer had said that Waine's success was exactly the memorial his mother would have wanted. "You could say that you were that memorial," Waine said to Francesca.

Francesca sat up and unhitched the sheet and paid attention to her sailing. They were heading through the sound on the north side of Shelter Island between the island and the North Fork town of Greenport. The airs were light and there weren't many boats out, but a ferry boat was making its way across from Greenport, and Francesca set a course to pass astern of it. When she was sure of her heading, she relaxed a little, though she kept the sheet in her hand. "I suppose that's a nice thought."

Waine was staring at the water.

"I suppose that's a nice thought," Francesca said again.

Waine stared on.

"Waine?"

And on.

"*Waine?*"

He started upright and smiled weakly. "I've had a tough week."

"You said that. Why don't you talk about it?"

"I don't really feel like it right now."

"You said that, too. I think . . . Well, it's none of my business, but . . ."

"But what?"

"Well, I just wondered if you shared your failures with your wife, as well as your successes."

Waine looked up at the sail, which was wrinkling slightly near the mast. "You're luffing." He smiled; he had just learned the term that morning.

Francesca glowered, but came off the wind a little until the sail filled and was smooth. "Don't show off. And don't change the subject."

Waine noticed the ferry boat, and wasn't entirely convinced that Francesca was going to miss it; he decided against saying anything. "Eventually, I did. Share my failures, that is."

"Well, eventually isn't good enough for me," Francesca said. "I need immediately. Keeping disappointment to yourself is as bad as keeping anger to yourself. It festers, and when you finally let it out, it's bigger and uglier than maybe it ought to be."

Waine stared at the water.

Francesca inhaled, ready to press her point, then decided to back off, and let her breath out slowly and evenly. She had said what she felt, and that was what was important. It might take time for him to be able to give her what she wanted, but time was what things like that most often took. She wondered, though, just what the disappointment was; hadn't he yet found out that a will existed that meant a victory for his clients, for him?

They passed just astern of the ferry and were buffetted by its wake.

"Speak of the devil," Francesca said, lifting her chin toward the ferry.

Waine looked among the passengers on the deck, half-expecting to see Aura, but he saw no one he knew.

"The man in the blue shirt and the white tennis hat is Vincent Clavin, the assistant chief of staff."

"Were we speaking of him?" Waine said.

Francesca laughed. "Mother and I were. The reason I'm so upset about the goddamned house isn't just that mother wants to sell it; it's that Clavin wants to buy it."

"Oh?"

"He's made an offer through mother's broker. It's just like him to . . . Oh, nothing."

"To want your father's house, since he couldn't have his job?"

Francesca looked at him narrowly. "Why did you say that?"

"I've heard they were rivals, as well as friends."

"You've heard right. I don't have to ask where you heard it. That hospital's a gossip factory. It's a wonder any patients get taken care of, what with everyone expending so much energy exchanging rumors . . . Speaking of which—" But before she could say that Eva James's condition was improving every day, in the hope that it would elicit from him some information about what was going on with Eva from his point of view, she saw an osprey, and pointed urgently, momentarily letting go of the tiller to do so, crying out an almost animal cry from deep in her throat.

They had rounded a point of land and were headed toward the Ram Island Causeway. Waine followed Francesca's point and leaned back as the huge bird flew directly above them, its wings moving not in a flapping motion but in a kind of rhythmic flexing—in, out, in, out.

"Oh, look!" Francesca pointed again.

And suddenly, there were two more ospreys, flying toward the one that had passed over them. The sky above them became a meeting ground as the birds swooped in grand circles around one another, calling out shrilly.

Then the circles became larger and larger until finally they burst apart and the birds flew off in tangents to the circles, the solitary bird continuing on northwesterly, the pair flying toward the causeway, dropping lower and lower toward the nests atop the telephone poles and landing on them with a suddenness that made the world seem to have been altogether deprived of motion.

Francesca landed on the causeway's beach and Waine hopped out and pulled the Sunfish up on the littoral. Francesca lowered the sail and they walked up to the road and along it toward the nests.

When they got close enough to see the bird's gleaming eyes, Francesca put a hand on Waine's arm. "This is their flight distance. If we get any closer, they'll fly away."

" 'Flight distance?' "

"It's what it sounds like—the distance to which an animal will let another approach before it runs. It won't run away altogether, just enough to get beyond its flight distance again. It's why animals can live in such proximity—in Africa, say, the zebras don't worry about the lions as long as they keep them beyond their flight distance. People have them, too."

"I was just thinking that," Waine said. "It occurred to me that my office is set up so that a new client is liable to sit in a chair that's quite far away from me—across the desk. Old clients tend to sit in the chair right next to my desk. The first would be flight distance, the second . . . I don't know what to call it."

"Polite distance, I think, is the sociological term. There's also intimate distance. That would probably be for the clients who sit on your lap."

Waine laughed, but remembered the day Bonnie Niles had moved from the chair next to his desk onto his lap. He'd asked for it, he supposed; he'd shown her to the chair next to the desk the very first time she'd come to see him. "I guess doctors are unusual, aren't they? They deal with people from an intimate distance right away."

"I never thought of it that way, but I think you're right. I'm always surprised at how quickly people develop a trust in me, but maybe that's the reason. They've let me inside their intimate distance—they've *had* to let me—so I guess they feel they ought to trust me. Maybe they feel they *have* to trust me."

"My mother felt that," Waine said. "She . . . misplaced her trust, I would say."

"It happens. Are you bitter about it?"

"I was."

"But not anymore?"

"I realized recently that a lot of the bitterness I felt I acquired from my father. I don't know that he was necessarily a reliable source. Also, I've begun to feel differently about doctors lately."

Francesca smiled at him and snuggled up to him, but she wondered how he'd feel about doctors—about her—if he found out she'd known about the will all this time and hadn't said anything. But why hadn't *he* said anything? She wanted to ask, but by this time she was sure that something was very wrong and that whenever she heard about what it was would be too soon.

A tourist who had been photographing the birds got too close to the nest and the osprey lifted off and soared down to a piling in the water of the harbor.

"*Voilà,*" Francesca said.

"It made a good picture," Waine said. In following the osprey, his eye was drawn up the slope of Ram Island, to the house that had belonged to Conrad and Edith James. In the bright sunlight, it looked desolate, a symbol of his failure. "There was a will," he said softly.

Francesca heard him and yet didn't hear him. But she couldn't ask him to repeat it, for she knew that he had had to tear it out of himself. She just waited.

The osprey returned to the nest, but neither remarked on it.

"There was a holograph will," Waine said. "Handwritten by Conrad James. It was in a box of papers in Eva's room at the Jameses apartment in New York. It was dated last summer. It leaves the estate to Eva and the custody of Eva to the Stewarts."

Francesca's lips moved, but nothing came out. *To the Stewarts? Not the Stewarts. No, no—not the Stewarts.*

"There were a couple of bequests, too," Waine went on. "One of half a million dollars to Lexington Hospital. Others to some other charities. It's typical of homemade wills; it raises as many questions as it answers. But to the central question—who gets custody of Eva—its answer is unequivocal. It was opened Friday by the Surrogate Court judge. Eva had known about it all along. It's just . . . Well, no one had asked her about it. She finally mentioned it to one of the doctors—Clavin, coincidentally. We all went up to the apartment—the judge, the Stewarts' lawyer, the Stewarts and I . . . And there it was."

Francesca felt faint and moved to stand in the meager shade of the telephone pole. Overhead, the osprey sat unmoving. *I'm inside your flight distance, bird,* she thought. *Why don't you fly away? Is it that I'm no threat to you? That I'm ineffectual?* She turned to face Waine, who was squinting up toward the Jameses' house on Ram Island. Having been inside his intimate distance, being any other distance from him seemed being very far away. "Is that it? Is there nothing you can do? You said there are a lot of questions."

"There are a lot of ways to challenge the will on a lot of grounds," Waine said. "There's the question of its authenticity in the first place, which remains to be established. There's always the possibility, with holographic wills, of undue influence—some kind of mental or physical coercion that deprives the testator of his free agency—" Waine scuffed at the sand that had drifted along the road, angry at himself for lapsing into jargon; it was a defense, he knew—a barrier against emotion. "And there are other grounds. But I'm afraid

Ted and Clara have lost their enthusiasm. They've been having a tough time. Ted sees this all as a symptom of his failure as a writer. He was beginning to feel that even if they'd won, he'd have lost. Lost his reputation, his credibility. In a way, it's just as well it's over for them.''

It was over for her and Waine, too, Francesca thought, for she didn't see how anything but discord could come of her telling him what she had done. She looked up at the osprey and envied its capacity for flight and its freedom from preoccupation with anything but feeding itself and its young, and with producing more young and feeding them. Who was the poet whose heart had stirred for a bird?

Francesca stomped in a small, angry circle. What did it matter, anyway? Poets—what did they know? What did a bird's heart stir for? Fish, a smaller bird, a rabbit, a snake?

A snake. That's what I am.

Stop feeling sorry for yourself, Francesca. You have to tell him.

I know.

Now's as good a time as any.

No. I'm not going to tell him now—out here, in the middle of nowhere. I'll wait till we get back to the house.

You just want to have someplace to run to.

What's so bad about that?

Nothing, except . . .

What?

. . . I thought you were through running.

Chapter 23

But Francesca didn't tell Waine right away. First there was the return sail to make, and the afternoon to get through. Beatrice Hayward was giving a lawn party—"for no good reason," she had said, but because, Francesca knew, it would be the last such party her mother would give in that house.

Everyone came—summer residents and year-rounders, close friends and mere acquaintances. Everyone looked beautiful. The women all wore filmy dresses and strode about proudly. The men were all in soft shirts and slacks and lounged with their hands in their pockets, admiring the women, the afternoon, the ambiance.

Francesca was the most beautiful of all. She wore a midnight-blue spaghetti-strapped top and a petal-hemmed skirt of wide blue and gray diagonal stripes. The top held her breasts the way sails hold wind, and she felt as though she was under sail, stepping barefooted across the lawn, her skirt swinging sassily behind her.

She saw the admiration in the eyes of many of the men, and she went often to Waine, to let them know that she was his, and, given how beautiful he looked in a simple royal-blue velour shirt and white sailcloth pants, to let the women with admiration in their eyes know that he was hers.

Beatrice Hayward saw Francesca's ritual dance and sidled up to her at a table full of hors d'oeuvre. "I get the sense that I should be getting an estimate on wedding announcements," Beatrice said.

Francesca sipped sangria and sighed.

"Or . . . am I wrong?" Beatrice said. "Is this just a front?"

"This is a lovely party, mother," Francesca said. She ducked her head, unable to meet her mother's eyes.

"And you feel you have in you the capacity to spoil it, is that it?" Beatrice Hayward said. "So you're being careful not to."

"Sometimes I miss Leeds," Francesca said. "His only concern in life was having a good time. He was perfect at parties like this."

"A perfect bore, you mean," Beatrice Hayward said. "What's going on, my dear? Is the handsome Mr. Ryan less than meets the eye?"

"No. Or maybe yes. I don't know. I think I'm fated to suffer permanently from some vague discontent."

Beatrice Hayward sniffed disapprovingly. "You should try just letting go for a change."

"'Letting go?'"

"Just fly, Francesca. Don't worry about how high off the ground you are. Don't worry about landing. Let the man take care of that."

"'The man?'"

"Waine. Whomever. And stop quoting me to myself. Just do as I say."

Francesca laughed. "It would be a switch, wouldn't it—to fly and let somebody else be at the controls?"

"You bet your sweet life it would be. You've achieved a great deal in your life, Francesca. You have every right to be proud—as a woman, as a human being. But you've gotten to where you are by walking a very straight, plodding, arduous walk. You deserve to skip a little. You deserve to dance."

And dance she did—the afternoon away, challenging the bees and butterflies with the ardor of her flight, leaving partners breathless and blinded with perspiration.

Only Waine could keep up with her, and her enthusiasm made him forget about weekday disappointments. Together they dazzled the guests with their twinned energies; they looked like sun and moon dancing together.

At last, they rested, and walked among trees on a quiet part of the lawn. Watching them, the other guests saw a couple, a pair, a union.

"I wasn't looking forward to this," Waine said, "but it's helped a lot."

"Good," Francesca said, who wasn't looking forward to what she had to do.

They walked arm in arm out on the concrete dock that ran out into Shelter Island Sound from her mother's beach.

"Thinking what?" Waine said after they had stood for a while, watching the descending sun turn the water of the sound and of Noyack Bay beyond a sparkling silver.

Francesca smiled and put her head against his chest. "Thinking that I'm very happy."

". . . but? I hear a but."

Francesca took a step back, lifted her chin bravely, and told him the whole story, determined not to let her eyes leave his, hoping his eyes wouldn't leave hers.

When she was done, she turned and looked out over the water. She was surprised to see the sun still there; or hadn't it taken that long, after all? Or had the sun set and risen again and traveled the sky again to the place it had been?

She turned back to Waine. His eyes hadn't left hers, but they had grown cool. "Thinking what?" Francesca said.

Waine made a small, irritated gesture with one hand. "Wondering whose side you're on."

His words went right to Francesca's heart and she hunched her shoulders in pain. "I'm not on anybody's side. It was the only thing for me to do, professionally. There's no doubt in my mind about that."

"But Clavin—why did you tell Clavin? Clavin's a close friend of the Stewarts."

"He's also the assistant chief of staff. At the time, he was acting chief of staff."

Waine kicked a loose shard of concrete into the water. "The professional thing to do would've been to call together the lawyers from both sides to hear Eva's story."

"I assumed Clavin would do that."

"Well, he didn't. Or not right away."

"Then accuse him of unprofessionalism—not me. And in any case, he did call you together."

"But not to hear what Eva had to say. He only told me—us—that Eva had spoken of a will. He didn't say anything about what Eva thought was in it."

"Maybe Eva was wrong about what was in it."

"And maybe the will is a forgery. Diana Stewart is Conrad James's sister. Siblings often have similar handwriting, especially if they went to the same schools." Waine pried loose another shard and threw it at the first, which floated on the water; he missed.

"I can understand that you're upset, but not that you're upset at me," Francesca said.

Waine turned his head slowly toward her and stared. "You withheld an important piece of information from me."

"Not so. I simply handed it on to someone else first—my superior, I might add. I fully expected that it would reach you eventually. I was in a difficult position. I did what I thought was right."

"Eventually is exactly when it did reach me." Waine said. "Not to mention in a different form."

Francesca sighed. "Waine, we're lovers. It's no secret; there are no secrets around that hospital. If I had told you what Eva said, don't you think the Stewarts and their lawyer would have had occasion to raise the question of conflict of interest? Even if I'd called the Stewarts' lawyer first, then told you, they'd still have raised the question. What Eva told me was what you and your clients wanted to hear; that I was the one she told would've looked very suspicious. And besides, if you think the will's a forgery, why don't you just round up the judge and go see Eva and get her to tell you what she thought the will said?"

" 'Thought,' " Waine said.

"Well, her father told her what it said."

"Exactly. But she didn't see what he'd written. What he told Eva he'd written is simply hearsay."

Francesca's stomach felt huge and empty. "I suppose it's just like Ted Hirsch's saying what Conrad James told him."

"Exactly," Waine said softly.

". . . and I suppose if I testified about what Eva told me her father said, that would be hearsay, too."

"Exactly," Waine said, more softly still.

Francesca sighed again. "Well, I'm sorry, Waine, but I did the only thing I could do. I'd do it again. If the entire hospital administration were out of town, and something like that happened, I'd tell the most senior person I could find—even if it was only the charge nurse on the floor—before I'd tell you."

"I gather that."

Francesca let her legs down and turned sidesaddle on the dock in order to see into his eyes; the rough concrete hurt her thighs. "Do you actually think I deliberately wanted to hurt anybody? I love Eva. I want the best for her."

Waine snorted, and nodded his head elaborately.

"What is that supposed to mean?" Francesca said.

"What is what supposed to mean?"

She mimicked him, nearly whinnying, and nodding her head violently.

Waine thought a moment, then said, "From your point of view, the best thing for Eva is to be with the Stewarts."

In a whisper, Francesca said, *"What?"*

"Clavin, the Stewarts—that's where your sympathies lie. To you, Ted and Clara are not the right sort of people. They're too simple—not to mention not rich."

Francesca let her head hang and swayed slowly from side to side. "Oh, Waine."

"I see it happen all the time," Waine said. "When push comes to shove, the rich side with the rich. They'll talk about believing in equality; they'll talk about believing that wealth isn't a measure of ability or deservingness, but when the time comes . . . In a legal situation, an ordinary person doesn't have much chance against the rich. The only way people like Ted and Clara can stand up against them is with as much ammunition as possible. You took their ammunition away from them. It's really as simple as that."

Francesca counted toward ten; she stopped at seven. "Let me get this straight: Do you actually think that if a patient tells me something—tells me without my soliciting the information—that I know to be important in some court case, that I should *not* tell my superiors?"

Waine just stared into the sun.

"Do you?"

With punctuating slaps of his hand on his thigh, Waine said, "If Eva weren't a patient, if she were just a friend, and you were visiting her and she told you about a will, whom would you tell? The mayor? The governor? The President? The police?"

". . . I'd tell the judge."

"Bravo. I wish you had told the judge."

"Brav*a*," Francesca whispered.

"What?"

"Nothing. I *did* tell the judge. Through Clavin."

"Through Clavin—who's not disinterested."

"I wouldn't know about that. All I know is that he was acting chief of staff at Lexington Hospital and that I'm a member of the staff at Lexington Hospital and that I—"

"Play by the goddamn rules," Waine said.

Francesca lifted her hands and let them fall. "Well, what's so bad about that?"

"Francesca, what is a hospital, anyway? It's not a society separate from the society outside its walls. Its patients are there for medical care, but they don't cede any rights by virtue of being patients—"

"Ah." Francesca held up a finger and nodded sagely. "This is all part of your anti-hospital routine, isn't is?"

"I don't have an anti-hospital routine."

"Oh, but you do. You may not say it in so many words, but you do. Your mother died in a hospital and you think the doctors messed up. We're not gods, you know; we just stumble around, feel our way, try to see what can't always be seen, poke a little, prod a little. We're more like plumbers than gods. Don't for a minute think I don't understand your frustration and bitterness, Waine, because I do. I feel frustrated and bitter about the vision that I could save that I can't save; I feel frustrated and bitter all the time. But it's different from your frustration and bitterness. You believe—and you're wrong—that doctors should know everything there is to know about everything; in fact, they can only know as much as they can about as much as they can. They're humans, just the way lawyers are humans. I have the same misconception about the law. I think the side that's telling the truth should always win; but it doesn't always happen that way, does it? Because it's about people, just the way medicine's about people; and where people are concerned, there's going to be fallibility. You have some strange notion that people can be infallible. I don't know where you got it. I don't know you well enough. That's part of the problem in all of this, isn't it? We don't know each other very well, yet we're . . . intimate. Look at us, having a fight at intimate distance. It would make more sense if we were at flight distance, lobbing insults at each other. But it's too late for that, I guess . . . All that really matters to me in this is that you accept that I *felt* I was doing the right thing. I don't care if you think it was the wrong thing; I don't care if you think it was wrong to feel it was the right thing. If you're going to be angry at me, be angry at me for the right reason—be angry at me because I did what I *felt* was right. Right for Eva, right for Ted and Clara, right for the Stewarts, right for the lawyers, right for the judge, right for society, right for the hospital, right for me. It's irrelevant, even, that you think it was wrong. What counts, what's going to make the difference between going on with this relationship or just breaking it off right here, right now, is whether you have sufficient respect for my right to do what I think is right—in this instance, or in any other instance."

And with that, Francesca stepped to the edge of the dock and dove into the water, cutting through the surface at a sharp angle so as not to hit the shallow bottom.

Of the merry-makers, only Beatrice Hayward saw the dive, for the others had turned their backs on the dock. She knew that it was not an act of abandon, but of despair.

Waine stood waiting in the sand as Francesca emerged from the water, her clothes clinging to her superb body. He had to lower his eyes as he spoke, lest that body lure him from the path he had chosen. "I'm going to try and convince Ted and Clara that they should stay with this case—"

"That sounds like a good idea," Francesca said. "I didn't like the idea of their giving up so easily—"

"—but it's going to be a long haul—and for them, an expensive one. They may not want to do it; the odds are pretty long . . . As far as you and I are concerned, I am in love with you."

"It doesn't always show," Francesca said. "Maybe love's like that."

"But I'm not sure we should see each other while this case is pending. I didn't ever consider the conflict of interest question before; it didn't occur to me that there would be any. I didn't think Eva was going to turn out to be such an important figure, and that your being her doctor, and my lover, would be a problem. I should've thought of it; I should've thought right away of talking to Eva, to find out if she'd ever discussed these things with her parents. But I didn't."

Francesca shrugged. "But you didn't."

"If I'm going to prove that Clavin lied—or at least withheld some information for a time, during which time the will could have been altered, or a new one made—I'm going to have to do it without using your testimony. As I said, it's hearsay; and it's also, I'm afraid, tainted—"

Francesca shivered, from the wind and from the sound of the word. "Tainted hearsay, my word."

"Francesca, please . . ."

Francesca turned away. Some of the guests were playing volleyball on a makeshift court; they reached for the ball like children for the moon. "I'm sad, goddamn it. Aren't you?"

". . . yes." Waine took a step toward her and put a hand on her shoulder, whose flesh was dimpled with gooseflesh from the wind. "Don't get cold."

Francesca shrugged his hand away. "No. Don't try to be soft with me. Be hard. Be the way you were out on the dock." She turned to face him, her chin up, her eyes on his. "You know where your bicycle is. I'm going to change out of these things. When I come down, I'd like you to be gone. I'll think of something to tell mother."

She turned and walked up the sloping lawn toward the house, her bare feet making lovely arcs as she walked, her wet hair falling straight, her wet clothes clinging to her, her heart nearly bursting.

Watching her, Waine thought his heart would burst, too.

Chapter 24

―――――――――――

"Francesca."

"Hello, Tim. Can I come in?"

"Of course, but . . ."

"Do you have company?"

"No. Come in."

Tim Ward stood aside and let Francesca into the hallway of his apartment on West Eighty-sixth Street.

"Is it very late?" Francesca said.

"It's after midnight."

"I need to talk."

"I gathered. The living room's straight ahead."

Francesca took a step along the hall, then stopped, looking puzzledly at a ten-speed bicycle leaning against the wall of the hallway.

". . . unless you'd rather talk here," Tim said.

Francesca smiled, but kept on looking at the bicycle, turning her head this way and that. "It reminds me of something."

"It's a lot like a bicycle," Tim said. "I'm often reminded of a bicycle when I look at it."

"I don't mean reminds me of something else. I mean it reminds me of something having to do with bicycles . . . But I can't think what."

In the living room, they sat in easy chairs at either end of the coffee table.

"What's on your mind?" Tim said. "Besides bicycles?"

"Do you have anything to drink?"

"Hard? Soft? To wind up or unwind?"

". . . scotch," Francesca said. "With ice."

Tim got up and got a bottle of Johnny Walker Black from a cabinet and two glasses and an ice bucket filled with ice from the kitchen. He put the bottle and the ice bucket in the center of the coffee table and a glass at either end. "Pour your own."

Francesca poured a half a glass and twirled the ice cubes with a finger. "How is it you never have women problems, Tim?"

Tim laughed. "'Cause I never have any women."

Francesca made a disbelieving face. "Come now."

"Never any I care about. I'm one of those perennial bachelors you read about and think, 'He must be gay.'"

"I don't know anyone who thinks that," Francesca said.

"I think my parents sometimes think it. After all, if I'm not, why am I not either married or knee-deep in blondes?"

"My mother, in effect, told me to get married this afternoon," Francesca said. "I was quite surprised."

"To get married this afternoon, or she told you this afternoon?" Tim said.

Francesca smiled. "Does everybody know about Waine Ryan and me?"

Tim shrugged. "I wouldn't say everybody. But I do, and I'm often one of the last to hear gossip."

"I *am* the last," Francesca said. "Well, in this case, you're the first to hear that we've broken up."

". . . I'm sorry."

Francesca could see Waine in her mind's eye, pedaling his borrowed bicycle down the road off the estate. "Bicycle," she whispered.

"What?" Tim said.

"Something about a bicycle," Francesca said. "I wish I could remember what it was."

Tim just sipped his scotch and watched her trying to remember.

Francesca finally gave up, with a shake of her head and a shrug. "Sorry. What were we talking about?"

Tim laughed. "Your shattered romance."

Francesca waved a hand. "Oh, that."

"Come on, Francesca. This is your old friend, Tim. You can tell me you're heartbroken."

". . . I'm heartbroken. It's somewhat a matter of principle. A professional difference." The scotch was going to her head and she let it. She didn't want to think any more. She had thought enough on the long drive back from Shelter Island.

"Are you hungry?" Tim said.

Francesca laughed. "I believe I am."

Tim scrambled some eggs and sliced some tomatoes and garnished them with salt, pepper, oregano and olive oil.

Francesca tasted the eggs. "These are great. Do you do windows, too?"

"I know—I'd make somebody a great husband," Tim said.

Francesca laughed. "I like you so much, Tim. I always have. I wonder why we're not in love, and never have been."

"Because we're friends, Francesca."

"Is it because we know each other too well?" Francesca said. "Is that it? Is it really only possible to fall in love with people you don't know very well? That's strange, isn't it—if it's true? We fall in love with strangers. Then we get to know them. And we find out that what we loved isn't all there is to them. We find out that what we loved is only a tiny, tiny aspect of them. What they really are may not be lovable at all. What they really are is almost *never* lovable. We fight off that knowledge as long as possible, then we tell ourselves that we've fallen out of love. But it isn't a case of that, is it? We probably never really *stop* loving them; it's just that they stop being strangers."

Tim lined up some tomato seeds with his fork. "What you're talking about doesn't really sound like love. It sounds like infatuation, like passion. Those things fade because they're reactions and reactions don't go on indefinitely. Love is something else. Love is an offer— an offer to stand by someone, to care for them, to nourish them, to give to them and to take from them, come what may. Think of a child: When you have a child, you can't know what he or she is going to be like—whether he's going to be smart or beautiful or athletic or creative—all the things you might like a child to be. If he doesn't turn out to be those things—if he turns out to be plain or uncoordinated or dull, you don't reject him, you don't stop loving him—"

"Some people do."

"But not people who really loved him in the first place, come what may. Love is an environment, a context in which someone can be himself and be sure of affection and trust. I'm not going to tell you that you didn't really love Waine Ryan at all, but it's something to consider. And you could also consider the possibility that you do love him and that you're just making the mistake of overreacting to things about him that are the very things that being in love with him should allow to be." Tim laughed. "Did you follow that? My syntax gave out near the end."

Francesca smiled. "Anybody's would. It's a complex topic." She gathered up the dishes. "I'll do these and get out of here."

"Just leave them," Tim said. "I don't do windows, but I never let my guests do the dishes."

At the door, Francesca ran her fingers over the seat of Tim's bicycle. "I wish I could remember . . ."

"You'll remember in the morning," Tim said.

She remembered just a few minutes later, driving down Eighty-sixth Street toward the park. It was a conversation she had had that morning with her mother. They had been talking—arguing—about her mother's selling the house and about Dr. Vincent Clavin's interest in buying it.

"Oh, well," Beatrice Hayward had said, "if Vincent buys the house, at least he won't have to come and get his bicycle."

"His what?" Francesca had said.

"His bicycle."

"I heard you, mother. What are you talking about?"

"That bicycle in the basement—by the boiler . . . ?"

"Yes?"

"It's Vincent's."

"Vincent Clavin's?"

"Yes."

"I thought it was our bicycle. Dad's."

Beatrice Hayward had shaken her head.

"It's Vincent Clavin's bicycle?"

"Yes, Francesca. My word, you certainly are going on about it."

"Well, what's it doing here?"

"He left it here, obviously."

"Left it?"

Beatrice Hayward had given her daughter a look. "It certainly didn't ride over here from North Haven by itself."

". . . when?" Francesca had said.

"When, what?"

"When did he leave it here?"

"I don't know—years ago."

"How many years?"

"I haven't the slightest idea. Years."

"Yes, but how many?"

"Francesca, really."

"I want to know."

". . . I don't know."

"You didn't try. Try harder."

"Francesca."

"It's important. I think."

"Important how?"

"I don't know, mother. I just *think* it's important."

Beatrice Hayward had picked up the book review section of the Sunday *Times* and had paged through it, clearly unconvinced that a bicycle could be important. Francesca had been about to protest when Waine Ryan had come down from the upstairs bedroom.

Then the sailing and the ospreys and the party and the argument and Waine Ryan had ridden off on *his* bicycle—or rather on the bicycle he had borrowed from Ted Hirsch. He had ridden up Driftwood to Midway, down Midway to 114, down 114 to the South Ferry Terminal, across to North Haven, down 114 again to Sag Harbor. Vincent Clavin would have gone the same way on his bicycle, except that he would have taken a right turn off 114 toward the town of North Haven itself. Except that he had not ridden his bicycle home. He had left it behind. When? Why?

Why was Vincent Clavin's bicycle so important?

Francesca sat up for hours in the living room of her tiny apartment, sipping scotch, trying to think why. She couldn't think why.

Chapter 25

Waine Ryan sat up until early morning, too, in the dark living room of his apartment, sipping a glass of bourbon, trying not to think about the past, trying to see into the future. The future was as indistinct as objects in the far reaches of the room. Nor would the past go away—certainly not the recent past, if for no other reason than that Waine was constantly reminded of it by the sunburn he had got while sailing with Francesca.

The phone rang three times as Waine sat there, but he wasn't curious about who might be calling. He knew that Francesca wasn't, and she was the only person he cared to speak to. He felt a need to call her and explain himself again, but he knew she wouldn't answer her phone and, after all, he *had* made himself clear.

"It wouldn't be fair to call her," Ted Hirsch had said. They had been sitting in Ted's car at the Bridgehampton railroad station, waiting for the train that would take Waine back to the city. "It's what we used to do when we were teenagers. We'd call up the girl we'd just broken up with to say we just wanted her to know we still respected her, that we still liked her, that we hoped we could be friends. All we were doing, though, was trying to set up a situation where we could see her again if we ever wanted to."

"I do like her. I do respect her," Waine had said.

"Look," Ted had said, "you told her you couldn't handle being with her right now. Having said that, you can't call her up and say, 'I still can't handle being with you, but I just want to repeat the reasons why, and tell you I still respect you and like you, and see how you are.'"

Waine fiddled with the lock on the glove compartment for a while. "You see my point, don't you, Ted? I feel that by getting involved with Francesca, I was very irresponsible. I feel I sabotaged my own case—your case."

Ted shook his head. "I don't see it that way, no. Diana clearly didn't know there was a will until she heard about it from Eva, via Francesca and Clavin. That she did something about it so quickly, so boldly, only means to me that she was thinking along nefarious lines already. She took the opportunity that was handed to her, but if it hadn't been handed to her, she'd have made her own. Your relationship with Francesca was just a bonus; she might've thought up something else that didn't in any way play on it."

"Maybe so, but it was just another chink in our armor. A great big one."

Ted lightly punched Waine's shoulder. "You fell in love. Since when is that something we can be in control of? I don't know you very well, Waine—not as well as Clara does—but I know you well enough to know you're a very principled man. The trouble is—your trouble is—you think love is a matter of principle, too, and it's not. Principles are based on reason, ethics, moral standards. Love doesn't abide by any of those things. Who was it who said, 'The heart has reasons that Reason knows nothing of?'"

"Pascal."

"Pascal was right."

The glove compartment had come open by this time and Waine was now working to make it shut; it wouldn't. Ted reached over and slammed it shut.

"Thank you."

"You're welcome."

"Sounds to me like you're saying I *should* call her," Waine said.

"Only if what you want to say is that you want to give it another try. Then call her, by all means. If all you want to do is repeat what you said to her over on Shelter Island, then have the grace not to call. The principle."

"I do want to give it another try," Waine said.

"Then call her. Let her know."

"I also want to win this case, Ted."

Ted shrugged. "It's a long shot, I'd say."

"It'll be an even longer one if I'm involved with Francesca. I'm going to need to call her to testify as to what Eva told her."

"You said that would be hearsay."

"At the moment, it's all I've got."

Ted spread one hand in front of him on the steering wheel and examined it, front and back, as if for cribs he'd written to himself. He sighed and let the hand slip off the wheel into his lap. "Let's drop the suit. Eva will be fine with the Stewarts. I mean, it's not as if we're talking about a baby. If she were younger, Sag Harbor would be a nice place for her to be, but she's getting to be an age where she can begin to appreciate New York. Pretty soon she'll—"

"Ted, you're just rationalizing. We're talking about what looks very much like criminal behavior. If you were serious about wanting Eva in the first place, then you can't want her to wind up in the hands of people like the Stewarts."

". . . you don't think they mean her harm?"

"I think they mean to try to get at her money. This

bequest to the hospital, for example. It's the kind of thing that can be easily skimmed en route to the recipient. My associate, Keith Rouse, has been looking into Charles Stewart's business. There's something fishy going on. We don't know what it is, yet, but it wouldn't surprise me if he was in some kind of financial difficulty."

Ted ran a fingertip around the steering wheel, then did it again, and again.

Waine heard the train coming and reached out and held Ted's hand. "At least give me a few days. A week. A week of looking around to see what kind of case we'd have."

Ted pursed his lips doubtfully.

"I won't charge you for it," Waine said. "I don't mean that condescendingly; it's just that . . . well, I feel I owe you some work; I got a little too much pleasure mixed up with business."

Ted shifted his grip so that he was holding Waine's hand. "You realize that you're the only one who feels that way. Nobody else heard about you and Francesca and said, 'Oh, ho, conflict of interest.'"

"Diana Stewart might have. If she knew about us, she probably thought we fit perfectly into her plan."

"That doesn't make you guilty of anything, Waine."

"A judge might not like the looks of it, either," Waine said.

"A judge. If the only people we were to displease in our lives were to be the Diana Stewarts and the judges, I think we'd have done well . . ." But Ted couldn't keep up the pep talk, and as he realized that he was going to be left alone with his thoughts, his face drooped. He gave Waine's hand a weak squeeze, then let his hand fall. "What a mess, hunh?"

"I've seen messier," Waine said. But on the train, heading back to the city, he couldn't think off-hand of a case that had been. He felt mired in events, unable to move, unable to think. He was glad to be on a train—something forthright and formidable that moved to its destination without deviating or dawdling. He hoped it would inspire him, but it didn't.

Waine went for a walk. He didn't have a destination, he just walked. As he got near Hudson Street, he heard a hubbub of activity—the low snarl of two-way radios, the shouts of men, the rumble of engines—the unmistakable sounds of a fire being fought.

Waine's brain made a leap. Had anyone been with him, he would not have said out loud the connection his mind had made; nor did he say it to himself. It wasn't a fact, but it was more than a conception; it wasn't something to announce, but it was something to act on.

Waine ran to the corner.

Bonnie Niles's restaurant was engulfed in flames. The big plate glass window at the front had shattered; the pair of windows in the second-story room that Bonnie used as an office gleamed like feral eyes. The building looked oddly like a jack o'lantern.

Waine ducked under a barricade the police had put up to keep the curious back. Given the hour, there was a decent crowd of spectators.

A hand thumped down on Waine's shoulder and a voice asked him what he thought he was doing. He turned to face a cop whose nameplate said *Nurse*.

"The owner of that restaurant is a friend of mine," Waine said.

"So?"

"So, I just want to make sure she's all right."

"You a doctor?" the cop said.

"I'm her lawyer," Waine said, half-smiling at the feeble sound of it. He wondered if he was having so much trouble communicating because he had had too much to drink, or because he truly couldn't make a valid connection between himself and Bonnie.

"Yeah, well, she's not going to be needing any legal advice at the moment, pal, so why don't you—"

"Waine?"

Waine looked past the cop and saw Bonnie sitting in the front seat of a police white top. The door was open and she was sitting sideways on the seat with her legs crossed; the curve of her calf made a pretty line against the door. Her left arm was across her waist and her right elbow rested on it, a pivot that enabled her to move a cigarette to and from her mouth with a minimum of motion. She had her hair piled up and held with a tortoise-shell comb. She wore a white cotton T-shirt that enhanced her breasts. So uninvolved did she look that she might have been watching grass growing rather than her livelihood being destroyed.

"That's her," Waine said to the cop.

"Who?"

"My friend. The owner of the restaurant."

"I know who she is," the cop said.

Waine looked imploringly at Bonnie.

"Frank," Bonnie called.

The cop turned.

"He's a friend. It's okay."

The cop looked at Waine and flicked a thumb toward Bonnie.

"Thanks," Waine said.

"Sure."

Waine went to the white top and crouched down before Bonnie. "You okay?"

"Did you notice his nametag?" Bonnie said.

"Yes. Are you okay?"

"Isn't that amazing? A cop named Nurse."

"Since when do you smoke?" Waine said.

"Just since the fire started. It seemed appropriate."

Waine stood up and put a hand on Bonnie's shoulder in a way that told her he'd be right back. He went over to the cop. "Has she seen a doctor?"

"Who?"

"Miss Niles."

The cop wagged his thumb toward Bonnie. "You mean . . . ?"

"Yes."

"No."

"No, she hasn't seen a doctor?"

The cop spread his hands despairingly. "That's what you just asked me, right?"

Waine considered punching the cop in the mouth, but decided against it. "I think she should see a doctor. She may be in shock."

"You a doctor?" the cop said.

". . . no."

"That's what I thought. I thought you said you were a lawyer."

Waine went back to Bonnie, crouching down before her again.

"Long time, no see," Bonnie said.

"Bon, let's take a walk over to St. Vincent's, okay? I think a doctor should take a look at you."

"Hey, I'm fine. I wasn't in there when it started. I was home in bed. You know, when I heard the engines, I knew exactly what had happened."

"So did I."

"Yeah? Well, we always did sort of think alike. On certain matters." Bonnie nearly flicked the cigarette away; then, as if intimidated by the presence of all the firemen, she put it out carefully in the ashtray on the dashboard of the white top. She brushed a strand of hair out of her face and looked sadly at the burning building. "The bastards."

"It's a message from your friends with the juke box, isn't it?" Waine said.

"How do you know about my friends with the juke box?"

"Archer told me."

"Did he? That blabbermouth."

Waine put a hand on her knee. "Bonnie . . ."

She looked at his hand curiously, as if it were some small animal of indeterminate friendliness. "I remember the first time you put your hand on my knee in public. We were at a party. I can't remember whose;

someplace up on the East Side. We were sitting on a couch and I was talking to someone standing next to the couch—No, not standing; sitting on the arm. And you wanted to introduce me to somebody or to listen to what somebody was saying, or something, and you leaned over and put your hand on my knee to get my attention. It made me feel so good . . ." She took his wrist in her fingers and lifted his hand gingerly. "We're not intimate anymore, Waine, so I don't think you're entitled. Old Frank there is getting the wrong idea."

Waine glanced at the cop, who was watching them interestedly. The cop smiled and touched a finger to the brim of his cap. "Counselor."

"Bonnie," Waine said, "there's no point sitting here watching."

"Oh, I don't know; it's kind of pretty. Everybody likes a good fire. And the firemen, Waine—they're so brave; they just walked right into it. I hope it doesn't spread. I'll be so unhappy if it spreads. People live on either side. They shouldn't have to suffer for my stubbornness. My stupidity."

Waine thought of a lot of vapid things to say: that the firemen would contain the blaze; that the arsonists would be caught and punished; that Bonnie's insurance would cover the damages; that she'd be able to remodel this place, or buy a new one, and would be back in business in a year; that it would have the fortuitous result of enabling her to make some changes the old place had constrained her from making. He didn't say any of them; it wasn't that they were arguable; it was that they were irrelevant. "Would you like a drink? We can go to my place."

Bonnie shook her head sadly but firmly. "As soon as I saw you, I thought, Uh-oh, here we go again. I'm vulnerable and he's strong and he'll help me through this night and the days ahead and I'll want to be helped because I won't be able to deal with this all by myself. I was really glad to see you—for just a moment. Now, I wouldn't care if I never saw you again. I wouldn't care if you just disappeared in—" she laughed "—in a puff of smoke—"

"Bonnie, I don't want anything from you. I just want to help you."

Her eyes were colder, more distant. "Of course, you don't want anything from me. That's the whole problem. You see everything in terms of what you can do for people; you don't have the least notion that anybody might be able to do something for you. It's the way the world works, Waine—give *and* take. But you won't take; you'll only give. Oh, you're generous, you're selfless, you're kind. But the effect of it, in the end, is that you wrap people up in your kindness—till they can't move, can't breathe. It's better to give than to receive—you didn't ever put it that way, but that's what you were saying. Well, that's not so. It's good to give and it's just as good to receive. It's good to surrender a little, now and then—to be vulnerable. It takes trust; it takes a real belief in other people's love for you. But you don't have it; you don't have that trust, that . . . that confidence in others. Maybe it's the business you're in; you're always dealing with people who can't reasonably tell the whole truth. If that's the reason, well, it's too bad. You're a good lawyer, but if being a good lawyer has turned you into a deficient human being, well, I think it's time you thought about going into some other line of work." Bonnie waved a hand impatiently, as if none of this was worth the time it was taking; she looked over at the restaurant. The flames had diminished; dark figures could be seen moving around inside. "It's probably just as well. I'd have had to give in to those guys eventually. There's nothing the police can do, really—except when they actually do something, something like this. And even then . . . I'm going to move out to California, Waine. Or maybe the Northwest—Washington or Oregon. I'll open a place out there. Or maybe I won't. But I'll at least have changed the scenery—" She pushed the heel of her hand against his shoulder abruptly, nearly knocking him out of his crouch. "Go away, Waine. Right now. Please. Hurry. If I need anything from you in a legal sense, I'll get in touch with your office. Now go. Go. Go."

Waine went, keeping his eyes down as he passed the cop, who touched the brim of his cap again. "Have a nice day, counselor."

Chapter 26

~~~~~~~~~~~~~~~~~~

When Francesca woke, she thought about Dr. Vincent Clavin's bicycle. Her impulse was to launch an expedition to determine the significance of the bicycle, but something told her that there was time—and that there were more important things for her to do first.

Most important was that today was the day she would operate to reattach the retina of Eva James's left eye. All indications were that the retina of the right eye was intact, but the retina of the left eye had clearly torn and she would have to reattach it, using the cryoprobe.

Francesca showered and dressed and made herself a bigger breakfast than usual. She gave herself some time to sit quietly after eating, then left for the hospital, taking a taxi.

Eva was still asleep when Francesca got to her room. She pulled a chair up to the bed and sat for a few minutes, her hand lightly resting atop Eva's.

You look very calm sitting there like that, her psyche said.

I feel calm.

Maternal, almost.

That's funny. That's what I feel—maternal.

That's not funny; it's logical.

Logical? I've never thought much about having children.

But you're thinking about it now?

. . . yes.

Well, you've never known a child as nice as Eva. She could charm the fangs off a rattlesnake.

There was a pause.

I wonder if I will, Francesca thought.

Will what?

Have children.

Of course you will.

By spontaneous generation?

Her psyche laughed.

. . . I do want a relationship with a man. I may not always act like it, but I do want one.

Do you want some advice?

Can I stop you?

(Laughter) Just give up.

Give up trying, you mean? That's encouraging.

I mean give up to the man. You can surrender to a man without surrendering your individuality.

"Surrender." That makes it sound like a war.

Only if you want to think of it as a war.

How else can I think of it?

Think of it—of a relationship—as a union of two people who can never, in fact, be truly united. They're different sizes, different shapes, different textures, different appetites, different intellects, different emotions, different gaits, different heartbeats, different enthusiasms, different backgrounds—

Ah.

Ah, what?

Different backgrounds. The key difference.

Is it?

I was thinking about the difficulty Waine has with it. Don't you see?

See what?

It's just his excuse.

Excuse for what? Acting like a brat?

Her psyche waited a moment, implying that there are brats and there are brats. *The point I was trying to make before you interrupted me was that given the differences between any two people in any relationship, the success or failure of the relationship depends on the extent to which each party allows himself to surrender. Most people can only surrender to a limited degree. They'll always hold on to something they think has to be theirs and theirs alone—if they're to be whole and therefore wholly contribute to the relationship. The fact is that that's the thing it's most important they surrender. And when they do, they'll find one of two things: Either they don't have to give it up at all; or, if they do, it's not that important in the first place . . . Take you and Waine. Your sticking point, whether you know it or not, is your independence. You think that having a relationship with a man means having to give up your independence. And look at the men you've had relationships with—men like Leeds (Pretty Boy) Cavanaugh, who basically doesn't give a damn for anybody but himself, and who thereby enabled you to be exactly as independent as you wanted to be. But Waine Ryan gives a damn about you, and the thing you'll be surprised to find is that having him around you and giving a damn about you won't limit your independence one bit. In fact, it'll make it grow . . . Waine has this hangup about your background. He had a bad marriage with a woman from a background like yours, so it's understandable that he'd be a little bit wary. He feels that he has to hold on to what he regards as his integrity. But what he'll discover is that it just doesn't matter—that no two people are alike, that coming from a certain background doesn't mean a thing, in the long run . . . So: If you're willing to surrender your independence, you'll find that you can be as independent as you want to be—because your independence will include being involved with a man on whom, to a certain degree, you depend. And if Waine is willing to surrender his position about your background, he'll find that it doesn't matter at all, that it isn't a position worth holding on to—because he'll be involved with a woman whose background has contributed to his wanting to be involved with her in the first place . . . You see?*

. . . if you're so smart, why aren't you—

Rich? I am. I'm you, remember?

I was going to say, why aren't you happy?

Ah, well—that depends on you. I'm you, remember?

"Dr. Hayward?"

"Good morning, Eva. How did you know it was me?"

"You feel good. Nobody feels as good as you."

"Today's a big day for you," Francesca said.

"I know . . . Dr. Hayward?"

"Yes, Eva?"

"My Aunt Diana says I'm going to live with her and my Uncle Charles."

". . . I'm sure they'll take very good care of you," Francesca said.

"But that isn't what my father wanted. He wanted me to live with my Uncle Ted and my Aunt Clara. It was in his will. I told you about the will. Did you tell anybody about the will?"

". . . yes, Eva, I did."

"I told Aunt Diana about the will and she said they found the will but it didn't say what I said it said. She said my father must've made another will after the first one, and didn't tell me about it."

"People often make more than one will," Francesca said. "They change their minds about things."

"My father would've told me if he'd changed his mind about something like *that*," Eva said. "And anyway, I heard Aunt Diana tell Dr. Clever—"

"Dr. Who?"

"Dr. Clever."

"You mean Dr. Clavin."

"Yeah, but I call him Dr. Clever."

Francesca had to laugh. "Okay, so you heard your Aunt Diana tell Dr. Clever what?"

"That the will was in handwriting."

"Longhand, you mean?"

"Yes," Eva said. "She told Dr. Clever that she has the same handwriting as my father, and not to worry because people would think my father wrote the will. But the will my father wrote wasn't in handwriting. It was on a typewriter."

". . . you're sure?"

"He *showed* it to me."

Francesca checked the clock on the wall. It was nearly time to begin preparing Eva for the operation. "Where did you hear them—your Aunt and Dr. Clavin?"

"Dr. Clever."

"Dr. Clever."

"Right *here*," Eva said. "My Aunt Diana thinks because I can't see that I can't hear. Dr. Clever kept telling her to talk softer, and I couldn't really hear them all that good. They weren't talking real loud; they were sort of whispering. But I could still *hear* them."

"People who can't see often have very good hearing," Francesca said. "You've had those bandages on for a while, so your hearing's probably improved a lot. They probably thought you really couldn't hear them."

"Dr. Hayward?"

"Yes, Eva?"

"I'm going to be able to see, aren't I?"

"You bet. Don't worry about it for a minute."

"Dr. Hayward?"

"Yes?"

"I don't like my Aunt Diana."

Francesca ruffled Eva's hair. "I'll tell you what. Don't say anything about this to anybody. I'm going to tell a friend of mine what you just told me, and he'll do whatever is necessary to make sure that this all comes out all right."

"You mean I'll get to live with my Aunt Clara and Uncle Ted?"

"I don't want to promise you anything, peanut. But let's hope for the best."

"I love you, Dr. Hayward."

Francesca held her breath, but she couldn't hold back the tears. "I love you, too, Eva."

". . . are you crying, Dr. Hayward?"

Francesca laughed through her tears. "Oh, it's good to cry now and then. It relaxes me."

Chapter 27

~~~~~~~~~~

Waine Ryan's intercom buzzed and he answered it. "Yeah?"

"There's a call for you."

"Phyllis, for the thousandth time, I'm not in today."

". . . why don't you go home, if you're not in? It'd be much more pleasant for me."

Waine sighed and clicked off the intercom and did what he had been doing all day—sat with his feet up on his desk, thinking.

What counts, Francesca had said, *what's going to make the difference between going on with this relationship or just breaking it off right here, right now, is whether you have sufficient respect for my right to do what I think is right—in this instance, or in any other instance.*

And Bonnie had said: *You see everything in terms of what you can do for people; you don't have the least notion that anybody might be able to do something for you. It's the way the world works, Waine—give and take.*

They had been saying the same thing, hadn't they?

They had been saying that what he had always thought of as self-sufficiency and an unerring sense of rectitude were merely facets of a mindless egocentricity.

Waine swung his feet down and got up and went to the window of his office, which looked down on Washington Square Park. A pretty young woman jogger in pale blue shorts and a royal blue singlet ran past, going at what he estimated to be a seven-minute-mile pace.

Waine felt like running after her.

He wondered if he could still run a seven minute mile. He wondered if he could still bench press his weight. He had stayed in shape, doing his daily exercise at home, but he had given up pushing himself to the limit, as he had done all through college and graduate school and even beyond. He told himself that it was because he had channeled his competitive instinct into his work, but he wasn't altogether sure that that was true. Perhaps he had lost his competitive instinct, and was merely getting ready to get fat and lazy.

Or maybe it was something else: Pushing himself to run seven minute miles, he had had to concede that there were people who ran six minute miles, whom he could never catch, never match. By giving up pushing himself, he had given up having to make the concession. He had done the same thing in his emotional life: By giving up working at relationships, he had given up not only having to make the compromises, but had denied to himself that the necessity to make them existed. In short, he had taken to living third class, among the dull and dispirited.

Waine turned away from the window, went to his desk, took his suit coat from the back of his chair, put it on, and went out to the reception area of the office.

Phyllis, the secretary, pointedly did not look up at him.

"I'm going to call it a day, Phyl," Waine said.

She nodded, almost imperceptibly.

"I guess I should look at my messages, in case there's anything urgent."

Phyllis pushed a thick stack of messages across her desk, gingerly, as if they were infected.

Waine picked them up and started to read through them from the bottom when he noticed the one on top. "Francesca Hayward? When did she call?"

"You'll notice," Phyllis said slowly, "that you are holding in your hand a standard office form used for making a record of telephone calls received in an individual's absence. In the upper right hand corner of the form, there is a box labeled *Time of Call*. In that box, in—"

Waine looked at his watch. "She called just a few minutes ago. That was her on the phone just now."

"You said you weren't in," Phyllis said.

"I was in for *her*. I didn't—Why didn't—When—What does this mean?" Waine read out loud the rest of the message on the slip of paper. " 'Conrad James typed his will, according to Eva.' " He looked at Phyllis. "Well?"

"Well, what?"

"What does it mean?"

Deliberately, Phyllis covered her typewriter, put away a folder, closed a half-open drawer, straightened her pens, removed her glasses.

Waine sighed. "I'm sorry, Phyl. It's perfectly clear what it means."

Phyllis smiled meanly.

"Ted, this is Waine Ryan."

"I didn't expect to hear from you so soon."

"What kind of typewriter did Conrad James use?"

". . . I beg your pardon?"

"What kind of—"

"I heard you, Waine," Ted Hirsch said. "What I mean is, why do you want to know?"

"The will we found in the Jameses' apartment was handwritten," Waine said.

"I know. You told us."

"Eva says the will she saw Conrad James put in the box was typed."

There was a long silence.

"Of course," Ted said at last.

"Of course, what?"

"Conrad never wrote anything by hand," Ted said. "Not a grocery list, not a note to Edith to say someone had phoned, not a postcard. When they traveled, he carried a portable typewriter along to make notes for book ideas with; he wrote all his postcards on it."

"A will's a little different," Waine said. "He might have felt the need to be a little more personally involved with it."

"Trust me, Waine," Ted said. "It's just one of those things that's not disputable. I remember very distinctly a conversation about it. I use a combination of longhand and typing when I write. I'll go along for a while on the typewriter, then when I get stuck, I'll write in longhand. The act of forming the words helps me form the ideas. Conrad felt exactly the opposite. I can remember his words: He said, 'I can't think in longhand. I get so involved in the esthetic considerations of penmanship that I can't concentrate on what I'm trying to say.' He blamed it on his schooling; he said the teachers taught penmanship as though it were separate from writing—as though it were, as he put it, 'merely decorative' . . . I don't know why this didn't occur to me before."

"You mentioned a portable typewriter. Was that what he wrote on?"

Ted snorted softly into the phone. "Just when he was on the road. No, Conrad was a very model of a modern major novelist. He wrote on a word processor. It's like a computer; you type on a keyboard and the text appears in front of you on a console, like a television screen. You make all the additions and corrections you want on the screen, then you press a button and the printer types out a perfect copy. Conrad said it made his work so much easier that he figured he'd be able to write two or three more books in his lifetime than he would if he used a typewriter."

There was another long pause.

"Hello?" Ted said.

"I'm thinking," Waine said. "I'll call you when I've thought a little more."

"Eva's operation was a success, by the way," Ted said. "Dr. Hayward called a little while ago to tell us."

". . . that was nice of her," Waine said.

"I thought so."

". . . I'll talk to you soon, Ted."

"Chin up, Waine."

"You, too."

Chapter 28

The next day, Francesca had lunch with her mother. Beatrice Hayward had come into the city for a final interview at the senior citizens' center whose director Waine Ryan had put her in touch with.

Beatrice Hayward leaned across the table and touched her daughter's cheek. "You look frightfully tired. I wish you'd take some time off. When was the last time you had a vacation?"

"Leeds and I went to Aspen," Francesca said.

"Did you?"

Francesca gave her mother a look.

"As I recall, you stayed only two days—you singular —then came back to look after one of your patients, leaving Leeds to his own devices."

". . . Mrs. Letterman's corneal transplant," Francesca said softly.

Beatrice Hayward took a bite of her cucumber sandwich. When she'd chewed and swallowed it, she said, "Your father was the same way. He'd overwork himself to the point where he'd have to be physically restrained from carrying on."

Francesca wondered: If her father was alive, would she be compared with him any less than she was now—just for the sake of politeness? She couldn't be compared with him any more. "And now you're about to join the club. I know you'll work at this new job of yours round the clock, seven days a week."

"I don't have the job yet," Beatrice Hayward said.

"You'll get it. You want it so badly."

"It's about time, wouldn't you say?" Beatrice Hayward said. "I have a lot of spunk left in me; it should be put to some larger use than just my own affairs."

"It's not as though you haven't been involved in things," Francesca said. "You've done an enormous amount of volunteer work."

"True," Beatrice assented, "but it's not enough anymore. I want to fully commit myself to responsible work and be paid for it. But we were talking about you."

Francesca gave her mother another look.

"You're not getting any younger, Francesca."

"Mother, really. Don't be fatuous."

Beatrice Hayward laughed so loudly that heads turned. "I do believe that's the first time anyone's ever accused me of *that*. I've been called a lot of things in my time, but never fatuous." She laughed again, even more loudly. "Marvelous."

Francesca sighed.

"When I mention your age," Beatrice Hayward said, "I'm specifically referring to having children. As a doctor, you must know—"

"I *do* know, mother. Can we talk about something else? Anything else?"

They talked about nothing else until they had finished their sandwiches, declined dessert and were served coffee—Beatrice's iced, Francesca's hot.

"What *did* happen with Waine Ryan that Sunday?"

Beatrice Hayward said. "That story you told me about his having had to go see a client—that was hogwash."

Francesca lifted her coffee cup to her mouth, but the liquid was still too hot, and she set it down. "We had a disagreement. An argument. A fight. We . . . broke up."

Beatrice Hayward patted her lips with her napkin. "I'm sorry. Truly sorry."

"I'll get over it," Francesca said.

"Of course you will—if you want to."

"What is that supposed to mean? I don't enjoy pining."

"I just wonder . . ." Beatrice Hayward shook her head. "Nothing."

"What, mother?" Francesca said evenly.

". . . It's too pat, too simple. You don't meet a man of that caliber and feel as intensely about him as you obviously did and just let him go out of your life because of some disagreement."

Francesca shut her eyes for a moment. She could picture Waine Ryan pedaling his borrowed bicycle down the path out of her mother's estate, riding down Driftwood to Midway, down Midway to 114, down 114 to the South Ferry Terminal—the same way Dr. Vincent Clavin would have ridden on his bicycle—if he hadn't left his bicycle behind.

What was so important about Vincent Clavin's bicycle?

"Francesca?"

Francesca opened her eyes.

"You haven't been listening to a word I've said," Beatrice Hayward said.

"I'm sorry, mother. You're right. I'm tired. I need some time off."

"How about Martha's Vineyard? We could go up there for a long weekend."

Francesca thought for a moment. "I think I'd like to go out to Shelter Island."

Beatrice Hayward leaned back in surprise. "The other day, you were saying you'd never go out there again—to spite me for selling the house."

"There's . . . something I want to do," Francesca said.

"Oh?"

Francesca looked at her watch. "I have to get back to the hospital, and you have to get to your interview."

Beatrice Hayward reached across the table and took her daughter's hand. "I was planning to stay in the city, but I could come out there with you, if you'd like."

"I'd like to be alone, mother. Nothing personal. I think I can manage to get the rest of the week off. With Eva James's operation out of the way, I don't have anything pressing on my schedule."

"This . . . thing you want to do? What is it, exactly?"

"I'm not sure," Francesca said. "I'm really not sure."

That night, Francesca dreamed that she was sailing on her Sunfish. There was hardly any wind. The high sun beat on the water as if it were a drumskin and reflected off into her eyes, her nostrils, her skin—so that Francesca felt full of heat. Twice, while beating upwind, she let herself over the side and let the boat pull her while she got wet. The water was warm, and full of jelly fish, but the evaporation cooled her for a time.

Then she had come about and was running before the wind, heading toward the North Haven Peninsula.

Some part of her that was not dreaming said—perhaps out loud—that Dr. Vincent Clavin had a house on the North Haven Peninsula.

In the dream, the peninsula was doing extraordinary things: The trees in the nature preserve at its north end were on fire; then they were simply shimmering in the sunlight. The beaches skirting the forest glittered with diamonds; then they were alive with flailing, dying fish.

The water that lapped up on the shore was metallic, like mercury; then it was crystalline, like glass. The sky overhead was a chasm into which Francesca felt she was falling; then it was a roof pressing down on her, threatening to crush her. Off in the distance, the ferry boats crossing the sound were white whales; an airplane flying overhead was a mantis.

This was no longer a dream; it was a memory, too. For something just like this had happened to Francesca once, sailing on a hot day in Noyack Bay. She had been stricken by the sun and experienced a disorientation that sometimes afflicts sailors when sailing with the wind behind them on an extremely hot day. As a result, she had fallen overboard.

She was dreaming again, and was falling overboard.

She fell slowly and luxuriously—as if, she imagined, she were falling through space, or descending back into the womb. The cool of the water salved the distress the heat had produced, and as she slipped down and down and down, her faculties regained their acuity, and she began to feel infinitely wise.

Above her, the Sunfish passed like a cloud across the sun, then glided on, derelict, but determined in its course.

Breathing became a problem—or rather, not breathing. She wanted to open her mouth wide and suck in sustenance. If she were going to keep on descending, she would need more oxygen than she had managed to gulp before slipping under the water.

Keep on descending where?

To the center of things. To truth.

That's absurd. This is no mystical experience. You're drowning.

Ah.

That revelation produced a determination not to drown—a determination that was confounded by the fact that the process of drowning was well enough advanced that reversing it required the expenditure of all the oxygen that was left in her lungs.

She expended it, and broke through the surface of the water.

Breaking through the surface of sleep, finding herself sitting bolt upright, covered with perspiration, Francesca understood something:

She understood the significance of Dr. Vincent Clavin's bicycle.

Chapter 29

~~~~~~~~~~~~~~~~~

"November 22, 1963," the old man said. He lifted his baseball cap by the brim, scratched his forelock, and put the cap back on, tugging it low and sighting out under the brim, as if at the past.

"It was a Friday," Francesca said. She was standing at the foot of a porch of a ramshackle old house built on an overgrown lot in an out-of-the-way corner of Sag Harbor. She was dressed for an expedition in a khaki safari shirt, khaki pants, sensible walking shoes; she had her hair tied up in a silk scarf.

"A Friday." The old man, who was standing on the porch's top step, lifted his cap again, scratched his forelock again, and put the cap back on, tugging it low but not as low, as if the day of the week had made a difference.

"According to the ferry company's work roster, you were on the five A.M. to noon shift."

"Five A.M. to noon." The old man left the cap alone this time. His eyes snapped back to the present. "Work roster? Where'd you get hold of a work roster?"

In a dusty file in a dusty drawer of a dusty cabinet in a dusty corner of a dusty closet in the dank basement of the ferry company's office, Francesca thought, remembering the feel of the dust under her fingernails and in her nose and throat and the dank in her bones. She had spent all day yesterday—her first day out on Shelter Island—going through dusty files. As to why the roster had been saved all those years, she had no idea; she had been afraid to ask, lest it turn to dust in her hands as she tried to decipher it. "What I'm interested in knowing, Mr. Parker, is whether you remember taking a man with a bicycle over to Shelter Island. It must've been around seven o'clock."

Parker felt in the righthand pocket of his gray cardigan sweater, then in the lefthand pocket. Not finding anything, or perhaps having determined that they contained nothing dangerous, he stuck his hands in the pockets and rocked back on his heels, then up on his toes. He rocked again, then came to rest and felt in the right pocket of his khaki work pants, then in the left, then put his hands in the pants pockets. "Who'd you say you were?"

"My name's Francesca Hayward."

Parker squinted at her. "Seen you around somewhere."

"My family's summered on Shelter Island for years."

Parker nodded dubiously. He felt in the left breast pocket of his khaki work shirt, then in the right breast pocket. He smiled smally, having finally found what he was looking for. He extracted it, but kept it hidden in his big hand.

Francesca checked a note she'd made for herself. "You were working that day with James O'Reilly and Fred Mazza."

Parker tugged the brim of his cap a little lower. "Jim's dead."

"I know."

"Cancer."

Francesca nodded.

Parker glanced over his shoulder toward the open front door of his house. He stepped down from the top step of the porch to the step below, offered Francesca a swift look at what he held in his hand—a cigarette—and returned it to the breast pocket of his shirt. In a whisper, he said: "Not suppose to have this. The wife'd have a conniption."

Francesca gestured toward her car. "We could take a little ride if you'd like."

He squinted at the car, as if the year and model made a difference. Then he straightened up suddenly, looking offended that she would think he would stoop to deception. "Say, what're you after, anyway?"

"November 22, 1963. A man on a bicycle—around seven A.M."

Parker lifted his cap, scratched his forelock and put his cap back on, tugging it to the lowest position thus far.

Francesca was beginning to understand what drives people to violence. "It was the day John Kennedy was killed," she said.

Parker looked at her pityingly. "Course it was. Everybody knows that. It's one of those dates you never forget."

Seeing Parker inhale preparatory to rattling off some other unforgettable dates, Francesca hurried to get her words in. "You probably remember a lot of things about that day. People tend to. They remember where they were when they heard about it, where they went after they heard, and so on."

Parker looked at her interestedly, as if expecting her to tell him where she had been, where she had gone, and so on.

"Do you?" Francesca said.

Parker raised the brim of his cap fractionally. "Heard about it at Jim O'Reilly's. Stopped there for a beer after work."

Francesca waited.

"Jim's dead."

"I know. I talked to Fred Mazza on the phone."

"Fred lives in Riverhead," Parker said.

"Right . . . I asked him if he remembered a man with a bicycle. He said he was piloting, and wouldn't have paid as much attention to the passengers as the deck crew—"

"Me and Jim were working the deck that day."

"And Jim's dead," Francesca said.

Parker stared, as if wondering how she could have known that. "Say, what do you want to know for, anyway?"

Francesca wrote her number on a slip of paper from her pocket notebook and handed it to Parker. "If you should happen to remember anything about a man with a bicycle, give this number a call." She started for her car.

"Say, miss."

She stopped.

Parker came to where she stood, glancing over his shoulder at the front door. "You wouldn't happen to have a match, would you? I clean forgot the matches when I came out here."

Francesca looked in her shoulder bag and surprised herself by finding a book of matches. They were from the restaurant where she and Waine had had dinner with Phil Archer, a hundred years ago.

"Much obliged," Parker said. He put the matches in the breast pocket of his shirt, then took them out and put them in his right pants pocket—as if on the chance that either the matches or the cigarette could be discovered he could aver his innocence by pointing to the absence of the other. "A man with a bicycle, you say?"

Francesca leaned against the fender of her car.

Parker lifted his cap, scratched his forelock and put the cap back on, resting it far back on his head this time, so that the brim pointed nearly straight up.

The new attitude gave Francesca hope.

"Lot of people go back and forth on bikes."

"But not early on a Friday morning in November," Francesca said. "And not in 1963. There weren't as many bike riders then."

"True enough. True enough." Parker jammed his hands in the pockets of his sweater and straightened his arms so that the sweater reached halfway down his thighs.

Francesca wondered how he could wear a sweater in this heat. Perhaps all those years of riding back and forth on the ferry had permanently chilled him.

"Yup," Parker said.

"Yup, what?" Francesca said.

Parker looked at her oddly. Didn't she know the object of her search when she came upon it? "Yup, there was a man with a bicycle."

Francesca felt warm and cold at the same time, and shivered.

Chapter 30

~~~~~~~~~~~~~~~~

"Starboard a touch, starboard a touch. Easy as she goes. Now to port just a hair." Parker leaned out the door of Francesca's car, a cigarette dangling from his lips, one eye closed against the smoke, muttering directions on how to negotiate a bumpy dirt road on the North Haven Peninsula.

"A *hair*, goddamn it."

Francesca braked the car. "You want to drive?"

Parker patted all his pockets. "Forgot my glasses."

"Then let me do it my way, will you please?"

Parker pouted. "We're close enough, anyway. We can walk."

They walked quite a way along the road, which turned first into a lane, then into a path, then into just a rut the width of a footstep, and finally arrived at a wooden shack at the lip of a small precipice that dropped down to a narrow beach at the edge of Shelter Island Sound.

Parker wagged a thumb at the shack. "Asa's place."

Only the filter tip of the cigarette remained, but Parker wasn't about to part with it.

Across the sound, Francesca could see her mother's house, sitting contendedly amid a copse of trees. She felt uneasy: Whoever lived here could, if he cared, know a great deal about her; had he seen her, out on the dock, arguing with Waine, diving into the water? had he thought it melodramatic, or only cryptic?

Parker stepped up on a wooden packing skid that served as the shack's porch and kicked at the wall of the shack three times with the toe of his big work boot. "Asa doesn't hear so well," he explained. "Feels the vibrations, though." He opened the shack's door and wagged a thumb inside. "We can go in?"

"Shouldn't we let him invite us in?"

Parker flapped his arms. "Told you, didn't I? Asa's crippled. In a wheelchair. Chair's too big to let him get at this door."

Francesca looked back at the rut they had followed. "How does he manage the chair through this grass?"

Parker rolled his eyes. "Told you, Asa hasn't been out of this place since 1958. That's when he got busted up. Out fishing he was. Best commercial fisherman between Riverhead and Montauk he was. A net got fouled and he—"

"You told me," Francesca said. "Maybe we should go in, now that we've, uh, knocked."

They stepped through the door into a dark anteroom littered with things they couldn't make out but that gave off a sense of having been accumulating for decades. They went up a three-step ladder and through another door, a door of less than full size, like a door on a ship.

Francesca was blinded by the light, and was then altogether disoriented to find herself, in fact, on a ship. Or—she saw as her eyes grew more accustomed to the brightness—on a facsimile of one.

The ceilings were low and heavily beamed. On the

walls were brass lamps and storage cabinets with brass handles. In the center of the room was a big oak table, bolted to the floor, as if to guard against its slipping in a storm; on the table lay some nautical charts, their edges floppy with use. Other charts were rolled up in pigeon holes in the table's base. Cut into the top of the table were notches for a plate and cup.

In front of the table was a huge wooden ship's wheel, its spokes polished from use. A pane of heavy-duty glass ran the width of the shack, from nearly to the floor to nearly to the ceiling. It provided the same view they had had from outside the shack, yet somehow intensified it, as if it were magnifying glass. The dock, for example, seemed to reach so far out into the sound that Francesca had little doubt that anyone standing on the narrow porch outside the shack's big window would have had any trouble hearing what she and Waine had said.

As her eyes got yet more used to the light, Francesca saw who the potential listener was. Seated before the window in an old-fahsioned wheelchair of cane and wicker, with wooden wheels covered with hard rubber tires, was a lean, long, whitehaired man in blue work-shirt and bellbottomed dungarees. He wore a blue seaman's hat, its brim pulled low over his eyes against the glare. On his lap was a long telescope with brass fittings. On his feet were sturdy black work shoes. The shoes—their soles were mint—said as nothing else about him did that his feet and legs were dead.

Parker went to the wheelchair, put his hands on his knees and leaned down to the man's ear and shouted—so loudly that glassware in one of the cabinets vibrated in consonance. *"Howdy, Asa!"*

Asa put a finger to the brim of his cap in salute. "Howdy, Bob."

"No," Parker yelled. "It's Jack. Jack *Parker*."

Asa saluted again. "Jack."

"Brought someone to see you, Asa," Parker shouted.

Asa touched the brim of his hat a third time. "Welcome 'board."

Parker bent closer and yelled louder still. "It's a woman."

"Ma'am," Asa said.

"Hello," Francesca said.

"She says hello," Parker yelled.

Francesca moved toward the men. "Mr. Parker, there's no need for you to interpret. I can ask him myself."

Parker waved a hand discouragingly. "This takes more lung power than you might think. Best let me handle it . . . Asa, this woman here, she wants to know about something happened out in the bay some time back . . ."

Asa tugged the brim of his cap a little lower, as if getting ready to set sail into the past.

"Sixty-three," Parker shouted. "November '63."

"Sixty-three," Asa said, a little disappointed, as if that weren't so long ago.

"November 22, 1963 . . . Day JFK got shot."

Asa twitched a shoulder, as if to say everyone knew that.

Parker shot a glance at Francesca. "Told you, everybody remembers that day."

"Maybe it'd be more efficient if I wrote the questions down," Francesca said.

Parker stood upright, frowned, raised the brim of his cap a little, frowned more deeply, pulled the brim of his cap lower. "Hunh?"

Francesca took out her notebook. "It'll save time."

Parker sighed and turned toward the window and looked out at the sound, shaking his head slowly. He turned back, lifted his cap, scratched his forelock, and put his cap back on, pulling the brim low. He wagged a thumb at Asa. "You mean write 'em out so he can read 'em?"

Francesca nodded.

Parker laughed a long, slow laugh, shaking his head

from side to side in time to it. He stopped laughing, unbuttoned his sweater, tucked in his shirt, buttoned his sweater and put his hands in the pockets of the sweater. "Asa's blind."

Francesca felt her face turning bright red. Wasn't she an eye doctor? She looked more closely at Asa and saw the vacancy in his stare. She stepped up close to him and bent to see into his eyes. "Cataracts."

Parker shuffled, a little embarrassed, now, at his gruffness. "Old Asa handles it so good, you sort of tend to forget about it, sometimes."

Francesca counted toward ten, stopping at five. "Mr. Parker?"

He took a step back. "Ma'am?"

"You told me Asa here has seen everything that's happened out this window since 1958."

"Since he got laid up, that's right."

"Everything?"

Parker went up on his toes and back on his heels. "Well, if I said everything, I wasn't exactly telling the truth. I mean, I wasn't exactly lying, either, since I didn't mean no harm by it—by giving you the impression that if you were interested in knowing about something that happened yesterday, say, or the day before, or even last week, then Asa'd be the man to tell you about it. No, if that's what you thought—if you thought Asa'd be the man to tell you about something that happened—"

"Mr. Parker," Francesca said. "Was Asa blind in 1963?"

Parker put up his hands in horror. "No. It'll be two years in August since Asa went blind."

Francesca knelt next to Asa's chair. "Asa?"

"Won't do no good," Parker said. He tapped his forehead. "Asa is getting a little soft."

This time, Francesca's count reached three. "Mr. Parker, why did you lead me to believe Asa was going to be able to shed any light on that day?"

Parker smiled. "Log."

". . . What?"

Parker struck a didactic pose. "Well, not being able to get around much, but being a healthy, active man till just a couple of years ago, old Asa used to enjoy keeping a log—a record of everything that went on on his doorstep, so to speak"—Parker tilted his head toward the window, and the sound beyond—"I've only seen a few pages of it, now and then, but I was real impressed by it—by the details—descriptions of boats, registration numbers, names, how they were rigged, how many people on board, wind and water conditions."

Slowly, lest the answer be too disappointing, Francesca said, "Where are they?"

With a showman's instinct, Parker stepped over to a cabinet built into one of the walls and thrust out a hand, looking like an emcee on a television game show, pointing out the door that the prize might or might not lie behind.

Francesca went to the cabinet, moving Parker out of the way with a gentle shove with the back of her hand against his arm. She opened the cabinet doors and surveyed row upon row of black leatherbound notebooks. She took one out and opened it and saw that its pages were covered, front and back, with a dense but elegant hand.

"Funny thing is," Parker said, "if old Asa were still chipper, I bet you'd find stuff in there about something that happened on his doorstep, so to speak, just yesterday."

Francesca could see that that was true—that if old Asa were still chipper, there would surely be something in his journals about her argument with Waine Ryan, out on the dock, a few days ago.

Slowly, out of a nagging fear that *the* volume she was looking for would somehow not be there, she took out book after book, checking the front page to find the inclusive dates.

When she found the one she wanted, she didn't open

to the important pages. She closed the book and held it in her arms, like a cherished memento.

She recalled telling Waine, that first time he had come out to Shelter Island, about her suspicions about her father's death. It had come out of her almost as an outburst; it had been something she had been compelled to do. It had been Waine who had compelled her—not by force, surely; not even by dint of questioning, for he had known only vaguely that there were questions to ask. What had compelled her had been the emanation from him of interest in her, in her life as she had lived it, in her essence, in her.

Holding the book in her arms, she realized that she did not want to read its tale alone—that it was a story she wanted to share with Waine Ryan.

Chapter 31

~~~~~~~~~~~~~~~~

Waine Ryan leaned into the wind that whipped down the East River, carrying with it just the slightest hint of autumn. He was standing on the heliport built on a pier that juts out into the river at the end of Wall Street, looking up at the sky, waiting for a seaplane—a seaplane Francesca Hayward had chartered to fly her back into the city from Shelter Island.

"I've found something—something important." That had been all she had told him on the telephone. She had said she had to hurry—that the seaplane was revving up.

Waine had found something, too. He had found it in Conrad James's word processor.

Before he had been able to find it, he had had to learn a little bit about word processors. By a wild coincidence, he had learned about them from Phil Archer, whom he had called because he remembered that Archer's brother was a salesman for a company that made small computers for use in homes and offices.

"What do you want to know?" Archer had said.

"It'd be easier if I just talked to your brother," Waine had said.

"What, you don't want to talk to me? I know as much as he does. More, I'd say, although I doubt if he'd say it."

". . . you?"

"What am I, stupid or something?"

"No, you're not stupid, Phil. But why should you know anything about word processors?"

"'Cause I've been studying about them, that's why."

". . . why?"

"Why? Because I'm not going to be a cop forever, that's why. Because one of these days I'm going to turn in my badge and gun and find myself a line of work where there's less chance the people I'll be dealing with will have an interest in shooting me. My brother and I are thinking of opening up our own business. This home computer industry's going to take off."

". . . when can we get together, Phil?"

"What's wrong with right now? Want me to come by your office?"

"Meet me at 275 Central Park West," Waine had said. "That's where the word processor I'm interested in is. Oh, and, uh, do you have anything that looks like a search warrant?"

". . . why?"

"Because I don't have a key to the apartment."

". . . what's going on, Waine?"

"Just something to flash at the doorman, Phil. It doesn't have to be authentic."

It didn't have to be authentic. The doorman barely glanced at it, and handed them a key to the Jameses' apartment.

The word processor was in the den. Archer sat down at the keyboard, picked up the instruction manual that lay alongside it, and began to read.

"We don't have a long time, Phil."

"I learned on a different model," Archer said. "Just give me a couple of minutes."

After a couple minutes, Waine said, "Phil."

Archer gave him a look. "There're two kinds of people in the world—people who read the directions and people who don't read the directions. I'm one of the people who reads the directions. You would seem to be—"

"Read the directions, Phil."

After a couple of minutes more, Archer put down the instruction manual, leaned back in the chair to tuck in his shirt, rubbed his hands together and tapped at the keyboard.

"Did you do it?" Waine asked.

"Do what?"

"Whatever you're trying to do?"

"All I did was turn the machine on," Archer said. "That was the easy part. Now comes the hard part. We got to find the right disk."

"Disk?"

Archer pointed at a shelf lined with what looked like 45 rpm records. "Those're disks. What I just learned from this manual is how to edit the program. That just means that when I put a disk in the disk drive, I can ask the computer to show me the directory for that disk. The directory is a list of everything that's filed on the disk. We'll have to go through all the disks and read all the directories to find what we're looking for. This machine has two disk drives, so I can go through the disks two at a time." He turned to look at Waine. "You haven't told me what we're looking for."

"A will."

"A will? Why would anybody keep a will in a word processor?"

"Am I right in my understanding of this thing?" Waine said. "You type something on it and it goes into the computer's memory, right?"

"Right."

"And then you can press a button or something and get a printed copy of what you typed, right?"

Archer patted a small machine, like a teletype, off to one side of the word processor. "Comes out on this."

"And what happened to what you originally typed?" Waine said.

Archer patted the word processor. "It's in here."

"Forever?"

"Or until you delete it from the machine's memory."

Waine thought for a moment. "The man who worked on this machine was a novelist. So I imagine most of the stuff on the disks is all part of a novel. Does that make things easier, or harder?"

"Let's see." Archer took down the rightmost disk from the shelf. "Let's assume this is the last one." He put the disk in the drive and tapped the keyboard, muttering to himself as he did. ". . . directory . . . space . . . A . . . colon . . ." He sat back, and after a moment, on the console screen, flashed the characters: "WIP-9."

"What do you think that means?" Archer said.

"Work in progress, number nine?" Waine said.

"Sounds right." Archer tapped some more keys, muttering. On the keyboard flashed a page of text. "Looks like a novel, all right."

"Now what?" Waine said.

"Now we go through all the disks, two at a time. If the directories are all like this—WIP number so and so—then we can probably say two things—either the novel is the only thing on each disk—"

"Or there are other things on the disk, but they aren't in the directory."

Archer smiled up at Waine. "You catch on quick, counselor."

"What if that's true? I mean, let's assume that the novel is on all the disks, but that there's something else that isn't on the directory."

"We can ask it to search for key words," Archer said.

"Such as?"

"You're looking for a will, right?"

"Right."

"Well, you could search for the word 'will.' Trouble is, if anybody in this novel says anything like, 'I wonder if it will rain," the computer will show us that entry."

"So let's think of a better word," Waine said.

"Like what?"

Waine thought for a moment. "Like Eva."

"Eva? E,v,a?"

"Yes." Waine realized he was holding his breath.

He didn't let it out until Archer had tapped at the keyboard, muttering.

On the console screen, this appeared.

8 July 1979

To whom, etc.

If I and my wife should die, all of our property, possessions, savings, assets, royalties, etc., will go to our daughter, Eva.

Her care and upbringing, assuming she is not of age, will be the responsibility of my brother-in-law, Ted Hirsch, and his wife, Clara.

Of sound mind and healthy body, I am, etc.

Conrad James

A small plane appeared, a speck of silver in the white sky. It flew past the heliport, heading out over the harbor, making a long, slow turn over Governor's Island, coming back up the river, getting lower and lower, hitting the water so gently it barely made a splash.

Waine moved out to the end of the pier, his hands in the pockets of his suit coat, trying to look nonchalant. His heart was pounding.

The plane bobbed close to the pier and a heliport worker climbed out on a wing, carrying a line with which to make the plane fast to the pier. When it was fast, he opened the plane's door and put out a hand to assist the plane's only passenger.

Francesca had made herself admire the scenery as the plane came low over the city, and had not let herself look for the heliport pier, and for Waine. The landing had been frightening enough that she had only been able to concentrate on it, using body English to help the pilot make it down safely. Now, stepping out on the wing, holding the hand of the heliport worker, she concentrated on keeping her footing and making it onto something firm and stable and unmoving.

When she had, she looked up. Waine was standing several yards from her, not moving, looking as though he awaited an invitation before approaching. He wore an olive-green double-breasted suit, his usual blue shirt, a yellow knit tie, his usual brown loafers. The wind tossed his hair this way and that. She felt a deep ache inside her, born of wanting something, yet feeling that events had made it unattainable.

Waine tried not to remark on the way the wind pressed Francesca's white cotton skirt against her long thighs, on the way her simple maroon cotton T-shirt held her admirable breasts, on how sensually the wind threw her hair about. He tried not to remember the way that body had felt, thrust against his, longing for his unmistakably, as his had unmistakably longed for hers. And even more, he tried not to remember how, in this woman's hands, he had felt his mind being made love to, as well as his body, and how he had felt that he was making love to her mind.

Francesca took a deep breath and walked toward Waine, her shoulder bag pushed back over her hip, in one arm a black leatherbound notebook.

Waine walked to meet her, nearly gasping with the shortness of his breath.

They stopped a few feet from each other. Their eyes were sad, though their mouths smiled slightly. They shook hands, and felt how far apart they had become, after having been so close.

"Hello," Waine said. "It's good to see you."

"It's good to see you."

"I have a cab waiting," Waine said. "We can go to my office, if that's all right."

"That's fine."

"Unless you'd like to get a drink somewhere," Waine said, wanting to suggest, but fearing to, that they go back to the top of the World Trade Center, to Windows on the World.

Francesca thought for a moment, wanting to suggest, but fearing to, the same thing. "Later, perhaps. Right now, I'd like to stay sober."

They walked off the pier, side by side, but not exactly together, each wondering if they would ever be drunk again, as they had been for each other.

Much later, after they had exchanged their incredible stories, it seemed impossible to speak. Waine stood at the window of his office, looking down at Washington Square. Francesca sat on a small sofa, staring unseeingly at the pattern in the rug. Down in the park, portable radios blared disco music; cars honked their way along the narrow streets; a battery of voices swelled up in discord. If either Waine or Francesca heard, they gave no sign.

After forever, Waine turned away from the window. "I guess the next step . . ." He paused, seeing Francesca shaking her head sadly back and forth. ". . . what is it?"

"I can't be businesslike any longer," Francesca said. "I know there's business to be done, but it can wait a moment. There's something I have to say first."

Hoping against hope that it was that she loved him, after all, Waine sat on the windowsill and waited.

"I did the right thing in going to my superiors about Eva," Francesca said. "The fact that Clavin was acting chief doesn't change that. I—"

"I know you feel that way," Waine said. "But—"

"Let . . . me . . . finish," Francesca said, with an edge in her voice she had rarely heard before.

Waine nodded, once, sharply.

Francesca thought for a while, then spoke softly, without the edge, but with something that warned Waine to listen very carefully. "I don't know where we stand. I don't know where our relationship stands. Too much else has been going on for me to think much about it. But I know one thing for sure: anyone who loves me has to stand by me even if he thinks I've done something wrong. I don't mean illegally, wrong; I just mean practically, pragmatically wrong—that I went about something in the wrong way. He's got to stand by me even if I go about things in the wrong way. Love can't be conditional on someone's being perfect. None of us is perfect and none of us has the right to expect it of others—perfection, that is. Whoever loves me has got to love me for reasons other than day-to-day performance; I'm not an expensive car; I'm not a championship baseball team; I break down; I win a few and I lose a few. And he's got to understand that, as I'll have to understand it about him." She ended on a rising note that seemed to imply there was more to come, but she felt she had said enough and she let the note hang.

After a time, Waine said, "I wish you hadn't said 'he.' You make it sound as if you're talking about being loved generically."

Francesca stamped a foot. "That's exactly what I mean, Waine. Don't go picking on the way I said it; pay attention to what I said. I'm no elocutionist, no orator; I'm a human being. I'm talking about what I *feel,* and if it comes out funny it's because it's felt, not crafted."

Waine turned sideways a little, and looked out the window. "Maybe it just isn't meant to be."

"Nothing's meant to be," Francesca said. "You have to work at it."

Waine nodded. "I know that about everything else in

life; I guess I feel love is one thing that should be magical."

"Too many fairy tales from your Arthurian mother," Francesca said. "Enchanted maidens and all."

Waine smiled, pleased that she sounded a little more relaxed. He wanted to propose that they relax even more—have a drink, have dinner; but he was afraid.

Francesca saw the fear, and behind it the wish to be close, quiet. "Let's finish up the business. There's a lot to be done. The fact that we have a professional relationship may be what got us into this mess in the first place, but we do have it, and it's a good one, so let's make the best of it."

"And then?" Waine said.

"And then?" Francesca said.

All that either had was hope, but neither was sure about the vintage.

Chapter 32

~~~~~~~~~~~~~~~~

Dr. Vincent Clavin had decided it was time for some changes. He knew it would be quite a while before he would be the beneficiary of Diana Stewart's manipulations, but that didn't mean he had to wait until then to begin to acquire some of the things that rightly went with the title of chief of staff.

He began by treating himself to a few baubles—a Baume and Mercier wristwatch, a pair of Bally loafers, a new pipe from Wilke. They were things that people might notice without reading into them any special significance, without wondering what it was he had to celebrate. He also bought a new Bancroft Super Winner squash racquet and a new pair of Tretorn tennis shoes.

The squash gear was not, to Clavin, an indulgence in the same way the other things were; a good raquet and sneakers were as important to him as a good scalpel and forceps. Squash was more than a game to him, more than just exercise; it was a test of the intellect and the emotions as well as of strength and touch; it was, in many respects, kinetic, three-dimensional chess.

Clavin played squash on the hospital's squash court at seven o'clock every morning with Kevin Markson, from Endocrinology. It was a ritual that had been going on for years. It had become so habitual that, this particular morning, Clavin was at the door of the squash court, as usual, before he remembered that Markson had telephoned the night before to say he would not be able to make it the next day. He hadn't been very forthcoming, and Clavin had guessed that it was woman trouble—not with Markson's wife.

Clavin decided to rally by himself for a while, and went through the door onto the court. He stood at the T of the squash court drilling alternating forehands and backhands off the front wall, getting set for each successive shot with footwork so quick and graceful that it seemed almost indolent, meeting each ball on the rise and driving it back with a power that made the court reverberate.

Chief of staff, chief of staff, chief of staff—the rhythmic sounds seemed to say. *Vincent Clavin, chief of staff, Vincent Clavin, chief of staff.*

Clavin heard footsteps on the stairs up to the spectators' gallery at the rear of the court. He heard the creak of benches as someone sat down.

Some intern, he imagined. Some ex-college jock thinking to get in a quick game before beginning his daily grind. He thought of the pleasure it would give him to beat some ex-college jock intern, who would be so impressed that he would have to admit to his peers that he had been soundly trounced by Dr. Vincent Clavin.

Chief of staff, chief of staff.

As last, Clavin mis-hit the ball; it spun off the wood of his new racquet and rolled behind him to the rear wall. He walked to retrieve it, head down, light footed, whistling softly to himself, as if he had no idea that there was anyone above him in the gallery, and no concern if he did.

"Good morning, Dr. Clavin."

A woman's voice. A nurse? Clavin, whose marriage wasn't any more inspiring than Markson's, and who could have done with a little woman trouble himself, constructed a swift fantasy of kindly offering to instruct some slim, quick nurse in the mysteries of squash, a lesson that would end with them locked together in passion on the floor of the court. He looked up, smiling.

"Hel . . . lo." The ellipsis was induced by the discovery that there wasn't only one person in the gallery, that there was a veritable crowd.

Francesca Hayward, who had greeted Clavin, gestured down the row. "Do you know everyone here? Waine Ryan, Ted Hirsch, Clara Hirsch . . . Dr. Finch you know, of course."

Clavin smiled weakly. "Gentlemen, and ladies. Wilson. What brings you out so early?"

"We wanted to talk to you privately," Waine Ryan said. "Dr. Finch mentioned your regular squash game, and we thought this would be a good spot. Dr. Markson was kind enough to agree to sit this one out, when we explained some of the circumstances."

There were ominous overtones in Wain Ryan's last word, circumstances.

Clavin's mind raced. "Let me come up there, so you don't have to shout." He scooped up the loose ball with a flick of his racquet, pocketed the ball, and went casually to the door, calculating that if he put his racquet and the ball on the stairs from the gallery, they would slow the first of his pursuers just enough that he could get a head start.

A head start to where?

The door was locked. Since it did not lock from the outside, that meant it was being held fast from the outside by some device that had no doubt been inserted while he was practicing and could not hear any suspicious noises.

Clavin backed away from the door and kept on backing until he backed into the front wall of the court. He slid down on the floor, his back against the metal strip that runs along the base of a squash court's front wall. Clavin was not unaware of the irony that the metal strip, which makes a loud noise when a ball strikes it, indicating that the ball is out of bounds, is called the telltale.

Waine Ryan was speaking, and had been for several moments before Clavin began to attend to the words.

". . . Hayward was in line to be chief of staff, and you were in line to be assistant chief. You were the same age, had the same background, the same credentials. You knew that if he got the job, he'd keep it for the rest of his career—and for the rest of yours. You knew that unless you went to another hospital, you were about to become permanent second fiddle . . .

"Unless something happened to him . . .

"November 22, 1963. Noel Hayward was taking a long weekend to close up his house on Shelter Island for the winter. You went out to your house in North Haven to do the same thing. His family was coming out the next day—a Saturday. I imagine yours was, too . . . It was unusually warm for the end of November, and Hayward saw a chance to go sailing one more time before putting his boat up for the winter. You were going to go with him. But your car broke down, and you couldn't get from North Haven over to Shelter Island. Hayward went sailing alone, he had an accident, he died. Ironically, you didn't get the chief of staff job; it had never occurred to you that the board thought of you *only* as a second fiddle; even if Hayward had retired for some reason, earlier than expected, you wouldn't have succeeded him . . .

". . . November 22, 1963. Here's what really happened. Your car did break down. We checked with the garage in North Haven. It's amazing what accurate records people in small towns keep, and how long they hold on to them. You took your car to the garage on the afternoon of the twenty-first, a Thursday. There was something wrong with the carburetor. The mechanic said it'd take at least a day to fix, because he had to send for a part. But after he'd driven you back to your house, he discovered that he had the part and he was able to fix it by that evening; business was slow—the summer crowd was gone and he had only local trade to deal with and there wasn't much of that. He called you when he finished the job and said he'd drive the car over if you wanted—his wife would follow in his truck and take him back—but you said not to bother. You said you'd get it the next afternoon . . ."

Clavin raised his head for the first time since he'd slumped down on the floor. Waine Ryan was sitting forward on the bench, his elbows on the ledge of the gallery; the others were sitting back, their heads bowed —not as if in prayer or out of embarrassment, but so as to concentrate better, without distractions, on what Waine was saying. Their averted eyes kept Clavin from feeling what he might have felt—that he was a specimen beneath a microscope, a rat in some test situation, a patient being cut open for the benefit of medical students, a cadaver. He did feel like the accused in a trial, for he had read or heard or seen in movies or simply sensed that juries were reluctant to exchange eye contact with the defendant.

". . . you didn't want the car because you wanted to be able to say that you hadn't had the car, and therefore hadn't been able to go over to Shelter Island to go sailing with Noel Hayward. But you did go over. You bicycled over. You took the South Ferry. That was a moderate risk, because the crew might remember you, but you didn't have any choice—it was the only way over. One of the crewmen does remember you. We found him by checking the work rosters of the ferry company. He didn't say anything about it at the time because nobody asked him and because he didn't see the connection. If he had, I suppose you could've said that you'd decided at the last minute to go sailing, that you'd called Hayward but he'd already left the house, that you'd gone over anyway, that you couldn't find him, that you'd left your bike there and hitched a ride back, that the crew hadn't noticed you coming back because you were in somebody's car. The reason you left your bike there, by the way, is that it had a flat—or rather, you gave it a flat. When we found the bike in the basement, the tires were flat; it could've been from sitting there all these years, but my associate here took the tires off and found that one of them had a flat. It wasn't a puncture, it was a gash—the kind you'd make with a knife . . ."

Clavin lowered his head again. He was shocked at how thin and bony his legs looked; all the youth he'd felt just a few minutes ago had left them.

". . . you and Hayward rowed over to West Neck Inlet to get his boat. You took it out on the bay. It was early; it was a Friday morning; there was no one else out sailing. You'd figured on that. What you didn't figure on was that someone was watching you from the shore—someone whose life in those days consisted of doing nothing but watching the boats on the bay, in the sound, in the harbor. He kept a log, a very thorough log . . ."

Clavin's mind had surrendered; it had given up trying to block the memories of that day. As Waine Ryan went on, the memories poured forth, putting flesh on the bones of the story he had reconstructed, adding colors, sounds, smells, sensations . . .

They were sailing before a brisk breeze, eight knots or so. Clavin was at the tiller, heading on a starboard tack. Noel Hayward sat on the cockpit, drinking coffee from the plastic cup of a Thermos bottle, his face tipped up to catch some of the wan November sun, talking about Francesca.

". . . it's strange to have her gone from the house,"

Noel Hayward was saying. "I know she's been away a lot during the summer over the past few years; I know she's just up at Barnard—a subway ride away; but I feel she's gone. Her room doesn't feel only temporarily empty; it doesn't feel as though it's waiting for her. It makes me feel old, I must say, having to face up to the fact that my . . . my little girl is a woman now. How is it you never had any children, Vince?"

"There were other priorities, then it was too late," Clavin said, not caring to say that the only thing he and his wife had in common was a feeling of revulsion toward children.

"It's never too late, as long as you take the necessary precautions," Noel Hayward said. "I wish now that Beatrice and I had had more kids, although I suppose that's just my fear of being abandoned . . . This is a nice wind; I'm glad we came out."

"Say, Noel—" Clavin squinted at the port side rigging. "—is that stay fraying?"

Noel Hayward put his cup down and followed Clavin's look. "I don't see . . ."

"Here, take the tiller."

Hayward heaved himself up. "No, you stay there. I'll have a closer look." He put one foot on the gunwale and balanced there, leaning back to see into the rigging. "Looks all right to me."

And to me. Clavin threw the helm to port, beginning a jibe. The boom swept nearly one hundred eighty degrees across the deck, whistling as it went, striking Noel Hayward in the back of the head, knocking him overboard.

Clavin couldn't look back. He told himself there was no need to look back. He trimmed the sail a little, lashed the tiller and went forward to see if there was any blood on the boom; there wasn't. He went back to the tiller, steered the boat into the wind and let it go into irons. He took off his boating shoes, tied them around his neck and dove into the water, making himself look for just an instant at where Noel Hayward would have been if he had stayed above the surface; there was nothing there.

Clavin swam to the North Haven Peninsula, put his shoes on and walked along the beach next to the bay. By the time he had walked a quarter of a mile, his hair and shirt and shorts were dry; his shoes still squished a little, but they would dry soon enough, and with an application of mink oil would be as good as new . . .

". . . you're probably wondering why the old sailor didn't say anything at the time," Waine Ryan was saying. "He was a bitter man. He was given a hard time by his insurance company over his fishing accident; he had a hard time in the hospital; he had a hard time generally. He thought that if the authorities thought to ask him if he'd seen anything, he'd tell them; if they were too stupid to ask him, then it was none of their business."

Clavin lifted his head and, softly, almost apologetically, said, "Why did he say something now?"

"Oh, he didn't," Waine Ryan said. "Or not exactly. Dr. Hayward—Dr. Francesca Hayward—found his log. She'd been on to you for quite some time."

Clavin tried to move his eyes to see Francesca, but they wouldn't go. He lowered his head.

"It was the bicycle," Waine Ryan said. "If you hadn't made inquiries about buying Beatrice Hayward's house, she wouldn't have mentioned the bicycle, and no one would've made the connection. You were asking to be discovered, I'd say. Amateur criminals often do."

Clavin laughed a swift, hysterical laugh. "And what now?" He held out his wrists, as if to be handcuffed. "Jail?"

"All I want," Waine Ryan said, "is a story in return for the story I just told you. I want you to tell it to a judge—a Surrogate Court judge. I want you to tell him that Diana Stewart forged Conrad James's will."

Chapter 33

Eva James opened her eyes the tiniest little bit. There was light; and there were colors. She could see. Dr. Hayward had been telling the truth all the time, not just trying to make her feel better. She peeked a little more, and saw her Aunt Diana sitting beside her bed in an orange chair. Oh, no. She didn't want to have to test out her new eyes on Aunt Diana. Eva shut her eyes and debated with herself about opening them again.

Now that she could see, she wanted to see Dr. Hayward. She wanted to confirm her suspicion that Dr. Hayward was at least as beautiful as Beverly Arnold, the singer who lived in Eva's apartment building, and probably more beautiful. Eva was getting annoyed, though, that Dr. Hayward wasn't there. She didn't understand why she had gone off so quickly after the operation to reattach Eva's retina. Another doctor—Dr. Ward—had come to see Eva and had told her that Dr. Hayward had asked him to say that she had had to go away for a few days, on a very important matter. Dr. Ward said Dr. Hayward would not have gone away if she weren't sure Eva was going to be fine. Eva wondered if the important matter had to do with her father's will.

There was no telling when Dr. Hayward would be back. And she could see. She had almost forgotten. She decided it was more important to practice seeing than to lie in bed thinking about it. Even if it did mean talking to Aunt Diana. She just hoped Dr. Clever wouldn't come in, even though she did want to see if he was as stupid and ugly as he sounded.

Eva opened her eyes.

Now that was odd. Where Aunt Diana had been sitting a new moments before sat a figure shrouded in black. The chair the figure sat in was black, too, not orange like the chair in which her Aunt Diana had been sitting. And the wall behind the figure, once blue, was now a dirty, dirty gray—almost black; and the window in the center of the wall, covered with closed blinds but still glowing with light around the edges just a few moments before, was a gray not quite so dirty.

Slowly, everything got darker.

And darker.

Eva screamed.

A million things happened at once. A million people crowded into the room. In the hubbub, Eva could separate out only three voices—those of Aunt Diana, of a man Eva was sure was very tall, of Miss Harriman, the nurse who was sometimes in charge of Eva's floor and always stopped to say hello.

"Nurse. Nurse. Nurse." That was Aunt Diana. Then she changed her cry to, "Doctor. Doctor. Doctor."

"Just keep calm, please." That was Miss Harriman. Miss Harriman then told some other nurses to do a lot of different things.

"Just sit down over here, Mrs. Stewart." That was the very tall man.

"I don't want to sit down. Get your hands off me, Mr. Ryan."

"I think you better stay right here, Mrs. Stewart."

"Oh, you do, do you? Well, I don't care what you think."

"Clavin's told us everything, Mrs. Stewart. You and I have to have a long talk."

Even in her distress, Eva wanted to know what *that* was all about. Her Aunt Diana didn't say a word after that.

Miss Harriman told still more nurses to do still more things. Then she seemed to be talking on the telephone. "Just find her. I'll take the responsibility." She hung up the phone noisily. "Damn. She's not at home."

"She's gone to her mother's house," said the man Aunt Diana had called Mr. Ryan. "She lives in the Village. Beatrice Hayward."

Miss Harriman dialed the phone. "This is Barbara Harriman again. Try Dr. Hayward at her mother's. Beatrice Hayward. In Greenwich Village."

Dr. Hayward? Yea! It had never occurred to Eva that Dr. Hayward had a mother. It was sometimes hard to imagine that any grownups had mothers and fathers.

Beatrice. That was interesting. In school, they had read a story about a man named Dante who was in love with a woman named Beatrice—a long time ago, in Italy. Dante was so much in love with Beatrice that he wrote a long poem about it.

Greenwich Village. That was interesting, too. Becky Morgan sometimes went to Greenwich Village to visit her aunt and uncle. They lived in what Becky said was a tiny little house like the kind you would expect to be made out of gingerbread and to find in an enchanted clearing in the middle of a gloomy forest. Her father had promised to take her there, but they had never gone.

Eva began to cry. It made her unhappy that she would never see her father and mother again. It made her more unhappy than the thought that she might never see anything again. She wished she could make a trade. She would be willing to see nothing at all if she could be with her father and mother, even if she couldn't see them.

The phone rang and someone answered it.

"Yes?" It was Miss Harriman. "Good . . . Good." She hung up. "Dr. Hayward's on her way."

"Yea," Eva said.

Miss Harriman and the very tall man laughed and someone rubbed Eva's head. She thought it was the very tall man.

Chapter 34

~~~~~~~~~~~~~~~~

Francesca Hayward sat in a cane chair in a gallery in the American Wing of the Metropolitan Museum of Art, facing the Sargent painting of the woman in the white skirt and her husband. Sunlight streamed through a window in the corner of the gallery and she put up a hand to shield her eyes; she was so tired that she felt her pupils would not have the strength to contract and that the sunlight would burn her brain.

There was no one else in the gallery and only a few people in the wing, for it was near closing time. Footsteps echoed purposelessly and voices flitted about in search of ears to hear them.

For not the first time since she had sat down in the chair, Francesca dozed. As was often the case after performing surgery, she dreamed that she was seated halfway up the steep row of benches in a classroom, listening to an introductory lecture.

Francesca strained to hear the lecturer, who spoke in a low voice. And she strained to see him, for she seemed to be seeing through the wrong end of a pair of binoculars. Or was the lecturer a woman? The voice was deep and neuter.

The lecturer had somehow moved to the top row of the hall, now, and Francesca had to turn to see him. Or her.

No—that was wrong. It was she who had moved—down out of the rows of seats and up onto the platform at the front of the classroom. It was she who was giving the lecture, standing behind a lectern with her notes spread out before her. She looked up at the eager faces waiting for her to impart more wisdom, and down at her notes; before her was not a drawing of the eye, but of a fully-rigged sloop.

. . . *the sheet is a rope attached to the lower corners of the sail, serving to move or extend it. The halyard is a rope used to raise and lower the sail—*

"Dr. Hayward," a student called. "Tell us about the time you fell overboard."

Laughter.

"Dr. Hayward," called another. "Tell us about the time your father *fell overboard.*"

"Dr. Hayward."

"Dr. Hayward."

"Dr. Hayward."

Francesca's head fell out of balance and she started awake. A cloud had covered the sun and the room was so dark that she thought at first that something had happened to her sight. She shut her eyes and rubbed them, making moiré patterns. When she opened them, the patterns persisted, then dissipated. When they were gone, she nearly cried out, for the man in the painting had stepped out of it and was standing before her, his arms crossed on his chest.

"Francesca."

No—it wasn't the man in the painting. It was Waine.

"I'm sorry if I startled you."

"No . . . I mean, sort of. I was asleep."

He turned a cane chair to face hers and sat down, leaning forward, his elbows on his knees, his hands lightly clasped, concern on his face. "You must be very tired."

Francesca craned her neck suspiciously. "How did you know I was here?"

"Just a lucky guess. At the end of a difficult case, I often take a walk across the Brooklyn Bridge."

"Do you really?"

"It's my favorite place, and it feels all the more special when a visit there has been well earned."

". . . Eva's going to be all right," Francesca said.

"I know. I talked to Dr. Finch."

"I transplanted a cornea."

"I know."

"The cornea is the central transparent portion of the exposed anterior third of the eye. It's clear because its fibers are in perfect alignment. It can become clouded —by disease, injury, a scar. If the clouding is in front of the pupil, it can mean loss of vision—"

"The pupil is the hole in the iris," Waine said.

Francesca smiled. "That's right."

Waine took one of her hands in both of his. "Let me take you home. You need some sleep."

"Eva developed an infection during the retinal attachment. Her cornea became clouded. I removed a piece of it and replaced it with a clear piece."

"I know."

"We got it from the Eye Bank. Someone donated it."

"I know."

"Someone dead."

Waine nodded.

"Poor Eva. No parents. How sad."

"The Stewarts are dropping their custody suit," Waine said. "The judge was a little perplexed at all the developments, but he seems willing to listen. He was peeved at not having been invited to see the word processor in action, but we're going to take him up there tomorrow."

". . . so you've won. How come you're not walking across the Brooklyn Bridge?"

"There are still a lot of loose ends. Ted and Clara will get custody, but it's going to take a while to work it out. Even though there was a will, after all, it was damnably vague because it was so terse, And there's the question of what to do about Diana Stewart. I'm trying to convince the judge to go easy on her. She could be charged with perjury, not to mention forgery, but I don't see the point."

"You're too kind," Francesca said. "She should answer for what she's done. And Clavin, too. Can he be charged with my father's murder?"

"The one eyewitness is a senile old man. He was lucid and alert seventeen years ago, but there's no way he can get up on a witness stand today and say convincingly that Clavin was one of the men he saw back then. Clavin was only vulnerable to the kind of drumhead court martial we gave him on the squash court."

There was a pause.

Waine looked over his shoulder at the Sargent painting. "They certainly look alive. I wonder what they're thinking."

". . . Waine?"

"Yes?"

Francesca shook her head. "Oh, nothing."

Waine squeezed her hand again. "You should get some sleep."

Francesca wriggled her hand free. "Stop saying that, will you? I'm not a child."

Waine ducked his head. "Sorry."

Francesca put her head back and studied the ceiling of the gallery. "We just can't seem to hit it off. We started out pretty well, but we got out of synch almost from the beginning."

Waine stood up and extended a hand tentatively. "Well, good-bye, then."

Francesca looked down, ignoring the hand, looking into his eyes. "Where are you going?"

"To my office—to take care of a few things. Then home."

She shook her head, annoyed. "I don't mean now. I mean . . . in the future."

Waine put his hands in his pockets and shrugged. "I don't know what you mean."

"The first time you came to Shelter Island—on your bicycle—I was down by the beach. I fell asleep in the sun. My mother came down to tell me you were there. I had a dream before she woke me. I dreamed I was sailing in a boat that had no sheet. The sheet is a rope—"

"I remember," Waine said.

". . . I've thought about that dream a lot. It seems to be an important dream. It seemed to be telling me something about my future; it seemed to be telling me that I shouldn't expect to get anywhere without . . . Well, it wasn't as though my boat had no sail; that would be a real frustration dream. You could sail without a sheet, if you were careful, if you kept the sail close-hauled and maneuvered the boom with your hand. The sheet broadens your range, increases your possibilities; it enables you to reach and run, instead of only beat. It's a tool—something that makes things easier. I've been sailing without one. I've been sailing close-hauled, upwind. You can go very fast upwind, because a sail is like an airplane wing. But it's only one direction. I've been sailing in only one direction. I want to change tacks, change my bearing, branch out, explore . . ."

Waine was sitting again, his elbows on his knees, his hands lightly clasped, looking intently into her eyes.

A guard came into the gallery and told them the museum was closing.

They made their way out, past the knights in armor, past the medieval chapel, under the great staircase, out into the main hall, out onto the steps. The day had been hot and the evening wasn't going to be any cooler.

Francesca stopped on the top step, leaning a hip against one of the metal bannisters. "I never thought of myself as following in my father's footsteps, but I think that's what I've been doing. The suspicion I've had all along that he didn't die the way they said was behind it, I think. Not that I ever did anything about investigating it; just that somehow by keeping his work alive through me I was keeping him alive—or at least keeping his memory alive. In a sense, it paid off. That his memory was still alive enabled me, with the help of the old man, to somehow remember that day, to see it more clearly, to reconstruct what really happened . . .

"That painting back there—the Sargent—I saw it differently today. I saw how much the woman is like me—dark, tall, competent. I saw how much the man is like . . . well, not like my father but like my father's ghost—watchful, a little dubious, maybe a little critical. He's been around me like that, my father has; he inspired me and he's also been limiting me. There are many things I have to do, and I'm now free to do them . . .

"I'm going to begin by taking some time off. I want to really examine this career of mine. I want to make sure I'm not on the same track Clavin got stuck on, that my ambition isn't so strong that it strangles my morals and my judgment. My father, after all, didn't get to be chief of staff-designate because he was a pussycat . . .

"I also want to think about some of the things you've said about hospitals. I read a terrible statistic the other day—that something like eight out of ten births in big hospitals are by caesarian section, because the doctors are afraid of malpractice suits if there're any complications in natural births. If I ever have a baby, I don't want it born by caesarian just because some doctor wants it born that way, because he doesn't trust enough in life. That's what being a doctor should be about, finally—allowing lives to be lived, not manipulating them . . .

"What do you think of all this?"

Waine scraped the sole of his shoe against the edge of the top step. "I hope you won't be offended, but I haven't been able to take it all in."

"It's a lot," Francesca said.

"And I've been thinking about myself, as well."

"Thinking what?"

"I don't think it would be fair to just plunge in and tell you about me when you've offered so much food for thought about yourself."

"So be unfair. Be unlawyerly."

Waine looked up and saw that she was smiling, so he smiled, too. "You're too good a doctor not to go on being a doctor, so I hope you don't examine your career to the point where you give it up. Work to change things, maybe—within the hospital or in a different kind of hospital or in a different setting altogether—in a clinic, in your own office . . . something . . .

"I don't know if I entirely understand your point about dreaming about sailing without a sheet. Maybe . . . Oh, nothing."

"What? Come on."

". . . maybe the point about the dream is that you can't do things on your own."

"Ah. I hadn't thought of that . . . Why did you hesitate to tell me that?"

"Because it's self-serving."

"How so?"

"I'm in love with you, Francesca," Waine said.

"Are you really?"

"Don't tease me."

"I'm not," Francesca said. "I don't think I've been very lovable. You were right, you know—about Eva? If I really cared about Eva, I should have come to you, and damn the protocol."

"I'm not interested in being right. And you did care about Eva. Do care. More than any of us, I'd say."

"Don't contradict me," Francesca said.

Waine laughed. "I haven't been very lovable either. This . . . attitude of mine about rich people is something I'm working to change."

"In this case, you were right. Diana Stewart's right up there with Lucrezia Borgia."

"Don't contradict me," Waine said.

Francesca laughed. Suddenly, she hoisted herself up on the bannister, lifted her feet and slid all the way down. She turned, triumphant, hands on hips.

Waine applauded.

"I had another dream," Francesca said. "Inside, just now, sitting in that chair in front of the painting. I dreamed I was giving a lecture to a class of med students."

"On?"

Francesca ducked her head. "It's embarrassing. It started out to be an ophthalmology lecture, then it turned into a lecture on sailing."

Waine walked slowly down the steps to where she was. "There's all kinds of teaching, you know? There's teaching a classroom full of medical students and there's teaching a classroom full of patients. There's teaching your friends. There's teaching your children."

"That's the second time you've mentioned children," Francesca said.

"No, you mentioned it the other time."

"So I did. So I did . . . Will you do me a favor?"

"Sure."

"Don't just say that. It's a big favor. Better wait till you hear it."

"Okay. I'm waiting."

". . . don't end this by asking when you can see me. I really need some time to think, and I want to do it at my own pace. I often don't do things at my own pace, and I think that's part of my problem."

"I think that's a good idea," Waine said.

"You're just saying that."

Waine shook his head. "No."

Francesca cocked her head. "Are you so sure I'll call you in the end?"

"No. Not at all."

"Really?"

"Really."

"That's good, because I'm not sure, either."

Waine smiled, but his heart hurt.

"It's hard sometimes when you deal with men like Clavin not to impose some of his awfulness on the rest of the male population," Francesca said. "I think men are to be guarded against."

"I think you're right," Waine said.

Francesca laughed. "Especially men who agree with you when you say men are to be guarded against."

Waine shrugged. "I can't win."

Francesca put a hand on his arm. "Oh, yes, you can. And you will. If not with me, with someone else. You're very special. Inspiring, even. The thing you said about teaching patients—that sent a shiver up my spine. Good women will want you. Right now, I have to do some thinking about my own value." She stood on tiptoe and kissed his cheek. "Thank you for coming to find me. For being concerned. For knowing where I'd be."

Waine touched her cheek with his fingertips. He couldn't trust himself not to speak about the future, so he said nothing at all, just turned and headed down the steps and walked south along Fifth Avenue, bending forward a little to cut a swath through the heat.

Chapter 35

~~~~~~~~~~~~~~~~~~

Before she took a leave, however, Francesca made very sure that Eva James's condition was stable. She also just plain enjoyed being with Eva.

"Are you married, Dr. Hayward?" Eva said one day. Just as she sometimes forgot that grownups had parents, she often failed to take into account that they sometimes had husbands and wives.

"No, Eva," Francesca said.

"How come? I mean, you're *beau*tiful."

Francesca smiled. "That's sweet of you to say, Eva. I'm afraid there's more to it than that."

Eva had already had an inkling of that. Her mother had told her that. "Do you have a boyfriend?"

". . . not at the moment," Francesca said. "How about you?"

There was Nathan Fain, who was in the fifth grade and played the guitar in his own rock and roll band. He had beautiful big brown eyes and curly brown hair. But Eva wasn't sure he even knew she existed. "Not at the moment."

Francesca laughed. "We should put an ad in the paper, or something. 'Two lonely hearts—female—seek two lonely hearts—male.'"

"What about Dr. Ward?" Eva said. Dr. Ward was *gorgeous*. "Doesn't Dr. Ward like you?"

"Dr. Ward is an old, old friend," Francesca said. "We've known each other ever since we were in medical school together."

Eva wondered if the fact that she and Nathan Fain were in school together meant they would never be boyfriend and girlfriend. "I like Dr. Ward."

"He likes you," Francesca said. "He told me so."

"*Really?*"

"Really." Watching Tim Ward fool around with Eva, Francesca had remarked on his gentleness and on his ability to just be with her, to listen to her, without asking a lot of questions. Most adults seemed to be constantly grilling children; it was no wonder that children preferred their own small worlds.

Watching Tim Ward with Eva, Francesca had wondered why she had never loved him. She told herself it was because she had known even back then, back in medical school, that she would need a friend like Tim Ward, now.

Does that mean you can't love your friends?

I do love my friends. The question is, can I be a friend with my lover?

Can you?

I don't know . . . A lover expects a lot; a friend can be forgiving.

Are you so in need of forgiveness?

I have been, I suppose. Not because I've been bad—because I've been . . . I don't know—distracted.

By?

My career. My fantasies.

Fantasies of what?

Traveling around the world. Doing great things. Being a great healer.

You are a great healer. That's no fantasy. As for traveling around the world, is that something you see yourself doing alone?

I don't know.

Think about it.

I am thinking about it, damn it. Stop interrogating me. You're just like an adult with a child.

I thought you were indulging in a little introspection.

. . . I am.

Getting your act together.

Umm.

. . . Well?

. . . No.

No, what?

No, I don't see myself traveling around the world alone.

Whom are you traveling with?

. . . I'm not answering any more questions.

(Laughter)

"Dr. Hayward?"

"Yes, Eva?"

"Do you think if I could be a doctor when I grow up, I could also be a writer?"

"Sure. You'd just have to learn how to use your time well. Being a doctor takes a lot of time. But lots of doctors write books—all kinds of books. Novels, like your father wrote, and books about medicine. All kinds of books."

"Dr. Seuss," Eva said.

Francesca laughed.

". . . is the reason you don't have a boyfriend because being a doctor takes a lot of time?" Eva said.

This kid is like a little adult, Francesca thought.

". . . I think the reason is that I haven't met anybody I really loved. I've had a few boy *friends*, but never a *boy*friend."

Becky Morgan once told Eva that if you stood on a street corner in New York long enough, you would see someone you knew. She wondered if you stood on a street corner long enough, you would meet someone you loved. "Dr. Hayward?"

"Yes, Eva?"

"If my parents were alive, they would like you."

Francesca put her head down so that it lay on the pillow alongside Eva's. "You're the bravest, dearest, most wonderful girl in the world. And you're going to be the best, most beautiful, most charming, brightest woman in the world. And I'm going to be very proud to say, 'I knew her when.'"

"When what?" Eva said.

Francesca laughed, and thought, *When she was innocent.*

And before she took her leave, Francesca made very sure that her mother was coping well with the revelation of how her husband had died.

"I can't say that I don't occasionally feel a very strong desire for revenge," Beatrice Hayward said. "Not that it would do any good."

"Clavin's through, he's disgraced," Francesca said. "He'll never practice again, unless he goes to Guatemala, or something."

"Oh, I know that. The trouble is, he was disgraced before he did this. I don't quite know what Noel saw in him to spend as much time with him as he did."

"He was a good sailor."

Beatrice Hayward snorted. "Heaven help us."

"And I think dad must've felt sorry for him, in some way," Francesca said. "He must've seen that his ambition was greater than his ability. Dad had a thing about lost causes, you know."

"That he did. That he did." Beatrice Hayward cleared away the dinner plates and brought dessert to the table they had placed close to the French window on the second floor of the West Tenth Street townhouse. She sat and looked out the window for a while, then suddenly shivered and hugged herself.

"Are you all right?" Francesca said.

Beatrice Hayward nodded. "I just felt a nip in the air. It's getting to feel like fall, isn't it? Always a season I've had mixed emotions about. So much going on—school starting for you, all kinds of cultural events around town, the thrill of a bracing fall day; and yet, a sense of sadness, of things slowing down, of dark . . . of dying."

Francesca got up and went to a hall closet and got a shawl and went back to the table and placed it around her mother's shoulders and stood behind her with her hands on her shoulders. "But this fall will be an exciting time for you. Your new job."

Beatrice Hayward nodded.

Francesca felt her mother's age beneath her hands and it frightened her.

Beatrice Hayward reached up and put a hand over Francesca's. "I don't mean this at all selfishly. I'm not one of those vain women who has to not only reproduce herself in order to be fulfilled, but has to see her daughter reproduce herself, as well—"

"But," Francesca said.

Beatrice Hayward laughed. "But I want you to be happy."

"Married," Francesca said.

"Oh, I know it's not all that fashionable, anymore. And, anyway, I don't mean married per se. But I do mean in love. It's important to me that my daughter be in love—and most of all, that she be loved. That you be loved. It's what got me through all these years alone, Francesca—the fact that I was loved . . ."

Beatrice Hayward went on, but Francesca hardly heard. She stared into the yellow pool of light cast on the street by a mercury street lamp, and realized that she had never thought of it that way. She had always thought that what was important was to love. Being loved was important, too—but it had seemed secondary, somehow—part of the process of loving. But perhaps it wasn't part of the process; perhaps it was a process in its own right. And perhaps, therefore, loving and being loved were aspects of a larger condition. What to call that condition? True love? That sounded trite. How about just love?

Whatever it was called, it was not something Francesca had known.

Or had she?

In Waine Ryan's arms—and, more importantly, in Waine Ryan's *presence*—she had felt herself to be in an environment separate from the environments in which they had found themselves—restaurants, apartments, automobiles, boats, and so on. Now that she thought about it, she realized that that environment had reminded her of the environment that, as a child, she had felt that she occupied—separate from the world around her. Separate but not isolated, not shut off—just . . . different.

Francesca remembered watching Tim Ward fooling around with Eva James and thinking that children preferred not to be asked a lot of questions. Most men were like that, too; they didn't like to be interrogated and they complained that women asked too many questions—and, especially, asked too many questions about what men were feeling. Did that mean that most men were like children? Well, no—because men ducked questioning out of evasiveness, whereas children ducked questioning because they simply had better things to do than to try to formulate lucid responses to the inane inquiries of others.

Just as staring at the pool of light caused Francesca's eyes to lose their focus, so concentrating on these matters made her brain soft and fuzzy. She shook her head to sharpen her vision, to clear her brain. She realized that her mother was still speaking.

". . . I think it's fine," Beatrice Hayward was saying, "that people your age are doing all the things they're doing, but I think it's going to be a damn shame if one of the results of it all is that the concept of romance gets lost. Plain old, mushy, tear-stained romance. God, what a wonderful thing it is. And it's in danger of being lost, because everybody's so . . . so so*phis*ticated . . ."

She went on some more, but Francesca wasn't hearing, again.

Sophistication, she had realized, was the key. There was a sophistication, a complexity, to the way men evaded questions, whereas children evaded them naturally, simply, naively.

The goal, therefore, was to find a man who, although he might not answer every question and might not like being asked questions, would react to them with a child's openness, not deviously.

Chapter 36

~~~~~~~~~~~~~~~~

Francesca went to Shelter Island. She swam and sailed and walked the paths of the Mashomack Game Preserve. She sat for hours on the dock of her mother's house or on the lawn, looking out over the water, watching the light change.

She borrowed a Jeep from a man who did yardwork for her mother and loaded Vincent Clavin's bicycle into it and took it to the dump. She laid the bicycle on its side next to the road and drove the Jeep back and forth over it until the bicycle was nearly flattened.

She rode her own bicycle over to Ram Island and sat and watched the ospreys. The ospreys sat and watched her.

She bought fresh fish each morning and ate it each night at the table on the back porch of the house, watching the sun set.

She drove to East Hampton and bought some canvases and paints and brushes. She set up an easel she had found in the basement, near Vincent Clavin's bicycle, and painted.

She blocked out a landscape—off toward Shell Beach and West Neck—but before she'd even finished she put a new canvas on the easel and painted a portrait—a self-portrait—not using a mirror—from memory.

It took her two days. The first day she painted for six hours, the second for eight. She painted outdoors, standing in the small grove behind the house, sometimes working in the sun, sometimes in the shade.

She sat up late into the night in the living room, looking at the portrait, which she'd propped up on a table. She wrote a story in her mind to go with the face.

Once upon a time, long before it returned to fashion, Francesca Hayward had a romance.

It began conventionally enough. She met a man whose looks she liked, and whose eyes said he liked hers. They looked each other over and decided they'd like to spend some time together.

They spent it conventionally enough, at first. They had dinner together; they went to a play; they took a walk in the park; they went to a museum.

One day, he said, "I have a proposal."

"So soon?" she said. They hadn't even kissed yet.

"Let's take off our armor." They were dressed in armor, from head to toe; it was each other's armor they had liked the looks of, really.

She hesitated, running a finger reflectively over the smooth, cold metal that enveloped her. She liked her armor; she had got it at one of the best armorers in town, as he had his.

"And throw away our swords," the man said. "And our lances and our maces."

She tried to see the expression on his face, to see if he were teasing her, but his helmet cast a shadow and she couldn't make out his expression. "How will we protect ourselves?"

"There won't be any need," the man said. "If we have no weapons, we won't need any defenses."

". . . Won't we be cold?"

Like a magician, he conjured up a pair of beautiful gowns—a white one, trimmed with royal blue for her; a blue one, trimmed with white, for him.

"They're pretty," she said. "But what about the others?"

"Others?"

"Our friends, our relations, people we work with. Even strangers. We'll stand out. They'll all have their armor on, and we'll be dressed in these flimsy gowns. They'll surely try to take advantage of us."

Without another word, he tossed aside his sword and lance and mace and stripped off his armor and slipped on the royal blue robe.

She caught a glimpse of his body; it was strong and smooth. She was amazed that he trusted her not to clobber him, right then and there—so amazed that she could not help but ask him how he could.

"Because I love you," he said.

"You don't even know me."

"You're thinking in the old way," he said. "I'm asking you to think in a new way. Or rather, I'm asking you not to think at all. It's thinking that gets us into trouble—thinking we know each other when we don't, when we couldn't possibly; thinking we're known, when we aren't, when we couldn't possibly be known."

"You want me to take off my armor *and* stop thinking?" she said. Her voice was shrill.

He ignored the shrillness. "Try it. Look—if I still had my armor on, and asked you to take yours off, you'd be right to be suspicious. But I've taken mine off, and thrown my weapons away. I can't hurt you."

She still hesitated.

"Don't think," he said.

She took a deep breath and shut her eyes and her mind. She threw her weapons to the side and stripped her armor off. While her hands were still over her head, he slipped the robe over her, covering her nakedness, warming her. She opened her eyes. He had a hand out, inviting her to take it.

She took it and they walked side by side down a broad avenue. Around them, people clanked and clattered; tanks rumbled up and down the streets; jet planes swooped overhead, belching fire from their exhausts.

He squeezed her hand; the pressure told her not to be frightened.

She wasn't frightened; she was giddy with the pleasure of not being weighted down. She began to run, pulling him after her. They ran side by side along the avenue. The clanking people parted before them; the tanks slowed to get a better look at their display; the jet planes yawed uncertainly.

At the end of the avenue was a green park. They stopped running when they got to it and walked slowly across the grass, getting their breath back, enjoying the cool feeling on their feet. After a while, they stopped and sat on the grass.

She had a sense that they were being watched and saw that all around them people idled, pretending to be looking elsewhere, casting glances at them from around the edges of their helmets.

"I feel sort of conspicuous," she said.

"You better get used to it," he said.

"I had a fantasy for a moment, when we were running, that I'd look back and see other people taking off their armor, climbing out of the tanks, putting on pretty robes, holding hands."

"A few people might be inspired by us," he said. "But it isn't our role to be revolutionaries. All we can do is do our best. It's all anybody can do."

She saw that around them on the grass crawled two babies, a boy and a girl, naked, pink and downy. "Those kids don't have any armor on. I wonder where their parents are."

He laughed. "We're their parents."

"That was fast."

He laughed again. "We're just daydreaming."

"We're having the same daydream."

"It's possible. Anything's possible."

Francesca woke from the dream that the story had become. She felt refreshed—not at all the way she usually felt when she fell asleep unexpectedly.

She got up out of her chair and went to the portrait and looked at it closely. She realized that what was so striking about the face was not that it was full of experience, but full of possibility.

Francesca walked out on the lawn. A fishing boat chugged through Shelter Island Sound, trailing a stream of gulls. Across the water, she thought she could make out Asa's shack, a darker place amid the dark of the trees of the North Haven Peninsula.

"Hi, Asa," she said softly.

Over on Shell Beach, a dog barked and a car's headlights flashed momentarily. She could hear the sound of a radio and the laughter of a teenagers' beach party.

She lay down on the grass and looked up at the sky. There were millions of stars. She remembered how as a child she had sometimes been afraid to look up at the sky on nights like this; the enormity of the universe had frightened her—the thought that it was so immense and she was so tiny.

She felt peaceful, now. It *was* immense, and she *was* tiny. But she and it coexisted, didn't they? And more than that, they harmonized.

Chapter 37

~~~~~~~~~~~~~~~~

Waine Ryan had many more formal lunches than was his custom, even though it meant having to venture out in the heat, even though he didn't like the feeling of being filled up in the middle of the day, even though it interrupted the rhythm of work.

He had lunch with Ted and Clara Hirsch, who had moved into the vacant apartment of a traveling friend in order to be near Eva. They held hands a lot and acted like newly-weds.

"Did Ted tell you the news?" Clara said.

"What news?"

"Didn't you tell him?" Clara said.

"I was waiting till we saw him," Ted said.

"What news?" Waine said.

Ted moved the salt shaker, as if out of check. "I'm a little embarrassed."

"Oh come on, tell him" Clara said.

"Well," Ted said, "one of the weird side effects of all the publicity about Eva and the will and so on has been that people who've never been interested in my work are suddenly very interested in my work—"

"He got a big advance," Clara said. "A very big advance."

"Congratulations," Waine said.

"I'm embarrassed," Ted said. "I can't help it. It has nothing to do with writing. It's commerce, public relations."

"That's what writing is," Clara said. "What did Conrad always say? 'It's not what you write, it's how well you talk about what you've written.' We're going to use the money to get an apartment in the city, Waine—so Eva can go to school here. We'll keep the Sag Harbor place for the summer."

"How are you, Waine?" Ted said.

"I'm okay. Busy."

"Are you seeing Francesca?"

"I've been very busy."

"We weren't going to ask," Clara said.

"But?"

"But this story isn't going to have a happy ending unless you two wind up together."

Waine picked up the menu. "I think I'll have the sole."

"He doesn't want to talk about it," Clara said.

"That's a good sign," Ted said. "If it were over for sure, he'd tell us. Then we'd have to feel sorry for him."

Waine had lunch with Archer, who took him to a place in Little Italy half of whose customers were cops, half gangsters.

"I'd feel safer if everybody checked his gun at the door," Waine said.

"Nobody's ever been shot here," Archer said. "Which reminds me, I saw your, uh, friend, Bonnie."

Waine waited.

Archer picked up the menu. "I think I'll have the veal marsala."

Waine put his menu back in the rack beside the salt and pepper shakers.

"What's the matter?" Archer said. "Not eating?"

"Not until you tell me about Bonnie."

"I was going to. I thought we'd order first."

Waine folded his arms on his chest.

Archer shook his head slowly. "You been out in the sun too much?"

"Phil."

Archer leaned back and tucked in his shirt. "She was thinking about going out west. Did you know that?"

Waine nodded.

"She changed her mind."

Waine waited.

"She's looking at a place out on the island. East Hampton, I think. Or maybe it's West Hampton. Anyway, the Hamptons. The guy's looking to retire and he's selling fairly cheap. She's getting a nice bundle from the insurance. It's seasonal, but she figures she can do enough business in the summer to maybe not have to work at all in the winter."

"Any leads on the guys who torched her place?" Waine said.

"A few. None of them's gone anywhere yet. They may never. Arson's that kind of business. Say, what's with your, uh, friend, the doctor?"

"She's still a doctor."

Archer rubbed his fingers together, demanding more. "Come on, don't play patsy with me."

Waine took his menu out of the rack. "How's the fettucini?"

Archer laughed and tucked in his shirt. "Congratulations."

"What do you mean?"

"You don't want to talk about it—that means it's serious. It's about time you got involved in something serious."

"And stopped living third class?"

Archer gestured around the room. "Hey, does this look like a third-class restaurant?"

He had lunch with Dr. Wilson Finch.

". . . What a whirlwind time this has been," Dr. Finch said. "And Dr. Hayward's been at the center of it. She's been very busy. She suggested we set up a committee of staff people to advise the board on who should fill Clavin's job. She wants it to be a permanent thing—a kind of oversight panel to look at all aspects of how the hospital's run. I think it's a good idea. She also wants to set up an education program for patients—lectures and counseling for people before they're even admitted, and while they're being cared for, and even after. It's quite exciting, and it gives me a great deal of pleasure that Dr. Hayward's the one behind it. I worried, momentarily, that the realization of how horribly her father died would have an effect on her."

Finch took a sip of his wine. "You and Dr. Hayward, I understand, were . . . involved."

Waine opened the menu.

Finch coughed apologetically. "Excuse me, if you'd rather not talk about it . . ."

Waine had lunch with Beatrice Hayward, in the cafeteria of the senior center where she worked.

"I have so much to thank you for," Beatrice Hayward said. "For helping me get this job—"

"You got the job," Waine said. "I just gave you a name to call."

"You might be surprised to know what clout your name had. You're a man for whom people have enormous respect . . . I also have to thank you for finding out about my husband's death. As horrible as it is to think that he was murdered and that his murderer is a free man, it's preferable to having had doubts all these years. Noel was not a careless man, although I suppose turning his back on Vincent Clavin was an act of carelessness . . . Did Francesca ever mention how much like Noel you are?"

Waine took a long time chewing something.

"I suppose that's a terrible thing to say," Beatrice Hayward said. "One doesn't want to know that one is *like* anybody. One wants to be unique—"

"I feel honored," Waine said, "to think I might be like a man who had you as a wife and Francesca as a daughter."

Beatrice Hayward blushed and poked at her food with a fork. "Well, you've turned that compliment around very deftly, haven't you? . . . Francesca and I are both very difficult women—whatever that might say about Noel. I was courted aplenty after he died, and I never encountered any man who was even remotely as capable as he was of dealing with us. I led Noel quite a chase before I married him, and the thing about him that finally impressed me was his ability to inspire me—to make me see that there were things I thought were worth doing that only I could do. You may not know it, but you've done that to Francesca. I don't know whether you've heard about what she's up to at the hospital—"

"I've heard a little."

"Well, you're responsible for it, to a large degree. I'm not here to tell you this in her stead; she'll tell you herself, in time—I'm sure of it. I'm simply here to thank you, on my own behalf, for having had the courage to stand up to her."

Waine laughed. "That doesn't exactly sound like what I did."

Beatrice Hayward shrugged, as if to say that if he didn't want to take the credit, that was his affair; *she* knew what she was talking about.

One day, Waine had lunch alone, on a bench in Washington Square Park, surrounded by young mothers with babies in strollers, pensioners, buffeted by disco music from gigantic portable radios. The heat was less oppressive and in the air was just a tinge of something that whispered of autumn. Waine had a hot dog with mustard and sauerkraut and a Coke. When he finished, he leaned his head back and enjoyed the feeling of the sun on his face and realized that he had not done any sunning since the day he had gone sailing with Francesca. A cloud blocked the sun and he opened his eyes a fraction to see how long its transit would be. It wasn't a cloud; it was a woman, who stood before him, her arms crossed under her breasts, her head tipped a little to the side. With her was a young girl.

"Handsome, isn't he?" the woman said.

The girl giggled. "Is that *him?*"

"I'm not sure," the woman said. "I've never seen him from quite this angle. If it isn't him, he really would do very nicely, wouldn't he? I mean, he's so good-looking. Shall we ask him?"

The girl giggled.

"I'll ask him," the woman said. "I have more experience at this." She bent forward from the waist. "Excuse me, sir."

Waine opened his eyes all the way and sat up straight. "I'm afraid I'm waiting for someone."

"Ah. Been waiting long?"

"It seems like a long time, but I guess it really hasn't been."

"So many things are like that. You think, Oh, dear, am I going to have to wait *that* long? But then, when the time's up, you find it hasn't really been that long at all."

"I guess the hardest part was not knowing that the time would be up."

"But you had faith?"

"Either that or I'm just a dreamer."

"Aren't they the same thing?"

The girl took a step toward Waine. "Do you know how many Americans it takes to change a light bulb?"

"How many?" Waine said.

"One."

Waine laughed.

"That's an American joke," the woman said. "I just

realized, you two haven't met. Eva James, this is Waine Ryan. Waine Ryan, Eva James."

Waine shook Eva's hand. "I did see you briefly in your hospital bed. I'm glad to see you out of it."

I want to thank you very much for everything you've done," Eva said in a sing-song.

"That was unrehearsed," Francesca said.

Waine laughed. "How did you find me?"

"We called your office," Eva said.

"Your secretary said you were in a bad mood," Francesca said, "and that whenever you were in a bad mood you went to Washington Square Park, because it's such an unpleasant place."

"Why do you do that?" Eva said. "Why don't you go to a nice place?"

Francesca patted Eva's head. "When you're older, you'll understand the pleasures of bad moods."

Eva ducked her head. "I don't like to be told I'll understand things when I'm older."

Francesca knelt beside Eva and looked her in the eye. "I'm sorry. You're right, it's a lousy thing to say."

To Waine, Eva said, "I'm going to be a doctor when I grow up."

"You'll be a good doctor," Waine said.

"How can you tell?" Eva said.

Francesca laughed. "You can't kid this kid."

Waine laughed. "I wasn't kidding. You'll be a good doctor because you have a strong grip. All doctors have strong grips."

"Does she?" Eva said, wagging a thumb at Francesca.

Francesca laughed. "Careful, counselor."

"She has a sensational grip."

Francesca ducked her head, embarrassed. "Oh, my."

Eva tugged at a strap of Francesca's pocketbook. "Are we going to go?"

"I don't know," Francesca said. "We still haven't asked him if he wants to."

"But you *said* he'd want to. You said he'd want to because all the loose ends were tied up."

Waine stood up. "I do want to."

Eva turned her back on them.

"Did I say something wrong?" Waine said.

Eva giggled. "I'm supposed to do this so you two can kiss."

Francesca shrugged. "That was unrehearsed."

Waine took her in his arms. They didn't kiss; they just pressed their hands against each other's backs, here, then here, then here.

"Oh, Waine."

"Yes."

They let go and each took one of Eva's hands and walked up to Fifth Avenue and hailed a cab.

"The Brooklyn Bridge," Waine said.

"You want to go to Brooklyn, you should say so before you get in the cab. If I go to Brooklyn, that means I either got to come back without a fare or I get a fare there and I end up driving all over Brooklyn when I don't want to drive all over Brooklyn. You want to go to Brooklyn, you should say so before you get in the cab."

"The Brooklyn Bridge," Waine said. "The Manhattan end."

"The Manhattan end of the Brooklyn Bridge?"

"Right," Waine said firmly.

"We're going to walk across," Eva said.

"Walk? What're you, nuts? What're you going to do when you get to the other side?" the driver asked incredulously.

"Nothing," Eva said.

"Nothing—that's exactly right. Nothing. You know why? Cause you'll be in Brooklyn, that's why. And there's nothing in Brooklyn. You're like that bear that went over the mountain. You know that poem, little girl, about the bear that went over the mountain?"

Eva sang her answer. "We're going over the Brooklyn Bridge, we're going over the Brooklyn Bridge, we're going over the Brooklyn Bridge, to see what we can see. To see what we can see."

Francesca and Waine smiled at one another and settled back in the cab. Their hands touched lightly. After a moment, they stopped looking at each other and concentrated on the long road that stretched invitingly before them.

Dear Reader:

Would you take a few moments to fill out this questionnaire and mail it to:

Richard Gallen Books/Questionnaire
330 Steelcase Road East, Markham, Ont. L3R 2M1

1. What rating would you give *With Eyes of Love?*
   □ excellent □ very good □ fair □ poor

2. What prompted you to buy this book? □ title
   □ front cover □ back cover □ friend's recommendation □ other (please specify) _____

3. Check off the elements you liked best:
   □ hero □ heroine □ other characters □ story
   □ setting □ ending □ love scenes

4. Were the love scenes □ too explicit
   □ not explicit enough □ just right

5. Any additional comments about the book?

   _____

6. Would you recommend this book to friends?
   □ yes □ no

7. Have you read other Richard Gallen romances? □ yes □ no

8. Do you plan to buy other Richard Gallen romances? □ yes □ no

9. What kind of romances do you enjoy reading?
   □ historical romance □ contemporary romance
   □ Regency romance □ light modern romance
   □ Gothic romance

10. Please check your general age group:
    □ under 25 □ 25-35 □ 35-45 □ 45-55 □ over 55

11. If you would like to receive a romance newsletter please fill in your name and address:

    _____

    _____

    _____